Den Smil series – Geopolitical Thriller

Secretariat PLOT

Conspiracy in the Arctic

SOUGATA

Fact sheet

- Word 'Arctic' came from the Greek word- **Arktos** (bear)

- Once upon a time the Arctic belonged to Tuniit **indigenous people** of paleo-eskimo and dorset culture. They were displaced by Norse invaders and Siberian immigrants and Inuit culture started emerging

- The Arctic Circle is home to 30% of untapped global **oil-gas resources**. The transpolar territory hosts a huge repository of **rare earth minerals** too. The **North Sea route** (via Russian coast) and the **NorthWest Passage** (via Alaskan North slope-Canadian coast) saves 40% time and cost of the present trade route between East and West.

- **The North Pole** means Sled, Kayak, Igloo, Northern light, Midnight Sun, white Beluga Whale, Caribou Deer, Sea Lion, Walrus, Reindeer, Polar Bear and Tundra.

- **Delicacies**: Akutaq- ice cream, Bannock- baked bread, Labrador Tea- made of Rhododendron leaf, Suaasat- staple food of seal meat, Maktaaq- frozen whale skin and blubber, White bean soup, Lapskaus- thick meat soup, Reindeer, snow crab

- **Polar Bear**- an iconic species may not survive beyond 2100. And by 2050, the entire Arctic will be ice free during summer

"Date for end of human race is still unknown but it is certain. Because the climate is changing"

Chapters

Casting

Den Smil : Lead character of the story. Den in his earlier career was an Airforce pilot and then war correspondent. He never had a smooth social family life. Despite the physical and emotional scars left by his past, he remains determined and resilient. His father- Smil Herz was a sugar farmer who got settled initially in Hawaii from Jerusalem. His mother was an American missionary. She left them long back soon after the birth of Den in Hawaii. Den and his father moved to Prague thereafter. Den was raised in Prague and is an official citizen of the Czech Republic at present. Den moved to Germany to complete his graduation before joining Airforce as trainee pilot. He is now at 32 and P-4 executive staff in United Nations – Secretariat department. He also served the UN Human right council as a 'special rapporteur' earlier.

Albert Guterres : Secretary General of United Nations. People usually call him 'Chief'.

Mike Power : Secretary of State of USA

Joseph Bolton : Security Advisor of USA

Remi Larsen : Director of CSIS (Center for Strategic & International Studies)

Sir Bill Jodman : Climate activist in Nuuk, Greenland

Ibrahim Helmy : Egyptian friend of Den Smil

Nikolay Ambrosov : Co-Chair in Arctic Council and Senior Researcher in CSIS. He is Interior minister of Russia and holds key position in supreme council of United Russia party

Alex Navani : Active non-communist political leader in Russia

Sumbat Tonoyan : Mastermind in uranium and nuclear smuggling. He usually operates from Batumi, Georgia

Dr. Hrant Ohanyan : Godfather in illegal trade of uranium and nuclear warheads.

Haile Mulu : Head of the UN Conference on Trade and Development in Ethiopia

Mett Fred : Prime Minister of Denmark

Kim Kielsen : Prime Minister of Greenland

Minik Kenoguv : Deputy PM of Greenland

Oskar Schober : Interpol Officer

Walter Bart : Journalist

Juha Olsen : Intelligence Officer in IcEye Earth observatory

Mrs Brown : Executive Assistant of UN Secretary General

Hazel Taylor : Daughter of David Taylor

Buljo Gaup : Ex Judge of the Supreme Court of Norway and was recently reappointed as a jury member of the 'Nobel Committee'.

Lieutenant General Morten Lunde : Head of the Norway Intelligence Service

Jeffrey Pence : Senior engineer in Gazporn. He is an instrumental founding person for Nord Stream gas pipelines

Kelvin Floyd : Computer genius and Hacker

'Polar Bear' operatives

C1 : ?

C2 : ?

C3 : **Vlad Medkev?**

C4 : **Dr. Mathew Bunn**

C5 : **Ted Mateen**

C6 : **Eric Nichols**

C7 : **David Taylor**. He is an experienced senior engineer in underwater construction

C8 : **Mac Metesky**

<u>'Codes'</u>

S_1.0 - 634736785939pb

S_2.0 - 741931772520pb

S_3.0 - 7417401152614pb

PR_I.0 - 7018511481139pb

PR_II.0 - 781428152100pb

PR_III.0 - 310508921011pb

COP24 - Climate conference of the United Nations (UN)

Katowice, Poland

"You are stealing our future," the little girl, **Creta**, was angry in her speech. Her whole body shivered with anger, but her eyes glittered with courage. She was a teenage Swedish climate activist who had created enthusiasm for the environment and against industrial pollution. The forum invited her this year for the COP24- the Climate Conference of the United Nations.

"We have not come here to beg the world leaders to care. You have ignored us in the past and will ignore us again. You have made enormous profits and let the earth and the poor suffer. We cannot solve this climate crisis without treating this as a crisis. To do this, we have to delete politics. Change is coming whether you like it or not, and we are running out of time." She continued her speech for another ten minutes. The entire audience amplified the clapping as she walked away from the stage.

The stage was shared by prominent Diplomats, Country Leaders, Policymakers, Scholars, Scientists and Climate Activists. The four-day summit was held in the 'International Conference Centre' at the heart of Silesia in Katowice. Today was day three. The day's first round was allotted for functional people like Scientists, Geologists, Environmentalists, and Engineers. Diplomates and Policymakers will submit their speeches in the second round.

Among the functional scholars, the last submission was from **Dr. Thomson Gorald**. Underneath data on oceans and recent research shows that the supply of a warm water stream to glaciers and permafrost is higher than earlier, and it is accelerating. Acceleration is caused mainly because of more industrialization and commerce.

"Ice is melting faster. The Arctic and Antarctic are the most affected regions. The Arctic is warming four times faster than the world average. We will see extreme weather conditions, excessive rain, severe drought, and scorching summers. The future is gloomy. Simply put, if we cannot restore the Arctic and Antarctic, our survival is at stake." Dr. Thomson submitted.

Next was **Mr Mike Power**, the present Secretary of State of the US and the former Head of the CIA. The present US Prime Minister is a climate denier. Last year he sent a low-profile officer to COP23 for the sake of attendance, which created protests and criticism. The US and China are strong business lobbyists. They have been pushing climate regulations and actions in favor of their industry and sometimes act in complete denial or withdrawal. This time Washington sent their strongest ambassador. The US is serious now. Foreign affairs and international diplomacy may be Mike's first responsibility. Still, as the most trustworthy right-hand man of the present PM, he intervenes in most of the critical dealings and agendas of the Government. Mike is the Defacto Commander.

Choosing Katowice for the climate conference was controversial but of equal geopolitical importance. Silesia happens to be a central cross-border between West and East Europe. Upper Silesia, along with its industrial city Katowice is in Poland, whereas the southern and eastern part of Silesia is in Germany and Czech. The cosmopolitan demography of Catholic Polish, German and Jewish minority is similar to the diverse ethnicity of Jerusalem. However, Jerusalem's 'Mediterranean' significance is mainly concentrated on marine trade and the choke point of Europe, Eurasia, North Africa and the Middle East. Poland's politics is different due to its complex and significant geography. Poland is in the proximity of the Baltic in the North and the Balkan in the South, along with the central border of West-East Europe. Katowice can be called the coal capital of Europe, hence one of the most polluted areas on Earth. Most environmentalists doubt that a climate conference held in the midst of the powerful Polish coal lobby may succeed. The coal lobby is not in support of policy-level decisions and investments to increase renewal energy. They foresee losing stake in the renewable energy business. Russia wants to push an alternative with a gas pipeline supply replacing coal mining in Upper Silesia. The US wants to hold on to the decision till the Poland election is over. Most likely, the present President will be reelected with the support of Washington and would continue with the coal lobby. Katowice is stuck in an ego fight between two stakeholder Nations- US and Russia. So, the climate pledge.

This was the time to launch the big code 'Green Climate Fund'. Mike was excited to take the oath, "we pledge to fight climate change strongly and honestly. A 133-page rule book is being published to execute the earlier Paris Agreement. This time it is more meaningful, more accurate, and stronger. We announce 100 billion to 500 billion contribution funds every year to developing Nations as an incentive to work for climate change. We, the developed nations, already support the mentioned cause and contribute deeply in the initiatives. We will be more committed this time," another big round of claps from the audience came in appreciation for Mike.

Mike announced, "The US is committed to the UN agenda and programs. My country, the United States, also pledged to work harder against the crisis. We presented our rationale for why we had to deny the Paris Agreement for climate change. We demand reforms to innovate methods and investments to keep parity between business and carbon neutrality. We do not believe that the immediate replacement of fossil fuel with renewable energy options will solve this crisis. Stopping shipping and banning coal or oil will not eliminate global warming. Alternatives need to be built on a proper scale to fulfill the global massive manufacturing demand. We do not favor stopping something but rather would invest more in the renewable supply chain of business to supplement."

***

"Please excuse me," **Den** came out of the hall. Mike was still talking. Time was monotonous since nobody would ultimately compromise the business for climate action. He wanted to come out of the suffocation for a few minutes. Although, he has been habituated since these last two years of his Secretariat job in the UN. He saw the nexus of world businesses, diplomacy, and politics from a very close proximity. This suffocates him the most. It is December in Poland. He took off his gloves to touch the real climate. The temperature lingers below freezing, causing a crisp chill to fill the air. Den stretched his eyes. The trees stand tall, adorned with a delicate layer of frost, their branches reaching out like intricate ice sculptures. The ground was transformed into a pristine white carpet. The weather was beautiful, but Den knew that the atmosphere was extremely polluted. The burning of coal from factories and mines caused a thick veil of smog around the city. All these are human made. Den lit a cigarette. He prefers Benson & Hedges. Den is chain smoker and usually smokes two cigarettes consecutively.

Inside the hall, the temperature was expected to be diplomatic. Hence it was warm, pleasant and artificial.

Mike had completed his speech. Now **Mr Nikolay Ambrosov** started narrating. He is co-Chair of the Arctic Council and Senior Researcher in CSIS. He is the Interior Minister of Russia and holds a key position in the supreme council of the United Russia party. He emphasized creating balance between marine life, inhabitants, and industry. He also covered labor welfare and job security via collaboration. The North Coast is ice-free, and this opened up better prospects for exploring more natural resources, scientific exploration and international trade. Russia urged to mobilize more labors to the Arctic coal mine belt from the Silesia oil fields. Russia also spoke in favor of a combination among climate initiatives, scientific exploration and business.

Nikolay said, "Better synergy can be achieved and job security will be maintained by an exchange program of labors between Silesia coal mines and the Arctic. With this, we will be able to provide a sufficient labor force in the Arctic region who, in turn, can volunteer in the climate change project. We seek support from Norway, International Community, IMO, and all stakeholders to smoothen this labor exchange program between Silesia and Svalbard. We pledge our resources not only to contribute to the climate change project but also to the Polar Code mission."

Den checked his watch. It was only twenty-five minutes since he came outside the hall, and he wished to spend some more leisure time, but he could not afford that. He was given this task by the Head Office to cover this event quite intensively. He already had some backlog and had to complete the full filing before he would report to his office by the day after tomorrow. He is presently stationed in Hong Kong. Although he was not missing anything as he was already connected with the hall through his ear stick. He also had access to live stream recordings of the session through the UN cloud. He came inside and approached the hall.

He was walking a bit casually. A stranger from the left corridor suddenly collided. "Sorry, extremely sorry young man," the **old gentleman** went into the hall. He perhaps came out of the washroom in a hurry and was nervous. It was a mere casual collision. Den didn't mind. Den still didn't realize that the gentleman was seated just in front of him. He entered the hall and took his seat. Den missed noting that another person, who was also outside and probably was in the washroom itself, just entered the hall silently within ten minutes and took his seat.

Tea break for 15 minutes

Most of the hardcore quick negotiations happen during this small networking break. Diplomats actively participate in engaging in this crucial business time. Den ordered a cup of green lemon tea.

Den has been observing his front seat for quite some time. That old gentleman has not taken tea or coffee. He was sweating in the cold. Den could make out from his body language that he was immensely nervous for some reason.

Den was engaged with **Ms Remi Larsen** for some time. Remi is the Director of CSIS. They both know each other and share a very close personal relationship. The old lady was giving some insights to Den about recent affairs. It was a casual discussion. Nikolay Ambrosov is another senior fellow in the same CSIS. Remi had serious ego problems with Nikolay automatically.

She whispered in his ears- "Den, I am afraid that Nikolay is very influential. Russia talks about the damage done by ice melting in the Arctic. But can you believe that global warming in the Arctic actually helped Russia a lot and some developed nations want to explore more profits and benefits in the similar line."

Den replied, "I completely agree. US policy has been reluctant for the Arctic for decades and hence could not leverage the gain yet. The West realized the value of this new emerging region very late. Russia is already in the commanding position."

"Labor exchange program between Silesia and Svalbard is just one part. They might have bagged better commercial benefits elsewhere. In fact, all interested governments are scaling up their policy and operation in the business of the Arctic. Nikolay is not reciting the full case."

"Do you mean the Arctic Trade route?" asked Den.

Remi replied after a long pause, "It is melting, Den. There are larger items. It is complex," Remi kept her silence.

***

Another incident had happened discreetly half an hour back. Two men in housekeeping costumes and badges entered the washroom just after that old gentleman came out of it. They put the "work in progress" board outside and locked the door from inside. There was already a housekeeping guy working inside the washroom. Before he got a chance to react, both the men caught him tightly and injected him. It was a V-series nerve agent and poison.

***

Tea break was over. Everybody went back to their seats. The session will start after five minutes. Den now observed that the old gentleman was still silent, introverted. He was not talking to anybody. He was busy sending some messages. Den gazed at him. He was busy in replying to somebody. He replied, "...*serious lie. It is also a hoax*".

Prelude of hoax

Svalbard

Three in the afternoon at Longyearbyen, Svalbard. An extremely remote inhabited place of Earth within the Arctic circle. This is called the roof of the Northern Pole. Svalbard is a sovereign land under the governance of Norway. Unlike other Nordic cities of Norway, like Tromso, Oslo is, where others are more jovial and busier during this particular early evening time, Svalbard is still quiet and slow. It has an Arctic climate. It is known for its extremely cold weather, which restricts Svalbard from building diverse infrastructure and urban livelihood.

On the other hand, it is Nature that really gifted Svalbard with loads of fossil fuel, coal, minerals, gold, rare Earth elements, whales, and marine resources. It is not just their old treaty for free industrial and economic activity among Arctic nations. Even in the present time, they manage equal traction from the world for their geographical significance. The northernmost township still remains Remilitarized land as an exception of the world.

But a slowdown has taken place. Most of the coal mines are closed in Svalbard. The economy is shifting towards tourism and research on natural resources. Climate scientists are equally active in this region. Svalbard is gradually evolving its geopolitics in a diverse direction. Choosing Svalbard for the global seed vault was not a simple unanimous decision, but there was another diplomacy behind this iron curtain. Russia's aggressive claim over the Arctic region and subsequent investment, submarine stations, military base and parallel western push on Norway to disrupt Svalbard in its own favor, put this region into more conflict, competition, and action. Svalbard became the epicenter of the north pole. This was not for conflicts but for prospects. A complicated conspiracy was planned to grab the prospects. The race for future geopolitical and economic supremacy was in making.

In the dim light of a late August afternoon, a sense of heightened activity enveloped the remote vicinity of the Global Seed Vault in Svalbard. The tranquil landscape was interrupted by the rhythmic thudding of military helicopters, their powerful blades slicing through the freezing cold Arctic air. Several military choppers landed one after another. Their destination was the 'Global Seed Vault'. This is of equal short proximity to Arctic World Archive, Svalbard Satellite Station and the airport. Armed guards were covering the zone in teams, but their purpose was not to protect the repository of the World's plant genetic resources. A crucial meeting would take place inside the deep chamber. The attendees were very influential and managed to get entry passes to go inside the seed vault. The tele connectivity, or satellite surveillance, was jammed intentionally for this meeting. The sun sank lower on the horizon, and daylight became scarce. Although, Svalbard is yet to move from its midnight sun to a long polar night. As the sun hovered just above the horizon, its waning light danced upon the pristine snow-covered landscape, lending an eerie atmosphere to the unfolding events.

The mastermind will fly from Olavsvern, a secret submarine base station inside a cave underneath the mountain in Norway. The strategic naval base was built after world war and during the cold war in anticipation of combat in case of a nuclear war or the next global warming break out. But the base could not flourish much because of the complexity of the project and bureaucracy involved. It was abandoned and then decommissioned. The deepwater cave facility above the Arctic Circle could provide a powerful base of operations for expanded submarine patrols in the resource-rich Arctic, where both Russia and America have been aggressively expanding their military presence. Both the superpowers are eyeing this Svalbard and increasing influence over Norway's government. Russia, US and NATO officials are trying to gain respective legitimate access. Both know the significance of this geography nowadays.

Another Chopper landed on the doorstep of the Seed Vault. The '**mastermind**' arrived with heavy guards. He was fat and had a beard. He was wearing a high-neck sweater with a woolen blazer, scarves and a hat. His code name was **C1**. He is a public figure and holds a very high government position. C1 usually attends these covert meetings in disguise. The core team had already arrived. **C3**- the supervisor was Russian by birth. He was the operation in charge and spearheaded the project '**polar bear**'. He was a special recruit. The core team and key instrumental people were also present in this working committee meeting except installation engineer **David Taylor** and instrumentation engineer **Kelvin Floyd**. **C2** was also absent. He does not attend these meetings. He operates behind the curtain.

The secret meeting was happening under the basement of the Seed Vault. The meeting started after one hour. C1 threw a paper over the table. This was the headline of Russia hosting the flag in 2007 beneath the sea of the North Pole. His chin was more tough now. He pointed out loudly, "This was great. We want more influence here. Change the world in favor of ourselves permanently. This is the center stage." The room was dead silent and everybody was listening to C1.

He continued his loud voice, "We have specific policy instructions for this global project. We will be able to hold economic and geopolitical dominance for a longer period of time if we are able to deliver this. For this, we need to buy multiple stakeholders and manipulate multiple authorities. We may have to camouflage a lot of systems and situations to change eyeballs. It is a serious, complex and classified project. Please cooperate with 'polar bear'. Payment terms were already discussed. This is pretty fat. Responsibility is equally high. Put your lives on the line."

C3 started addressing the attendees, "Project brief was already shared earlier with all of you. For confidentiality and dependency, tasks are not discussed to-gether. Each task is splitted into several orders so that the respective owner has access only to the respective goal. I will transmit the action plan shortly. Nobody will speak in a personal handset. Syndicate will provide a separate handset and SIM. By the way, **Mr Taylor (C7)** could not make it today. He is an old gen-tleman. He was given the charge for site installation. He has experience in marine construction in extreme weather. He will be introduced to the team in due course. We can introduce the rest of the team here."

The other three key incharge were also present. **Dr. Mathew Bunn (C4)** was incharge of design and development, **Ted Mateen (C5)** was Instrumentation incharge along with Kelvin Floyd, **Eric Nichols (C6)** will take care of supply and logistics.

The attendees were served with canned Tea and packed Cakes.

C1 addressed the team again, "Gentlemen, the next climate conference is going to be held in Katowice by next December. Time is crucial. The more we delay, the more we lose. Governments and businesses are investing in this project with a clear agenda. We are answerable for the return. A lot of things are interlinked and time-bound. One thing gentlemen, everybody is accountable, you are recruited with a heavy price. Please cooperate sensitively. Syndicate will not tolerate double cross. Respective responsibility and delivery is a must. Remember, everything is changing. Climate is changing us fast, but we will change the climate faster," C1 laughed loudly.

He indicated a secret plan. Political business for global supremacy is ruthless. Since the plan was big, the conspirators had to make the blueprint complex.

Canada

Dr Xiangguo Qiu was removed from a National Microbiology Lab in Winnipeg, Canada. She was interrogated in private for an unsolicited shipment to Wuhan in China with virus samples of Ebola, Nipah and Corona Sars. She was married to a Chinese scientist **Professor Keding** who was in charge of virology in a Wuhan Lab. This was a Category A substance that was supposed to be properly labeled as 'UN 2814 infectious substances affecting humans. It was also supposed to be packed in a refrigerator flask with special conditions. The capsules were originally transported from Texas Medical University to Canada for warehousing. For all these, they had to follow a strict procedure and check. The system was compromised, false labeling was done and it was smuggled to Wuhan.

A pandemic genocide was planned with a clear agenda of global lockdown, landslide price of oil along with stockpiling at such cheapest ever rate and a pharmaceutical gameplan on antivirus manufacturing. The estimated profit was planned to be invested in the project 'polar bear'. A chain of interlinked conspiracies, but the virus capsule was stolen before the schedule and mishandled in a Wuhan wet market at the time of delivery. The virus broke out in the wrong place.

Saudi Arabia

American and European policy on the Middle East never depended solely on the White House Senate. There has been a panel of lobbyists who intermediated between bureaucrats, businesses, Kings, Prime Minister and Congress. Journalist- **Mr Jilani Khashoggi** is a key lobbyist of the US with the Saudi Royal family. Khashoggi is a media adviser to Prince Turki in Faisal, the former head of Saudi Arabia's intelligence service and the country's former ambassador to the United States. Presently Mr Khashoggi holds a senior position at the Washington Post.

He is very close to the Arab King, but this family relationship deteriorated after Prince Soleman took charge.

Riadh, under the new leadership of Prince Soleman, changed its stand and decision to diversify from oil to survive economically and to defy the spread of Arab springs. They are looking beyond stereotypes. But this large-scale economic and political ambition cannot be achieved by simple steps. The Prince is interested in investing in the business of the Arctic. Obviously, it is not through a straight route. The Arctic is a new future and the new yardstick of global supremacy. Opportunist countries are moving fast to grab advantage of possible corners and miles of the Pole.

The conspiracy program 'polar bear' had a vast and wide budget. Half was sponsored by a few Governments and business houses. Half was planned through the revenue of vaccination. This was the dirty part of the story. A Sars Covid virus was manufactured with the vaccine formula in the making. The revenue would support the malfunctioning of the present Arctic and would create a new Arctic. The ambition of a new World order was conceived. This was a political decision. The game plan was straightforward. Saudi Arabia was investing to buy its future and hence invested heavily on 'polar bear'. but they were just one party to the consortium. It was still difficult to imagine who the other sponsors were.

Prince Soleman wanted to move fast, but Khashoggi opposed and complained to the King. Both parties could not agree to several terms. For the Saudi Prince, it was an immediate business agenda, but Khashoggi took it personally. His personal hatred toward Prince Soleman was maturing into a personal rivalry. He went all out publicly to criticize Arab policy. Khashoggi started blackmailing the Prince. The Prince identified this as a threat and prospective diversion. Journalist Khashoggi managed to access more information about the Arctic mission. He knew the bad secrets, but he didn't know that he was included in the hit list soon.

Assignment | UN Secretariat

Hong Kong

Den was surfing the world news in his cubicle. He was tired from the trip. Before Poland, he was in another continent covering another agenda. After he returned from Poland, he had no time for sleep. He and his team had to complete all of the reports on a war footing because COP24 was a big event, and the world was eagerly waiting to hear the formal UN version and policies after that.

Den Smil is a P-4 grade professional staff in the executive office of the General Secretary. He is presently located in a duty station in Hong Kong. Den joined the UN only two years back. Although he was associated with the peace keeping force and UN human right council for quite some time. He was a young Airforce pilot and a freelance war correspondent in earlier days.

The desk phone rang! It was a video call from the General Secretary of the United Nations- **Mr Albert Guterres**. Den calls him '**Chief**'. He went inside a meeting cabin.

"Hi, Sir."

Chief didn't react. Chief was absent-minded for a few seconds.

"Oh yeah, Den, how are you doing? I am sorry that you just returned from Poland and I am asking you for another trip immediately. But I urge you to get your next engagement very soon. It may interest you, my dear friend. There is urgency to this task."

Den was morose, "Ok, Sir. No issues. Could you kindly elaborate?"

Chief demonstrated several important leads. "The Russian Navy announced plans to procure at least 30 Poseidon- nuke powered unmanned underwater vehicles (UUV), which will be deployed on four submarines, two of which would serve the Russian Northern Fleet and two the Pacific Fleet. Several complaints are lodged in our security council by the US and NATO against Russia on the subject of a labor dispute and forced labor mobilization between Silesia and Svalbard. We hope this would not fuel new conflicts in the Polar Circle, but we fear that it may escalate to the international court. We have to stop these nuances. The Department of Peacekeeping has a recommendation to send you there to negotiate. They are not sending any intelligence analysts. You fit well for this job. We cannot move this politically but can fix it diplomatically. I hope you understand what I mean here! There are enough series of arctic conflicts. Let us not afford further escalation on the subject and lose more momentum. The UN and developed countries have pledged more investments. We have many more plans to fight climate change. Conflict is an obstacle to achieving that goal, and we have to solve this quickly," the Chief said.

"Yes, Sir, I understand. What do you want, Sir?" Den asked.

Chief replied, "We want the Svalbard and Arctic clean."

Den completed the conversation and came out of the cabin.

***

Den got a private pin. It was Mike- "I am in Hong Kong. Meet me in person. It is urgent. Meetup in 'Sky100' at 10 pm." Den got a sense that Mike didn't want to disclose now. Mike was calling to meet face-to-face. He confirmed to Mike that he will be on his way shortly.

Den reached early. It is an observation deck on the 100th floor of the skyscraper. It is the International Commerce Centre in West Kowloon. There is a cafe on the rooftop. He had to wait since Mike was yet to reach. He was looking through the glass wall towards Victoria Harbour. It is not a British colony anymore but still remains one of the busiest trading and shipping hubs of the world. However, there are controversies around the corner because of issues of corruption in dredging and the gradual decrease of water depth. The tip of the South China Sea is heavily polluted because of the dense traffic and commerce. Tourist spots, water taxis and water ballet shows are closed because of the partial lockdown in Hong Kong. Mike arrived after fifteen minutes. They sat on the corner sofa and ordered Glenfiddich & Cantonese pork wontons. Mike strictly instructed the attendants not to disturb them for the next one hour.

Mike started, "I am here for a couple of days for some work. Labour conflict in Svalbard is true. People are worried, but going to Svalbard has no meaning since we should not interfere in the labor conflict with Russia. We can blow this issue to the public through our media to keep pressure. Do not get trapped in the Russian conflict. Chief is wasting time there. Chief was saying that he wanted to engage you in the task. At present, we have more serious issues to address. I told Chief that he should change your plan and rather solve shipping conflicts. Solving shipping conflicts is a solution for the future arctic trade route."

Den nodded his head. He knew that Mike was very logical.

"I was arguing with Chief on the subject. Our priority should be to resolve Chinese Arctic aggression. It is not a good sign that China is planning the arctic silk road with Russia. China must be highly interested in Russia's natural gas on the north coast, but their recent aggression to declare themselves 'near the Arctic state' is not a good sign. There are some complaints from IMO and the Arctic Council on this subject. People are exploring canceling the permanent observer status of China. Restrict China as much as possible from the Arctic Circle. Cover Beijing and Hong Kong extensively. China would soon invade here either by law or by force. China is playing with double swords. One target is definitely Hong Kong, Taiwan and the South China Sea. Another target is the North Pole. There are serious concerns, and we are raising this to the Security Council," Mike continued.

"I also heard a little about this. 'Maersk', even after a successful voyage on the north coast in collaboration with Russia, suddenly announced that they wanted to go slowly toward the Arctic. It is very surprising."

Mike smiled, "This is not strange at all. China has really increased its influence over Greenland. They influenced Denmark to compel Maersk in deciding to stop preparing for an Arctic route. Actually, China's largest container shipping company "COSCO" has bigger plans and wants to capture the maximum shipping orders for the Arctic future trade route. They are clever and starting it now. Den, I hope you understand that we together have to stop this dominance. This is the immediate task. The Arctic trade would benefit the world, but one dominant ally of Russia and China should not grab all the benefits. We want our pie. This is high time for capacity buildup.

The order was served interim. Both cheered the pegs and intensed the discussion with low voice.

"Are you meeting some critical guys here in this regard?" Den asked.

"Yes, of course, but I feel that we can keep surveillance. Den, better you be our eyes. You have been working in Hong Kong for quite some time. You have access to important officers in the territory. We must know their investment and strategic plan for the polar region, or else we cannot counter them timely."

"You want me to spy on them?"

The meeting went on for an hour.

It was just half an hour since the meeting was over. But Den was still carrying a hangover. Mike departed by giving him a peculiar task. The world should restrict China at this moment from an over-aggressive establishment in the Arctic Circle. Parallelly he really had some doubts about the purpose of going to Svalbard to negotiate with the Russian government and authority to solve the Svalbard situation. It was his official assignment, after all. He knew the seriousness of the geopolitical prospect in the Arctic. He was not able to fix his mind. He lit a cigarette.

Den's mind was disturbed and tired. On the one hand, he has been given an official assignment by Chief to counter the labor dispute created by Russia in Svalbard within the heart of the Arctic Circle. On the other hand, Mike had some merit in unofficially investigating the Chinese plan for the Arctic. The Arctic polar region is gaining momentum, and there has been a sudden jerk in the recent past. It is beneficial for the UN to know more information and gain deeper access to confidential and controversial actions which may be going on undercover. The UN is interested to know whether these activities damage climate or peace. Their core work does not succeed if they can't control diplomatic conspiracy. This is required beyond stereotype Secretariat execution. Den could not decide whether he should immediately fly to Svalbard to solve the problem or stay back in Hong Kong for damage control! He still did not know that a heavy storm was coming which would melt his life forever.

He went to a nearby pub and ordered two pegs of whiskey again. He saw the watch. It was 1AM at night. He could comfortably call Remi if she was still in Europe. It might be evening there. He rang, "Hi, Remi. How are you? Is it a good time! I want to meet you."

"I am in Canada for a seminar and have some programs for the next couple of days. Is there any urgency Den?"

"I'll meet you the day after tomorrow evening. I will catch a flight. I need your help."

"I am in Iqaluit, Nunavut. It will take you some time to get here. Weather is not easy here now. It is already 15 degrees below freezing. Are you sure, Den?"

"I will manage Remi, thanks."

Den trusts Remi. He wanted to discuss the situation in detail. He sent his travel indent to admin. The UN Admin will arrange his flight, booking and stay.

Nunavut

Wednesday 2 pm. 'Nunatta Sunakkutaangit Museum' in the capital, Iqaluit, on Baffin Island.

Remi understands the Arctic very well. She is very active in this region and holds responsible portfolios both in the Arctic Council and IMO. The World keeps talking about climate change but does nothing. Remi believes in working in the field. Her team works closely with the indigenous people of this northernmost geography. She came to the museum curator to collect a few belongings of old local people. The Arctic Council is going to conduct an exhibition in London on polar habitats. This will showcase to the World how serious the civilization is about Arctic climate change. The mega event is scheduled after the upcoming ministerial meeting of the arctic council in June. Council sent her to Nunavut. She was also collecting primary information for her upcoming research paper on "Arctic Business". The "Economist" will probably publish this.

Remi was sitting with Dr. Thomson. Dr. Thomson is a Geophysicist at Norwegian Polar Institute in Tromsø. As a specialist in sea ice and climate, he has contributed to several projects and reports of the "Arctic Monitoring and Assessment Program (AMAP)". Both are colleagues in the same field and friends for common interests. Dr. Thomson gives some statistics on ice melting and greenhouse gas emissions. It was a casual discussion.

"Do you really think, Remi, that Polar Code is successful? It already failed to address greenhouse gas emissions. The report says that the DOD (Department of Defense) of the US emits the most GHG (greenhouse gas) in the world through War. Only the Pentagon emits more GHG than the whole US. I feel developed countries should contribute more quota for carbon credit, and they should be serious about it. The northern coast of Russia is already ice-free. Northwest Passage will be left with 50% of ice by 2030. Research says by 2050, even the North Pole and the entire Arctic will be ice-free in the summer," said Dr. Thomson

"I agree. Developed countries are hypocrites. They are not even ready to accept the seriousness of climate change. Paris's climate change withdrawal by the US was not at all acceptable. They are not contributing enough. Moreso, it is surprising that the US is not serious about climate change action but has increased its seriousness in the Arctic regions so suddenly. It is peculiar," stated Remi.

"The US wants to restrict its immediate competitors Russia and China in the region."

Den arrived and went inside the museum.

"Welcome, Den. I am not surprised that you ultimately could make it. You are always stubborn" Remi said, smiling.

She introduced Dr. Thomas to Den. One attendant offered him a cup of tea. They chatted for a few minutes. Dr. Thomson departed.

Remi realized the seriousness of Den coming to the far Arctic. "What is the matter, Den?" she asked as both of them walked out of the museum.

The landscape was adorned with majestic snow-covered trees, their branches bending under the weight of the glistening white snow. As daylight wanes, the hues of the sky shift, displaying a kaleidoscope of soft purples, blues and greens. They were approaching the long polar night. This was a frigid January month in the North West Territory of Canada. Streetlights were switched on throughout the days of winter.

Den got straight to the point. He expressed his concerns about the new assignment in Svalbard. "I feel that shipping conflict in the Arctic is a priority. Mike is wise. Let me consult with Chief once more. Chief may be offended. I want your input, Remi. I am not able to decide the priority between Hong Kong and Svalbard. What is going on here?"

"One thing is common in either agenda. There is business in the Arctic. Please come with me. Stay here for a couple of days and then decide. Dr. Thomson will also accompany us. We are planning a round trip through important Arctic Ports. There is a sudden surge in infrastructural development. Old ports are privatized and getting upgraded. New deep-water ports are being built in the Arctic ring, especially in NWP and NSR. There is a big business plan. The business has the lowest priority in terms of the environment. We want to evaluate the status. Join us."

"Yeah, there is a surge in military activity as well. Russian State military shipping company 'Oboronlogistika' has become very active and frequent these days in delivering goods to Russia's new Naval bases in the High Arctic. Even the US is ramping up. The US is planning a huge defense bill, especially for the Arctic, to build ports, manufacture icebreakers and establish military bases. I have information from some trustworthy sources that Vt Halter is going to get a few hundred million orders for icebreakers. There are serious activities."

"Good, you realized that all routes lead to the North Pole, whether it is Svalbard or shipping conflict or something else," Remi smiled again.

Preparation for Long Shaft

Arctic

Den applied for a ten-days leave and informed Chief that he had a personal emergency. Nobody knew that he would actually be accompanying Remi and Dr. Thomson for an expedition in the Arctic. Remi knows the nerves and blood of the polar circle. Den needs to spend some time in this region to understand more. There are events behind the curtain which are still unknown.

Den made a huge mistake. He already informed the UN admin for going to Iqaluit. His flight and where he was staying were arranged by the UN admin, meaning he might be tracked. He forgot that he kept the audit trail.

***

At the same time, in the Arctic, other activities were going on in secret. Goods for the few last consignments were being mobilized.

Barrow, Alaska

Gobin was waiting for the arrival of an important consignment. He has been posted on the north slope for the last two weeks and managing secret consignments through the north slope route. He is working in port as a technical hand, but he is mainly engaged in something else. Good mobilizations were happening from Nome, Alaska, to Barrow through the Bering Strait. His responsibility was to ensure a safe delivery. Actually, goods will be transferred from the submarine to the unmanned Poseidon underwater. Gobin is a local asset for 'polar bear'. He ensures logistics and rations. He, along with his men, were waiting on a boat in mid-sea. He was waiting for the arrival of the whale.

***

Taylor was sleeping in his berth. A submarine sleeper's berth is half-rack and is usually very narrow. Taylor is familiar with staying in submarines through his past naval experience and other expeditions, but he does not like this anymore. He is older now, and he feels suffocated and lonely in the berth. He was an important crew member in 'polar bear'. His was the engineer in-charge of shaft construction under the ocean. This was an Ohio class 175-meter submarine. This can carry 140 crew, ten missile tubes, and 100 torpedoes. But for now, this was carrying some equipment that needed to be delivered to specific sites. They started from Amchitka Island near the Bering Strait and were heading towards Barrow.

The crew were working in the sonar control room upstairs. The boat came to a place where they needed to station for a while and wait for the next signal. This was close to the continental shelf of Barrow, and the water depth was not too great. The whale arrived and came to a standstill 150 meters beneath the water's surface. This depth was risky as countries like China, Russia and the US have their own surveillance satellite to scan underwater up to 200 meters below. In fact, recently, China, through its Project Guanlan and the US, through NASA and the Defence Advanced Research Projects Agency (DARPA), achieved 'LIDAR' technology to detect submarines and other underwater objects up to a 500-meter depth.

Gobin got the signal from the submarine's crew. Fish nets were arranged over the water's surface to look as if they were fishermen and had come to hunt. Fish nets were specially designed to disrupt satellite surveillance. The fishing arrangement acted as a camouflage and created disruption for laser beams, so satellites could not understand what was going on beneath the sea.

One Poseidon came from the other side and moved closer to the hull of the submarine. Poseidon is an unmanned underwater vehicle. Large subs cannot move much in the Arctic passage because of the fragmented sea route. Even small ships also face challenges in passing through this route without an experienced icebreaker. So, Poseidon will carry the containers and deliver them to the destination site.

A two diver crew came out of the lockout trunk from the dry deck shelter. One diver was holding a remote control. He navigated the Poseidon to the storage shutter, getting the transhipment ready. Poseidon plugged into the storage shutter lockout trunk of the sub. Both the doors opened, and four containers were transferred from the sub to Poseidon. The storage shutter closed down, and Poseidon was pulled off. The diver crew then navigated Poseidon to its earlier position. They released the Poseidon as its autopilot mode and came back into the sub.

The sub will now head to Nuuk, Greenland, to drop off Taylor. Taylor has been stationed in this region for quite some time. He was taking care of constructing four shafts underwater and three secret petroleum reservoirs. He was originally from Nome and very familiar with the Arctic conditions and its extreme weather. On the other side, the carriage Poseidon was moving towards the 'Northwest passage'. It will deliver the first container to a site near the entry point of Northwest Passage between Blank Island & Melville Island, where the Northwest passage connects from Beaufort Sea to Baffin Bay. The Poseidon will have to deliver the other two containers to different sites around the Northwest passage.

IcEye Head Office, Espoo, Finland

Juha Olsen is a Section-3 intelligence officer. She works in the analytics division for North Pole geography. 'IcEye' emerged as a new reputable player in the field of Earth observation. They have their own SAR (synthetic aperture radar) satellite and collaborate with others for the task of maritime surveillance. They closely work with NOAA for vessel tracking, ice monitoring, and earth observation.

A yellow trigger rang in her computer, notifying her that the system captured some repeated events. Surveillance works in a methodical value chain. Nowadays, the imagery, or intercepts, are programmed with artificial intelligence. The system showed imagery similar to a submarine or marine vehicle. The location was spotted near Northwest Territories of Canada, 250 meters under the sea ice. This also had a previous trail of similar objects that had come to the same location earlier. Data said this was a small submarine. Previous logs say that the same sub has been visiting the same place for quite some time, and surprisingly, this stopped every time in specific locations in specific underwater depth. Juha became curious and started analyzing both imagery and data in detail. She studied the information for three hours and concluded, with immense surprise, that the sub ultimately stopped every time near a civil buildup. There was no human trail. This did not appear to be a SPAR platform or Floating Ice platform of any oil exploration, but this seemed to be the roof of a shaft. The shaft might be long and deep, but this could not be judged by a satellite bird's eye angle. This needed to be analyzed by data from a nearby acoustic transponder.

There were three lockout hatches visible on the shaft roof. Everytime the submarine seemed to reach the rooftop lockgate of the shaft and waited for a few minutes before the same departed from the location. Juha was sure by this time that this was suspicious activity and this needed to be flagged red. She found out from data that a nearby transponder was deployed by NOAA. Before she officially reported this to NOAA and asked for their help, she decided to check informally first. She approached her connection at NOAA and tried to investigate further. She needed more data to collaborate before final flagging.

After two days, Juha was able to collaborate with her connection on a final draft. She was astonished by the fact that all the three activities were very similar and the locations were spotted in Northwest passage. More specifically, all three spots were in 'Qikiqtaaluk' (Baffin region's coast of Greenland) and 'Kitikmeot' which are the heartland of NWP Trade route.

The second most interesting observation was that the moving submarine seemed to be a Russian Poseidon, but there was a little difference in shape and outer body. One cannot easily differentiate this, but an expert and experienced eye can catch the difference. This is rather similar to NOAA's small UUV fleet. Juha red-flagged the findings and reported them to the IcEye authority for further judgment.

She did not know that her effort will not even be considered but will rather be treated as a leak. The report was first classified by the authority with immediate effect, and then Juha's assignment was changed. She was not even aware that the spiderweb was bigger than she could imagine. The 'polar bear' cannot allow a single leak or probability of a leak. The team has deep roots and is operating on a large scale. They have connections in most of the government departments and locations to influence and manipulate anything they want.

***

Taylor just woke up. He managed a quick nap in the cabin. He took a cup of coffee from the vending machine and came to the sonar control room. The Navigation Controller, the Sonar Supervisor and the Diving Officer were leaning over the plotting table. They were busy managing the depth and direction. Other crew members were engaged in their respective consoles, and ballast tanks were getting ready as the sub was diving deep. There was a long and thick ice slab, and the sub needed to bypass this by diving down 1000 meters deep.

***

The sub reached its destination. The station was at a 700-meter depth and connected to a Floating Ice SPAR platform. This was one of many oil exploration stations by Zonmobil. Zonmobil has been very active in this Polar region and has quite a few stations for oil and gas exploration. They privately allowed a station for the submarine to connect to. Zonmobil has a vested interest in it. The submarine will be on standby here for some time for refuel and technical checks. There will be an exchange of a few crew and staff. Taylor and a few other staff took the lift and came upstairs to the surface deck.

Taylor went to his cabin. He has a workstation here, and being a senior engineer for the undercover mission, he hasd workstations in other oil rigs as well. This undercover racket spread its coverage throughout the region, and the entire system was compromised. He opened his laptop and switched to a different user. Different user means this leads to an encrypted cloud login where he signed in as C7. Each of the members has this private communication channel.

There was a video call from C3. Taylor needed to call him back. Taylor started up the video call.

"What's the update C7? We are not happy about the speed of withdrawal."

"Shafts are installed. That was the priority," Taylor said, frustrated.

"You were recruited not only for the installation of the base, but withdrawal is equally important. Timely withdrawal of the specific oil rigs was the agreed task for the investor. The company has to re-use the asset. The migration process is still slow. It is going as per your old age!" C3 seemed to be annoyed with Taylor.

Taylor yelled, rolling his eyes. "Please understand that there are some serious bottlenecks, hence the delay. Work is going on in full swing. I already reported the progress and action points last week. A few stations are almost on the verge of closure. Work is in progress for other targeted rigs as per the plan."

"Work is extremely slow on the west coast of Greenland. This is a core area of NWP, and we can't afford any mistakes out there," C3 shouted.

"We are waiting for a critical decision to be made. The committee is aware of this complexity. This zone has quite a number of oil rigs. We just cannot withdraw one or two specific stations, whereas the others continue to run with prospects. Both the Greenland Government, through its NUNAOIL arm, and other private JV partners have a vested interest in the zone. The latest licensing round for new underwater mining in the Southwest and West Coast of Greenland was just completed, and it is not easy to convince all the stakeholders. We are negotiating and still searching for a reason to escape. We are trying really hard."

"China has a vested interest, but they have a good investment in Greenland. Don't expect cooperation from them. Even Denmark's lobby, especially the President, may not at all cooperate to build pressure on Greenland."

Taylor tried to argue, "Only Zonmobil is cooperating. Most of the target rigs belong to their operation. But the other strong competition, Cairn, who is already active in the Southwest zone, is interfering with buyouts. They create many hurdles in our ability to withdraw!"

"We cannot take this lightly. Denmark's Prime Minister- **Mr Mett Fred** is also choking us. We will separately take care of him soon."

"I don't think that Denmark has any role here!" Taylor said, trying to defend Denmark.

"You concentrate on your job. Use your mind. We are running out of time. Create an oil spill! We will spread the news in the media that, technically, this can't be repaired, and the company decides to withdraw. Now, do not cry that an oil spill would damage the environment and marine life. Give up this bullshit and do what's needed. Do you have any idea how much and how thick these companies are getting paid to compromise the existing business in terms of the withdrawal of a few stations? We have an alternative, better, arrangement for them," C3 smiled.

"I am trying to fast-track, but I cannot satisfy all the parties in the consortium," Taylor replied.

"The investor list is big. The consortium is formed out of several powerhouses, and as you know, they are big brothers. Their governments bet big for a larger piece of the profit pie, and they may lose patience if we do not complete the program timely and effectively. All of us are hypothecated to their investment commitment. It is a complicated consortium. So do it fast. We cannot lose them, but we do not mind losing you."

They discussed for another few minutes before completing the call. Zonmobil officials will be meeting 'Nunaoil' engineers and some Government diplomats in Nuuk. C3 instructed Taylor to meet them in person and manage the situation.

Taylor's mood was off, and he unloaded his anger on some of his team members. He told the station masters to finish the job as soon as possible. He was also worried about the Denmark PM for a reason. He felt that he himself should attend the site immediately. Before that, he must attend the meeting of Zonmobil and Nunaoil with the Government officers. He made the arrangement and called a helicopter for Nuuk.

***

On the other side, Poseidon completed the last trip in delivering the other consignments to the designated destinations.

Leads | First Round

Nuuk, Greenland

Den ordered a hot chocolate. He was in the cafe of the Katuaq Cultural Centre. It was extremely cold outside. Arctic areas are fully ice covered in January. The long polar night makes the peak winter more extreme. Remi, Dr. Thomson and Den were staying in 'Nuuk City Hostel'. There were quite a few hostel accommodations in Nuuk for explorers and tourists. Remi had an appointment at the National Library, so she left the hostel earlier that day. Dr. Thomson went to the middle of Baffin Bay for his research. They arrived yesterday from Iqaluit and planned on staying in Nuuk for a couple of days.

A group of tourists were also sitting inside the cafe. They were talking among themselves about a nearby incident. There was a public protest going on near Nuuk Cathedral. Den decided to check it out. It was a five-minute walk. He headed towards the commotion. He was now able to hear the noise of the crowd. There was one gathering near the 'Statue of Hans Egede'. This is on the hilltop, just after the Nuuk Cathedral. The weather was very foggy, and visibility was poor. He sped up.

There was a group of local Inuits showing agitation against the police. Den tried to understand the reason for the protest. He asked a local guy.

The local person replied in broken English, "Sir, there is an oil spill nearby. One boat caused the accident. They went into the sea for whale hunting. Three people are seriously injured and were taken to the hospital. The other survivor claimed that it was not a simple accident. The fishermen saw a submarine coming out of the sea. The submarine and the boat collided. They both argued, and suddenly, an oil spill started with a subsequent fire. But before that, somebody shot at our men. They had a pistol."

"Shooting?" Den was surprised by the shooting.

"Yes. One fisherman was seriously injured. All of us now assembled here to protest. The administration is trying to defend the situation."

The protest escalated when the Police started beating a few protesters. The mob became more furious. Den realized the degree of trouble. He went to a senior police officer and showed his ID card. The police officer allowed him to address the crowd and try to get them to calm down, but Den made another mistake by disclosing his identity. This would be reported later, and he would be kept under surveillance by Greenland government.

The crowd was still vocal. Someone shouted, "We know that this was not a simple accident. This is all because of American-Chinese companies. This is manmade." The old gentleman came with a placard. It is written, 'Oil companies and shipping companies are vampires! The government became the broker of Zonmobil, Cairn, Maersk, COSCO and all these private giants. They are climate traders for profit!'

He again voiced his protest: "On the front stage, they pledge for environment protocol, but on the backstage, they only mean business. They are destroying our land!"

The crowd supported him loudly. The police were still trying to convince the protesters to calm down. The policeman whispered to Den, "He is a local teacher- **Sir Bill Jodman**. We see him in all environmental rallies and activities. Locally, he is a respected and influential figure."

Den also observed that the person was accurate. The other normal people would have simply called out 'companies', but this person called out specific companies. The person was well informed about Greenland and its surrounding industrialization.

Den assured the crowd that police and local administration would address all the concerns of the local people and protesters. Police will cooperate and investigate. However, Den was not a party to this incident. He engaged himself from the moral ground. He was curious about Sir Jodman.

Den went over to him and exchanged his card. "Sir, I admire your concern. I am not from this region. I came here as a tourist along with an expedition team. Can we meet, Sir?"

At present, Sir Jodman was jittery and annoyed. He hesitated for a while and then invited Den to his home at noon after lunch.

***

Information on Nuuk agitation was reported. Deputy PM of Greenland, **Minik Kenoguv**, was accumulating all the information. Minik was closely tracking the situation so that it did not feel much for further protest.

Greenland is the constituent government of Denmark. The PM of Greenland- **Kim Kielsen** and the PM of Denmark were not in favor of agreeing to the US's proposal of buying Greenland from Denmark. Although Deputy PM Minik was in favor of trade-off. He wanted to ruin the existing governments and take over the power by himself. Naturally, he became part of the nexus. Minik was well aware of the fact that the recent oil spill was man-made, and this was done by Zonmobil intentionally. Minik, along with top officials of Canada, were controlling safe passage for the 'polar bear' and ensuring the secrecy from the public. For any such confidential task force, recruiting the correct asset is very critical. They trade-off. They buy the person either with money or ambition. Minik had a vested interest in altering the legislative Government of Greenland.

Minik keeps an eye on Sir Jodman and hates his rebel attitude. They are not in good terms. The presence of one UN personnel- Mr Den Smil was also reported. Minik, for further validation, passed the information to C3. For Minik, 'Den Smil' was a new person.

***

The housing at Nuuk is colorful. Most houses have gabled roofs. Usually, supply stores, churches, schools and social architecture are painted red, hospitals are yellow and municipal buildings or any other government buildings are blue. Sir Jodman stays in a posh colony. These houses have hip roofs and little expensive construction. Most of the upper-class of Nuuk stay in this part of the city.

Den knocked on the door. Mrs Jodman opened the door. Den greeted her, "Madam, I am Den Smil." He told her his purpose for coming.

"Come inside. Please wait here. Sir is with someone. His friend had come to meet him. Please excuse him for a few more minutes," Madam went inside the home.

The drawing room was small but neatly organized. A wooden desk, adorned with neatly arranged journals and books, occupied a prominent position in the room. The walls, crafted from sturdy timber, exude a natural charm that blends harmoniously with the surrounding Arctic environment. There were four armchairs placed near a crackling fireplace. Den chose one to sit comfortably. Now, he will have to wait. The fire's gentle warmth provided respite from the biting cold outside, while the dancing flames created an ambience.

A mild voice was coming from upstairs. This was a duplex hut. There were two voices. One was of Sir Jodman. He was talking to someone who might be his friend. There might be a casual discussion between two friends. Den concentrated on the bookshelf. He took out a journal.

A sudden loud word startled him. "I am not responsible for this mishap! Although I was asked to do it, I was not in favor, but somebody had done this oil spill before my team did. That Russian wolf," the gentleman abused someone with a loud voice. This was an unknown voice and might be of the friend.

Sir Jodman replied, "You still have time, Mob. Come out of this nuance. You were dragged into the crime."

Den understood that the friend's name was Mob.

"I hate Russia," Mob shouted.

"But your immediate authority is a Russian! Give up this hatred, Mob. You are an old man now. You should be a sensitive person."

There was silence for a while.

"You are hiding," Sir Jodman continued.

"So what! I have my own commitment and will do my task."

"What kind of task is it? I may know half of it as you tell me the portion of it from time to time. I am sure that you are also exposed to half of it. Whoever recruited you, do not trust them fully. Ultimately, you guys are destroying the natural environment for the sake of business. You also know that it is your employer corporation that did this man made oil spill. This is not just one. They keep doing these things to achieve their business goal by whatever means. They do not care."

Den was waiting. He lost concentration in the IMO journal. He was listening to an interesting conversation.

"Environment! Climate! Earth! Who cares!" Mob wondered. "I was present at the Poland climate conference, and I will probably take part in the upcoming COP25 in Italy as well. I know that all these are a hoax."

Den was astonished to hear that the stranger was present at the Katowice climate conference in Poland.

Mob continued, "Developed countries are hypocrites. The US not only denied climate change by withdrawing from the Paris Agreement, but they also continued ignorance of all previous environmental policies and carbon credit. Other superpowers, China, Russia, the UK and France, reduced their carbon contribution, and they arrange such stage shows every year on a large scale. I already told you that this is a hoax. On the contrary, they among themselves create a business nexus and leverage underground. We cannot break this business syndicate. Life goes on. This is practical. I get paid. I am doing my assignment."

"On the other side of the coin, there is war and conflicts. Whom do you trust? All are battling for their own interest in the Arctic. Instead of renewable energy, they all are investing in more oil and gas exploration, new icebreaker fleets and cargo ships. Do not be a party to this. Care for the next generation, Mob." Sir Jodman said.

"Jid, don't blame me. There are multiple criminals. I am doing my job. You know I hate Russians. I also do not support the way the US deployed a permanent military base along with Nato troops in Poland. The US is investing in 5G infra in Poland and convinced Poland to support sanctions on Iran and Russia. The fact is, the US will keep the economic restriction on Iran and Russia by all possible means because Iran is influential in the Suez Canal trade route, and Russia controls the northern sea trade route. Both of the trade routes are the present lifeline of maritime shipping transport and commerce globally," Mob said.

"This was done because Russia was constantly increasing its influence over Poland and East Germany. Everybody is getting aggressive. If the US loses Germany, the US will keep Poland at any cost to their favor. It is the obvious choice," Sir Jodman argued.

"Of course. Global business has now evolved beyond the traditional European market. China is the largest exporter. The US is the largest importer. China is playing a big bet on Italy and Greece to increase its influence in Europe. It is a debt trap. The US may compromise Europe partially and prepare more for East and Pacific markets. Russia is finding its way to survive in the new pattern of market economy. There are tensions in the Middle East and Eurasia. Everybody is exploring new combinations of geo economy. So, our project at this juncture is extremely meaningful. Europe is a mess. A new market is required. So is a new trade route."

"So, Europeans don't invade others anymore? Rather, others are invading Europe? Times are changing!" Sir Jodman said sarcastically.

Den came close to the door to hear the conversation clearly. Although the voices were not very loud, Den was able to make it out. It was also interesting that the friend of Sir Jodman was extremely updated. It seems that he was engaged in a particular assignment that might be linked to this Arctic circle. This indicates a complex geopolitics in the backdoor.

"NATO is losing its relevance to defend Western European countries from Russia because the position is changing. There is a strategic formation of artificial conflicts in Europe, so a few European countries are looking for alternative investors. Brexit was a natural choice. The European Union or the West European countries need an alternative rescue package. This is a new rule of invasion. China may not like to confront East Europe and keep space for Russia. Rather, China finds alternative routes and tricks for going to Western Europe. The US and NATO will restrict Russia from Western Europe and compromise some space for the benefit of China. There will be a new combination and consolidation of powers in Europe soon," Sir Jodman said.

"No, there will be a change of power," Mob replied.

"Either way, whether it is consolidation or change, the world wants alternative routes and benefits for business. The Arctic is the new frontier. Greenland, Iceland, Norway and Denmark within the Arctic Circle are recent investment zones. But we have to defend our own sovereignty too. Why do we lose our land to foreign business Invaders everytime!"

"You are not losing, Jid. You are selling. Somebody is buying and paying the price."

"The indigenous people are paying the price of life. This is only because they are not clever. They still do not know the tricks to compete with the corporations." Sir Jodman said, frustrated.

"We cannot deny this truth. You are correct, Jid, but business must go on. Somebody has to grow at the cost of others. Everybody and every country is compromising for something."

"So, who has been compromised the most?"

"Canada. It is not their survival. It is their growth ambition." Mob replied.

Both were taking slight pauses during the chat. They might be having some drinks.

Sir Jodman took in the view. "Canada is developing with a new speed," Sir Jodman flouted, "huge no of ports throughout the north slope and northwest territory is being made. Don't you think it is US debt? Or you call this US donation!"

"The US is a businessman and never invests without having a proposal of sufficient return. Although there are several lobbyists. Arctic countries are divided. Economic sponsorship and political influence from different allied nations are key investors for the Arctic."

"These combinations are really interesting, Mob. Russia has deepened its influence in Norway and Svalbard. The US is trying to penetrate Greenland and hence created pressure on Denmark. I wish Nuuk becomes independent from Denmark one day." Sir Jodman said with a hope.

"We are opening up for a new trade sea route. Greenland and its parent Denmark government will play a significant role in this. Preparations for this are going on."

"The oil spill is the preparation!"

"The oil spill is nothing. The game plan is big. I am apprehended for change of both Denmark and Greenland governments. This will be decided very soon." Mob reacted.

"Where is your private meeting?" Sir Jodman asked.

"I am not supposed to disclose that. It is dangerous. It will be closely held between investors."

"You should say that the conspirators will assemble for a global crime."

"Whatever it's called, fate will be decided. This is going to be held in Svalbard."

"You are completely sold out, Mob. You are aware of the risk, and you still continue to be a party to this! Don't you know that Mett is under immense pressure?" Sir Jodman asked. Sir Jodman was angry.

There was silence for a while, and then Mob replied, "Mett is not safe."

"Nobody and nothing is safe in your business. Mett himself is not sure if he will be reelected as Prime Minister in the upcoming election in Denmark. He is still defending selling Greenland to the hands of the business mafia. He may not hold it for long. We actually do not battle for land because ownership of land is political and hand-exchanged. This land belongs to Nature, and we should save this land before it gets completely ruined and exhausted by diplomats. It is not global warming. It is not climate change. Ownership of the Arctic is getting changed. New owners are changing their landscape from Nature to business. The Arctic is burning. Realize that fast." Sir Jodman was exhausted.

There was silence for a longer minute. Mrs Jodman might have entered the room and reminded Sir Jodman that a guest was waiting. Sir Jodman was forgetful. Now he asked his friend to wait for some time since he had to attend to his guest.

Den tried to digest what he had just heard in the last fifteen minutes. His presence was a coincidence. He realized that his visit with Remi and a trip to the Arctic might be accidental, but he was able to witness some signals of geopolitical chaos which was going on behind the curtain. At this stage, it was difficult for him to correlate all the facts, but by this time, he was able to decide that he had to find out the means to attend the secret meeting of Svalbard. He could smell the importance of the meeting. Chief already gave him an assignment for Svalbard. But he should not open up everything to Chief at this stage. Who knew the consequences that could happen? Nobody was trustworthy.

Sir Jodman entered, "Hey, young man, I am sorry you had to wait. I had a guest and was attending to him."

"No issues, Sir. Thank you for agreeing to meet."

"What can I do for you?"

They both started a casual discussion. Den's agenda was different. He already got a sense that the stranger Mob was one key asset for the said business syndicate, which was in the secret task to change the industrial fate of the Polar region. Mob knew some classified information. This might be an industrial, political nexus. He should trick Sir Jodman into reaching out to Mob at any cost.

Den played the climate card. "Sir, we need your support for our research. My friend Ms Remi Larsen is writing a book on Arctic and Arctic business. We are helping her gather information. Dr. Thomson of Tromso University has also come along with us."

"Oh yeah, I heard about Dr. Thomson. But you said you are working in the UN!"

"Yes, Sir, but this is not my UN assignment. I was a war correspondent earlier and now work in the UN. I often volunteer for this kind of activity. The Earth is a priority."

Sir Jodman looked at Den brightly. He was impressed by Den. He offered, "Can I prepare you tea?"

"No, Sir, thank you. You are an eminent climate activist in this region. So, I thought of meeting you. It is my pleasure."

Den knew that initial ice-breaking was important. He just could not jump into his agenda, so he was trying to engage Sir Jodman casually for the first few minutes. He knew that he had to trick Sir Jodman emotionally, or else Jodman would not open up.

"Greenland is getting deeply impacted by global warming. Still, this region is very active with industrial outfits. Nowadays, this is accelerated. What is your opinion, Sir?" Den pushed his question.

"Industry is not just a simple hypocrisy. Industry often hides and lies as well. They do business, after all." Sir Jodman replied.

Den tried to push Sir Jodman more, "Surely. Business and politics go hand in hand in this kind of pact. So, do you witness political influence here?"

"Of course. It is not about Greenland but the entire polar circle. Arctic affairs are not like they used to be. Only a few years ago, the remote region on top of the world was comfortably quiet. Isolation from extreme weather was a blessing. Today, it is increasingly embraced by disturbing and inter-state tension. The Arctic is no longer only regional affairs. It has become the epicenter of big-power politics. It is climate change that is the main driver of new prospects and damage. Business classes are leveraging this at full speed. Unless the right decisions are taken, the Arctic could ultimately slip into bigger unrest." Sir Jodman said.

"Are the right decisions being taken?" Den pushed further.

"Yeah, why not? World powers are very serious. They do climate conferences every year," Sir Jodman showed his frustration with this sarcastic comment.

"What do you think? Yesterday's protest was a routine affair! Day by day, this land and water are getting colonized by private investors. We already lost it. There is no way back. The territory has shown her prospect, and automatically, we lost all our rights to new invaders! They will capture us!" Sir Jodman was breathing hard.

Den got the opportunity. This was the right moment to penetrate someone's mind. Sir Jodman was psychologically weak at this emotional moment.

"Sir, your eyes are trustworthy. I want to support your movement," Den mellowed down his voice. "In the coming week, Svalbard will celebrate its 100-year anniversary of the 'Svalbard Treaty' over a few days. A few diplomatic programs and functions are organized. Parallelly, Svalbard is undergoing a lot of political disputes and conflicts. I am assigned by the UN to get involved there. I have news that there is a confidential meeting organized among a few corporations and country officials. At the backdoor of the trade fair, some governments or somebody might have plotted a conspiracy. An investment consortium was formed to capture the Arctic. I have yet to get a detailed outfit, but it is clear that they will finally authorize their blueprint in that meeting. If they succeed, it will change the fate of Earth. There might be representation from your Greenland as well."

Den wanted to judge if Sir Jodman was surprised to hear 'Svalbard meeting' from a stranger. Sir Jodman still did not know that Den had already heard their conversation where Mob mentioned this top-secret meeting in Svalbard.

"How do you know all of this?" Sir Jodman was surprised. He was still looking at Den through his thick spec glass.

"Sir, if you all want to defend the sovereignty of Greenland and the Arctic Circle, help me with the information that you know. The more you suppress, the more you lose your land. I am trying to get an entry route for the Svalbard meeting. It is a must. Please keep in your mind to share important leads with me if you come across anything."

***

Sir Jodman was nervous. He tried to correlate his friend's version with this stranger's. Den was a stranger to him, but the facts coincided. He was failing his nerves. He could not disclose the coincidence that his own friend was present in his house at this moment, and his friend was one participant in the confidential meeting at Svalbard. He could not open up upfront to a stranger that his own friend might be a party to the conspiracy.

He replied after a while, "Mr Den, better if you come tomorrow. I am in a hurry as my guest is waiting in the living room. Kindly excuse me. Let's discuss this tomorrow."

Den thanked him and departed. His job was done. He was able to push Svalbard into Sir Jodman's mind. Den was tensed on the fact that the circumstances were dragging him into an unknown agenda of global conflict. This resembles his earlier days of investigative journalism and field coverage of crisis zones. He could smell a mole in the system. Something was going wrong.

***

Sir Jodman updated his friend that his recent guest- Mr Den Smil was aware of the Svalbard meeting.

***

Den updated Remi on his recent introduction with Sir Jodman and his findings.

"I shall find out the coordinates of Mob. He was one delegate at the Poland climate conference."

"But how do you manage information for the Svalbard meeting?" Remi asked.

Den admitted that this was tough. Something was being cooked. Time was less, but he had to manage an entry pass at any cost.

***

Den and Remi were having evening tea. Tea time in Nuuk during the winter evening serves as a cherished ritual, a time to pause, connect and find solace in the simple pleasures of life. It is a moment to appreciate the beauty of the Arctic surroundings while creating lasting memories and fostering a sense of community in the heart of winter's embrace. The room was adorned with thick rugs and plush cushions, offering a cozy retreat from the crisp cold of the evening. A small table was set with delicate teacups, moose burgers and a traditional cake made with dried berries. Remi and Den were enjoying the evening.

The bombshell quickly came thereafter. Dr. Thomson came from outside screaming.

"What happened, Thomson?" Remi wondered. Den kept the cup over the nearby table.

"You have not heard yet? Turn on the news immediately! Iran Army Chief Sulemani was killed by a US drone attack. The PM of Denmark, Mr Mett, was also killed in a car accident!" Dr. Thomson yelled.

"What!" Remi switched on the television.

Den tried to guess the consequences of the accident. Even with his mobile kept on the nearby table, he missed the update.

All channels were covering the news of both events. Sulemani was head of the Kurds group and the Iran Revolutionary Army. He was very popular inside Iran. He fought against ISIS and was stationed in Iraq. Iran is expanding, and the situation is vulnerable. The US made a quick decision to eliminate him. The attack on Sulemani was straightforward. He was spotted by a US drone and hit by a missile.

The sudden car accident that killed Mr Mett was very unfortunate. The convoy was coming from Sweden via the 'Oresund Bridge' and heading towards Copenhagen when the accident happened. The bridge over the Baltic Sea has a unique stretch of four kilometers, which goes under the sea through the underwater 'Drogden Tunnel', where the accident took place. Mett had a meeting in Malmo with Swedish and Finnish diplomats in the presence of NATO senior officers. There is international pressure on Sweden and Finland to join NATO. A US lobbyist was trying to push these Nordic countries to leave war neutrality. Russia influenced Mr Mett to intermediate the lobbyist. The Russian PM had a close relationship and tie-up with Mr Mett and the Danish government through the present Nord Stream gas pipeline project. This new Nordic friendship became stronger when they got German support. It was a natural phenomenon that Washington was not taking lightly, but geopolitics is not simple either. International friendship doesn't go hand in hand with simple, clear bifurcation of parties. Reality often differs from perception in politics. Truth in this case is stranger than fiction.

Everybody was silent in the room. There was only sound from the television and a slight sound of a gentle cold breeze outside. Remi broke the ice-cold silence.

"Are these two incidences correlated?" Remi asked.

"Certainly not. The US couldn't take the risk of killing two targets at the same time," Den replied.

Reporters on the news started assessing different possibilities of the attack. Remi and Dr. Thomson were also debating on the motives and possible scenarios amongst themselves. Den became aloof for a while. He was wondering if all these were interconnected and whether they had a common purpose.

He was not able to find any correlation. There has been tension between Iran and the US in recent times. Sulemani was a popular leader and a strong man in the Army. The US didn't want to take too much of a chance and delay their next move. The more they delay, the more they put Israel's election at risk for going beyond their control. Sulemani was one mastermind in the Arab Spring. Sulemani was fighting his own battle in Iraq to push America out of the Middle East's war terrain. He also might have been a big threat to disrupt the Golan's height of diplomacy in Israel and might have created problems for Jerusalem. He was a priority candidate on the superpower's killing list.

On the other hand, Denmark is neither a war zone nor a politically conflicting region yet. Den doubted if it was only a mere car accident, though. He recollected the conversation between Sir Jodman and his friend Mob. There was already a hint about a threat to the Danish PM's life. The stranger Mob was a key link. He surely knew a lot of undercover secrets. Den's immediate task was now to talk to Mr Mob by some means.

***

Early in the morning the next day, Den went to Sir Jodman. He rang the doorbell.

Sir Jodman himself opened the door, "Oh, please come inside,"

He was having breakfast. He offered white bean soup to Den also.

"No, Sir, thank you. I came in a hurry," Den replied.

Sir Jodman looked at Den curiously. Den came to the decision that he should be frank and upfront with Sir Jodman this time, or else he couldn't push Sir Jodman to connect him with Mr Mob.

"Sir, I came to surrender," Den tried to break him emotionally.

Den continued, "I represent the United Nations. We failed in a lot of areas. We could not save the 'Polar Code'. We couldn't save Greenland nor the Arctic because we could not save Denmark."

Sir Jodman's eyes were upset. He was not able to express a reply. It was probably anger and sorrow.

"Can I offer you tea?" Sir Jodman asked.

"Yes, Thanks." Den agreed for a cup of tea. He wanted to spend some more time with Sir Jodman.

Sir Jodman was completely silent. This was a typical stage of psychological breakdown. Sir Jodman silently poured tea into the cups and offered one cup to Den. Den had a hunch that Sir Jodman would open up shortly.

"Sir, thank you," Den took his first sip, "The entire world is morose about the death of Mr Mett. We are surprised that people were desperate to kill Mr Mett whereas we do not see him as a global threat."

Sir Jodman now seriously looked at Den, "But it was a car accident."

"Didn't you know that Mr Mett was not safe? He was killed!" Den exclaimed.

"Do you know what you are saying, young man?"

"I have information. There is a threat to the Arctic. I do not know if these are correlated, but I am getting a hint that Greenland is sitting over a melting volcano of ice. If this explodes, this will change the fate of the Earth. There is a game plan, though."

"Who are you?" Sir Jodman was firm this time and asked directly.

"I work in the secretariat department of the United Nations. I was a war correspondent for a few years. Then I joined the United Nations. Please extend your help to me. I want to dive deep into this conspiracy. My sense is that a massive conspiracy is being planned. Let's volunteer to investigate the secrets. Trust me, I will not let you down. You are serious about saving the Earth. This is a high time that you should save without any delay!"

Sir Jodman heard Den patiently and then replied after a long silence, "What do you want?"

Den told everything to Jodman to gain his trust. He started from his original assignment given by the UN Chief for going to Svalbard. Svalbard is the epicenter of the Arctic Circle and may come across political instability very soon due to Russian diplomacy and activity. Countries are aggressively trying to control the Arctic for future economic power. The Arctic is also a top priority for the UN to keep the region insulated from economic and war aggression. The sovereignty of Svalbard is very critical for keeping the peace and neutrality at the North Pole. That is why the UN is serious about saving the Arctic.

He also elaborated that the US principal state secretary- Mike Power asked him to be engaged in a Chinese camp to gather information on their shipping strategy and conflict. China is increasing its aggression and activities in the polar region. For both the US and the UN, the respective authority wants someone to accumulate sensitive information. Ultimately, this intelligence will be used for the benefit of the peacekeeping agenda of the Arctic Circle.

He also told Sir Jodman that he took unofficial leave to accompany Remi. Den being in Greenland was very coincidental. They were in Iqaluit before coming to Nuuk. Remi and Den both had plans to make a round trip within the northern territory for a couple of days. He got involved by chance. He also admitted that yesterday, he could hear part of the conversation between Sir Jodman and his friend Mob.

Den thought that Sir Jodman would get excited after hearing all of this from him, but Sir Jodman was still reserved.

Sir Jodman kept eating and completed the fruit salad. Den was a stranger to him, but he understood that Den might be an effective person at this stage who can solve some critical conflicts. With his help, Sir Jodman could try to change Mob's mind back to goodness. Mob is his close friend, after all, but he cannot just disclose everything to this stranger about Mob. He hesitated to decide.

"You can go now. Excuse me, I am not feeling well. I have a little fever and need rest," Sir Jodman said, tensed. He was not able to decide. Even If Mob was part of some crime or secret task, his heart did not approve of blowing his friend's cover.

"Ok, Sir. Whenever you feel ready, please call me. Your friend Mob knows a lot, and he can lead us to key findings in the secret mission. Please think about it, Sir. I hope you understand that we do not have much time. Good day," Den said as he departed.

Sir Jodman saw Den going till he was invisible in the mist. He also had a secret. He hid that Mob, Mett and himself were close friends. After the Denmark incident, Mob was broken down. Sir Jodman knew that for now, at least he could influence Mob to realize that he was on a dangerous team. His team leaders were planning a nasty game, with or without him. They were brutal, clever, and ruthless. They probably killed Mett first and now will kill the Arctic.

Sir Jodman rang his friend and mentioned the scope of using Den Smil, a UN official who would volunteer to get involved in this situation, to investigate. He tried to convince Mob that the syndication for which Mob works was doing a double cross. There might be a specific motive behind the assassination of Denmark's PM, which might be directly linked to Mob's secret task and the recent spate of industrial politics in the Arctic Circle. Together, they could find out the nexus.

***

Mob was mentally devastated. He had hints from the syndication leader that very soon, the constituent governments of Greenland and Denmark might be seeing a change. He could not believe that something of this stature would happen. Sir Jodman asked Mob to take Den Smil along to the Svalbard meeting. Mob might not be able to handle it alone. Better Den Smil would accompany him as a support. Sir Jodman was sure that in the secret Svalbard meeting, the syndication was going to disclose and discuss a few crucial actionable plans. They would surely discuss openly and in detail with corporate investors and political state heads. If the mastermind key head will be present in person, both Mob and Den Smil will get a chance to witness the detailed game plan. They should not miss this opportunity. There was a high chance that in the meeting they will witness a lot of known faces of world politics and business houses which were under masks. Mob understood the intensity and agreed to take Den Smil alongwith.

The fact was, it was not just an unfortunate accident but the Danish PM was assassinated. There was neither any immediate proof, and nobody knew that this was just one part of the bigger conspiracy. Apparently, it seems that some isolated events were not correlated, but the conspiracy of geopolitics was never linear. The complexity spread across geography, and connecting the dots of the string was equally complicated.

Mob made a huge mistake. He rang the syndication leader and got into a confrontation. He was equally morose on his friend's death. He accused the leader of being directly involved in killing Denmark's PM. He lost his patience and temper. And he decided to attend the funeral of his friend. This would not go well for the fate of Mob. The relationship of Mob with his syndication leaders has not been great recently. The leaders started doubting his loyalty. The direct confrontation would lead to a fatal consequence. The private employer would have simply taken off the job. This time, the syndication would take his life. They will never keep the risky asset.

Leak and Mislead

Ethiopia meeting

The escalation of tension between the US and Iran put all the intelligence agencies of the world on their toes. Tension escalated further to a probable revenge attack by Iran for the assassination of Sulemani by the US military. On the other side, the world was extremely confused because of the ambiguous attempt on peaceful Denmark. Speculation was flying about whether it was an accident or an assassination. People failed to find out the motive and links. Intelligence agencies and Interpol started a marathon investigation around the globe using Interpol, which was used for linking up available information and crime records.

Although there was no clear motive to doubt the accident, experts tried to link up and invent political reasons. This was a peculiar situation. On one hand, there was speculation of a terrorist attack, and governments were clashing amongst each other with diplomatic accusations. The US pointed a finger at Russia and China. Russia and China pointed a finger at the US. There were several schools of thought for the involvement of Israel or Saudi Arabia. One accident changed the equilibrium between countries.

Intelligence agencies were collecting numerous amounts of information. The intensity of the field investigation had gone up heavily across the world. 'Polar bear' will now move slowly and more consciously. The recruits and assets across different regions would not be able to move as easily now. Even the logistics and communication channels were required to be rearranged. Several important tasks were kept at a standstill. The risk was higher now. C1 instructed for an urgent meetup. C3 called for an immediate field meeting.

The syndication aggregated each possible leak. They not only depended on field information but also collaborated through satellite surveillance. A confidential report was prepared and sent to C1. The report alarmed suspects and spotted a few of them as a threat.

Sleipner Gas field station, North Sea

The syndicate assembled in the gas field station in the middle of the North Sea. A large gas pipeline project is serving energy from Norway's continental shelf to England. Mastermind C1 doesn't go to all the meetings. He usually dictates from behind. C3 spearheads the field meetings. First, they addressed the pendency of the project. Although the mobilization of goods in the sites already took place, rig withdrawal activities were on hold after the Denmark incident. Leaders decided to compromise some sites and keep the debris and half-broken platforms untouched underwater. There was less time to complete the mission, and the work was very risky in this situation. Rather, they will explain the situation to the companies in the upcoming 'Svalbard meeting'. Companies will demand compensation or equivalent benefits.

"Only balls and switches are pending to be delivered. All other important action points are almost on schedule," C3 was addressing the meeting, "but time is running out. We need to be fast but cautious. We are changing routes and some responsibilities. The Denmark incident brought significant opportunities for us. Now, we can surround Greenland, but this is a classified objective, and we are not discussing this here. Let us concentrate on the mission. A report has come where we see some leaks. Taylor is one. We are replacing him."

C3 then introduced **Mr Mac Metesky** and resumed his speech, "Mac is younger and has extensive experience in underwater mining, installation, and machinery. We recruited him from the 'Langeled Gas Pipeline Project'. He is officially working for Gassco-Statoil and is stationed in the Sleipner gas field. He is now our asset and will devote some crucial time for us," C3 smiled towards Mac.

C3 continued, "Although a major portion of Taylor's responsibility in building the underwater shaft is already achieved, Taylor is too old, and he has not been reacting correctly in the last few days. We can give him up at this stage. He knows everything, and he also knows who C1 is. He is considered a threat now. We will take care of him. Cooperate with Mac. We were informed of another gentleman named 'Mr Den Smil' who is a UN officer and is visiting our region quite frequently. He is sharp, and he is collecting information. We will need to be mindful of Mr Den."

After Minik, Greenland's deputy PM, reported all the incidents and events of Nuuk, they put Den under surveillance and did another background check. It was revealed that Den took leave from the UN for a few days and has been visiting the Arctic region. Before Nuuk, he was in Iqaluit. Den's travel itinerary was managed by UN admins, and they leaked this information. The syndicate has deep assets in satellite vigilance. Staff of satellite stations work for the syndicate. A political group controls the satellite networks of different agencies. This has deep roots. In the background of their information-sharing protocol and agreement with different countries, they actually camouflaged the system with a different purpose. The law makers hid sensitive imagery as per their choice and decision. These classified leads are immensely valuable, and they use this under their own control and discretion. This vigilance report depicted the detailed movement of Den. This also reported his meeting with Sir Jodman and his stay in Hans Egede with Remi Larsen and Dr. Thomson. Den didn't even realize that he was being tracked.

"We have plans for both Taylor and Den Smil. One has lost his value, and the other one is a threat. We will eliminate both. But before that, we will trap them and play a game," C3 smiled cleverly. The meeting continued for another hour, detailing pending tasks. As per instruction and plan, they also changed the venue of the 'Svalbard meeting' to Ethiopia.

***

Den was winding up from Nuuk. Remi and Dr. Thomson will catch a flight tomorrow for their next destination in Iceland. And Den will fly back to Hong Kong. He decided to pursue the task given by Chief for Svalbard. Something is going on there. He was arranging his bag when he got the call from Chief. Even though the signal was not strong, they were still able to talk.

"Den, where are you?" Chief asked with annoyance in his voice. "You just took leave, and there is no trace of you since then! We need you urgently. There are situations. We have the Security Council meeting in the coming week. You already know that I have an assignment for you. An important task."

"Sorry, Sir, I was engaged in something serious. I am winding up to join back. Please guide me on my Svalbard assignment."

"No, there is a change in plan. You do not need to pursue the labor dispute case in Svalbard anymore. There is a new priority that needs immediate attention. We got a lead that a special meeting is being organized in Ethiopia, and few corporations along with their delegates will join together there, some political diplomats may also attend. We are not sure whether they are assembling there for smuggling or something else, but the intelligence report said that agenda is big. A few international trade agents will also participate. A secret syndicate is planning a business for something and this may not be clean. The source of this information is genuine, so we can't miss this opportunity. This will be a huge intelligence input. I am not involving the CIA or MI6 in particular because there can be the risk of double agents. Involvement of CIA or MI6 may escalate the issue further so we should avoid at this moment. This can be managed in a better way. I know a trustworthy Interpol officer who will join you."

"Me?"

"Both of you will go. The Interpol agent will be your backup. He will introduce himself to you in the meeting where both of you will go in disguise."

Den smiled with surprise and curiosity, "You are the Secretary General of the UN. Our job is not to investigate. Our job is diplomacy. We frame policy for Humanity and Nature. Don't you think you are taking unnecessary and additional risks, Sir?"

"We don't frame policy. Break that myth. We do paperwork. And we do this paperwork for member countries. Go beyond this Secretariat capacity and save the world. This may be the last chance before it is too late. I cannot do this in my personal capacity. I request you to volunteer this unofficially." Chief was very emotional in his last few words.

Den replied, smiling "I am not any field correspondent anymore!"

Chief replied with his common polite voice, "I trust you. You can do this."

He came outside the hostel. All the benches were wet and filled with thick ice. He entered the 'Skyline bar' of the Hans Edge Hotel. He needed some isolated time for himself. He ordered whiskey.

Den's mind was absent. Chief is well-connected to bureaucrats and intelligence agencies across the globe. His chair managed to bring him closer to information circles, but Den was not able to trust anybody at this time. His mind was losing information, and all seemed to get mixed up. He tried to reconcile this. He opened Evernote on his handset and started jotting down incidents that had occurred. He started with his conversation with Chief after coming back from the Katowice climate conference. Chief first demonstrated the priority for Svalbard. Now this got rescheduled. Now, he had to go to Ethiopia. Den did not know if Chief was aware of the 'Svalbard meeting' earlier. He also did not know whether the venue changed from Svalbard to Ethiopia or if there were two separate meetings. Arranging entry passes was a separate challenge, and how Chief would manage the same, remained a mystery. Den was trying to stretch his brain to discover at least a few answers, but the questions and doubts were unanswered.

Remi was reading something very deeply on her laptop. She was sitting in the rooftop lounge of the hostel when Den entered.

"China's Wuhan city ultimately started reporting that there was a virus outbreak. Several people are affected, and a few are already dead. They are calling it Coronavirus," Remi said.

Den nodded his head at what he just heard.

"Sit Den", Remi said seriously, "This seems to be free-flowing, and we see more damage coming."

"Is this serious?" Den asked.

"This is only the tip of the iceberg. This is going to be a pandemic. It is not only China. Italy and Greece also started reporting an outbreak."

"This shows people fly very frequently between these three countries," Den smiled.

"Italy and Greece are new Chinese colonies."

"I have a discussion about another pandemic." Den briefed about his findings to Remi.

Remi endorsed that future conflict is imminent for the Arctic Circle. She was not sure about the specifications, though. All the major muscles, i.e., the US, Russia, China and Nordic Europe, were turning their focus and budget towards the North Polar region. The Arctic is the new battlefield.

"Remi, I am serious. Something wrong or bad is happening on an international scale. I seek your engagement to de-root the agenda. Let us find out. You have good access to polar information through your official association and personal connections. I am sure that the upcoming Ethiopian meeting will unmask a lot of clues and people if Chief is right."

"Very difficult. Whom do we trust? this is going to be a complicated affair. This requires a methodical investigation, a large team, deep assets and official machinery. Every step that you take and every person that you interact with has the risk of double-crossing us, resulting in fatal consequences. Can you imagine if the cover is blown?"

"Let's not give them a chance to change the fate of Earth."

The next day, Remi and Dr. Thomson departed. Remi went back to her home in Oslo. Den stayed back in Nuuk until further orders were given. He was not going back to Hong Kong now for the risk of catching the virus. In the interim, he enquired about the injured fishermen in the hospital and checked with local police for updates on the investigation. However, there was less probability of any complaint being lodged or any true investigation because police filed the case just as a mere accident. The witness's report on the submarine and the bullet injury was not considered. He went to the hospital but was not allowed to meet the victims. Local police said that the oil spill was now under control.

Den also went to Sir Jodman's house. He was not feeling well that day. His wife opened the door and informed Den that Sir Jodman was bedridden due to a high fever and breathing trouble. Den was not sure if Sir Jodman was trying to avoid him, so he texted Sir Jodman about the 'Ethiopia meeting'. Den needed to know whether the venue was changed to Ethiopia or if there was a separate meeting in Svalbard. It was critical. He also asked Sir Jodman about the way forward and scope to connect with Mr Mob. Hopefully, Sir Jodman would see his WhatsApp in time and reply. Den would just have to wait.

He received a message from Chief that night. Chief asked him to meet **Ms Haile Mulu** in Addis Ababa, Ethiopia. She is head of the UN Conference on Trade and Development in Ethiopia. She is also the Ambassador of the African Union. The meeting is going to be held very soon. Chief will communicate with him privately. His flight tickets were booked.

Addis Abada, Ethiopia

Den reached Addis Abada. For the next couple of days, Den roamed around the city. He went to Meskel Square, St George Church and Mount Entoto while he was waiting for his gate pass. He came to Ethiopia with a single purpose.

Madam Mulu offered him a meeting with the **PM of Ethiopia, Mr Adil Ahmed**. It was a high official diplomatic meeting for their 'Renaissance Dam'. Ethiopia was building this dam over the Nile River to become a hydroelectricity exporter and supplier to the neighboring countries Sudan and Djibouti. This would boost their economy. The project was almost 80% completed, but Egypt was protesting against this project and escalated the issue to international forums. The US had shown interest in acting as a mediator. The US PM was going to hold a joint meeting between Ethiopia and Egypt in the coming weekend. PM Adil didn't want third-party intermediation but ultimately agreed to sit across a common table of agenda. After the meeting in the morning, there will be a diplomatic get-together in the evening. Madam Mulu was invited. She managed permission to include Den.

The US PM had come along with the Head of State- Mike Power, Chief of the Royal Navy and the NATO Admiral. They had a meeting in the morning. The Egyptian president, along with his team, had come, but only four people attended the first round of meetings, which was arranged in Lake Tana. The US PM, Mike, the Egyptian president, and PM Adil boarded a small cruise in the lake and discussed it in isolation. The second round of meetings happened in Mekelle. This border city of the Tigray region had been an epicenter of a long-standing regional conflict between Ethiopia and Eritrea. The Tigray People Liberation is a local rebel group fighting for regional sovereignty from Ethiopia. They will also play a critical role in stabilizing the region. Stability is important for commerce. Peacekeeping is often a balancing act. So, the intermediary was trying to moderate all the parties to a mutually amicable agreement. A few secret dealings were an inevitable part of this. They did a press meeting after that, but it was very general. They told the media to keep patience for the next few days for the conclusion and final submission. Often, this kind of negotiation is complicated and based on so many options of deals, pressure tactics, etc. The countries just cannot concede so easily. They take their time to analyze the benefits and usage values, and then they mutually agree. In some cases, one party wins and another party compromises.

***

This was a high-voltage dinner party. The venue was the African Union's headquarters in the capital city of Addis Ababa. Other than the US, Egypt and Ethiopia, the Leaders of Eritrea, Sudan, Djibouti, Somalia, Saudi Arabia, UAE, Israel and France were also invited. The US and France were the only odd men out of the lot because all the other countries belonged to the local territory of the Horn of Africa and the Red Sea- the busiest sea trade route in the world.

France is an important partner of Ethiopia and is building the Ethiopian Navy from scratch, so France was invited. China is equally important and a legitimate contributor to the Suez Canal trade route with its huge strategic military presence in Djibouti and Ports in Egypt. Surprisingly, China was not invited. This might be because the US didn't want them in this specific diplomatic agenda of the Ethiopia and Egypt escalation. Although the Egypt PM didn't turn up. They were upset after the morning's meeting. The wind was not in their favor.

Madam Mulu and Den got out of the car and showed their pass. Nowadays, each delegate receives a QR code on his own mobile. Guests can enter only after a QR code and facial recognition match. Den was new to this part of the globe, so he did not know the people. He could recognize **Yazeed Al Habib**. He met Mr Yazeed a couple of times at the UN general assemblies and other international summits. Yazeed Al Hamid is the head of the Local Holdings Investments Division of Saudi Arabia and is instrumental in building foreign investment for Neom City. Den knows French President Mr Macron. He went up to Mr Macron and exchanged pleasantries. Madam Mulu engaged herself with Israel's PM in a casual discussion. Den was not able to find Mike. The US PM and Mr Adil were also missing from the hall. They all came together after a few minutes. The room temperature perhaps increased by a few degrees as the US PM stepped into the hall. He came along with Mike. This is the natural dynamics of a world superpower. Den saw him during several international meetings and seminars over the last few years, but they never interacted in person.

"I heard you were on leave," Mike came up to Den with a smile and welcomed him.

"I just joined and came here for this meeting. How are you, Sir?" Den said with a smile.

"Well, I am fine. So you are here for a couple of days?"

Den felt that this was not the forum to discuss his real purpose. He trusts Mike and might inform him in due course.

"No, Sir, I have to stay here for a few more days. I have an engagement with Madam Mulu."

"Ohh, I see. Chief is constantly changing your assignment," Mike smiled, "he is keeping you busy and will make you a globetrotter."

Den smiled in return. Mike leaned in and whispered, "Meet me separately. I need to talk to you."

An attendant offered a mocktail. They both picked up the glasses.

"The US PM would love to meet you, Den." Mike wanted to introduce Den to the US PM. The French president, the Arab prince, two other diplomats and Mr Adil surrounded the US PM, talking. Mike introduced Den to the US PM. Den greeted him with a gesture.

"I heard good things about you," the US PM said.

"My pleasure, Sir," Den replied.

"Are you posted in Hong Kong?"

"Yes, Sir"

"Good now that the Hong Kong protests are under control. China made a mess of it."

Den didn't reply. Forceful invasion into other sovereign territory does not always happen by arms, but sometimes by law. They discussed a few other things for a few more minutes.

Madam Mulu introduced Den to Mr Adil and Eritrea's PM. They were talking about the local situation of the region and the peace treaty. Mr Adil is instrumental in convincing Eritrea to agree on a mutually beneficial, peaceful and commercial deal. For this peacekeeping game-changing work, Mr Adil is getting praise from across the world. The relationship between Eritrea and the landlocked country Ethiopia has not been stable for generations. Things escalated since the start of Renaissance Dam in 2011. It was speculated that Egypt attempted to stop this project with help from Eritrea. The project lead was killed, and this led to further unrest on the bank of the Red Sea. After Mr Adil joined as Ethiopia's PM, he somehow managed to meet with key people across Eritrea and Sudan. They came together to stabilize the land and build a peaceful and ongoing commercial atmosphere for the benefit of a stable Red Sea Trade Route. He won a Nobel Peace Prize for this. Although the balancing game in global politics is never permanent. It is a temporary arrangement for a greater purpose.

Mr Adil and Eritrea's PM greeted both Den and Madam Mulu. Mr Adil has a smiling face all the time because he benefited the most from this deal. Egypt Leaders were missing from today's dinner. In world politics, often, a deal is worked out to be one-sided. Recently, the US announced a peace deal between Israel and Palestine by offering East Jerusalem to Palestine as per their long pending demand. The fact remained the opposite because Israel's settlement in East Jerusalem was still not made illegal. Nobody knew who coined this beautiful term 'peace deal of the century', whereas nobody even invited Palestine to make it a deal. Jerusalem was already announced as Israel's capital without even discussing and negotiating with local stakeholders. The US, in its mission of cementing influence throughout Mediterranean entry points, obviously could not compromise to lose its friendship with Israel. It seems they were ready to polarize the issue and give up Egypt willingly because they arrived deep inside the Red Sea with a stronger presence and a new relationship with an alternative ally, Ethiopia. Diplomacy of this stature is often based on closed-door politics.

Mr Adil invited Den to his home along with Madam Mulu. It seems Madam Mulu was on good terms with him. Mr Adil described the importance of the Renaissance Dam for the region to Den. The Djibouti PM also joined the gathering. They discussed several topics, from the Yemen crisis, the pirates problem of Somaliland, the prospect of Sudan's breadbasket dream and the probable bridge in the choke point of the Bal al Mandab strait between Yemen and Djibouti.

Mike has been trying to get a chance to speak to Den in isolation. Den was also curious to discuss updates with Mike on the recent assassination in Iran and the accident in Denmark. Mike got him alone in the corner of the hall while he was drinking warm lemon water.

"So, you are coming from Hong Kong?"

"No, I took leave for a few days. Sorry that I could not pursue your task yet. I will think it over."

"Forget China for the time being. There is a virus outbreak in Wuhan. We will engage you later. China is not safe right now, but here, the situation is eventful."

"Sulemani was a very popular figure there. Iran must be preparing for revenge. What's the matter that it was required so urgently?" Den asked

Mike looked around the corners. He was cautious.

"Top terrorist leaders often gain popularity within his own territory and declare himself as a rebel. This is common, but we didn't touch him because of his popularity. Sulemani was the strength of Iran and its strategic expansion. He was the mastermind behind Iran's attempt to provoke and disrupt Aden of the Gulf. Iran was making aggressive moves against Saudi and the oil movement. This was high time to eliminate the source without any delay," Mike whispered so no one could hear him.

"What about Denmark?" Den asked.

"That is a real mystery. All the intelligence agencies are running behind the resolution. Even my CIA is clueless. No rebel group has accepted the responsibility, nor are we able to find or link the motive of any country. It seems to be a simple accident."

"Is there any connection with Greenland?"

Mike looked at Den for a few seconds, "We offered a package to buy Greenland. The US PM and I had spoken to the Denmark PM several times on this. The deal was not easy. The discussion will resume soon from scratch. We offered from the perspective of US priority in the polar region. If we look forward to the future, the Arctic Circle is one of the top priorities of a few states at this moment. We need this at any cost."

"Who is the immediate threat?

"Russia."

They both understood that this was not an ideal time for this discussion. There was a gathering. France's president came closer. He came with Djibouti's PM and a few diplomats for a casual interaction. Mike and Den stopped talking. They engaged with the delegates.

Stability in Ethiopia and Jerusalem is necessary for the benefit of the Horn of Africa- the most important oil and trade corridor of the world. The region is getting upgraded in terms of importance with a new project by the Saudi Prince in **Neom-the future city "Line"**. The convergence of the Red Sea-Suez Canal and the Mediterranean Sea never lost its glory or significance for global commerce, but a PlanB was getting ready elsewhere.

***

Dinner time. The world is very vast. Multiple events were going on in different parts of the globe at the same time. Some events were in public, while some events were covert. Who knew, some of them were programmed to make international allies and enemies more complex. On one side of the coin, this was named geopolitical warfare, but on the other side of the coin, there were dangerous game plans.

China

Dr Kin was a whistleblower in China and was the first person who revealed the outbreak of coronavirus in Wuhan. Nobody noticed that he himself was admitted to the hospital with the infection. China covered it up, and Dr Kin was injected to death.

Canada

National Microbiology Lab. Two separate centers were working throughout the day and night shifts. One batch of scientists were working to create the antidote for the Covid-19 virus. Very soon, the world will demand this medicine in huge quantities. Another center was working on test kit preparation. If an epidemic grows, the world is going to face a scarcity of test kits. They wanted to get ready with both test kits and medicines well in advance with large scale production. There was a huge business opportunity. Dr Xiangguo Qiu was already fired for her secret dealing to ship the virus ampule and formula to China. Now, another Chinese fellow scientist, Dr Sheen, was also caught leaking data on an antidote. She was also sacked.

*****

C3 received an update that switches were delivered successfully and installed in the shafts. The movement has not been made public yet. They could make the satellite imagery and vigilance intelligence classified about this movement as far as possible. This went well according to the desired plan. They were on schedule. C3 reported to C1. Now it was time for final action.

For any final action, money is the confirmation. In 'polar bear', money came in the form of investments. Corporations and countries invested in the project. Investors should not back out in the last leg. So, all the stakeholders were called to the 'final meeting'. They will take the final call before the final button is pressed.

*****

Everybody greeted each other before they departed from the dinner party. Den was coming back with Madam Mulu. Madam Mulu was driving the car. Den looked beyond the window. He couldn't get a chance to discuss the secret meeting with Mike. He opened WhatsApp but didn't write anything. Communicating through the open internet was not safe. He was also thinking about Mob and Sir Jodman. They still hadn't replied yet. Mob said he was present at the Katowice climate conference meet, but as per the roster, there was no one named Mob. Remi might be working to find out and accumulate information. At present, there was no single clue to link up Denmark's incident with anybody. He tried to think more deeply. A lot of work was pending. He did not even know who the Interpol agent at the meeting will be. He was yet to get an entry pass. The car was driving fast. With the windows closed, Den felt suffocated. He was not sure if this suffocation was due to the present tension and complexity of time. He picked up a water bottle from the holder and sipped it twice.

Just then, Chief called. He asked Den to go to Saint George Church in Lalibela tomorrow at noon and wait for a kit. Den turned down the volume. He was sitting just beside Madam Mulu.

"See the news, the Egyptian PM is doing a press conference live. He is categorical that if there is a blockage of a single drop of Nile water flow to Egypt, they will compensate with blood. It seems the negotiation was not very fruitful."

Den just nodded his head.

Chief said, "Our security council received two applications. These will be discussed in the next general assembly. Greenland and Taiwan filed for independence and sovereignty. China completely stopped the supply of rare Earth metals to the US, and this fueled the trade war to the next level."

"What do you mean, Sir?" Den asked.

"Smell the change. One more thing, the Russian president was in Budapest recently. He praised the Danish Government with an open heart, saying that they are a true international partner. They ultimately took the right decision in protecting their own interest and the interest of other European partners."

"Yes, I saw. The Russian gas pipeline project 'Nord Stream2' was on halt for some time due to Danish objections. Fifteen days back, the Danish Energy Agency (DAE) withdrew the objection," Den said.

"Who?" Madam Mulu asked while she was driving.

"It is Chief," Den continued. "Sir, do you see any Russian connection with the death of the Denmark PM?" Den yelled into the phone.

"I don't know! Attend the meeting and keep your eyes and ears on alert. I must tell you that the world is undergoing a critical phase of change with more intrinsic and vulnerable international relations. There must be a purpose. It is all a sleeping time bomb."

Lalibela, Ethiopia

Eleven monolith churches were built during the very early years of Orthodox Christianity to recreate the Holy City of Jerusalem. The other churches are also nearby and interlinked with tunnels and trenches. Lalibela is one of the genius architectures of ancient times. This is UNESCO's world heritage site. Lalibela is located on hills, and it takes two hours from Addis Ababa. Den reached the location before the meeting time and came to the Eleventh Church-Biete Gabriel-Rufael as per the plan. He had to wait. There were no tourists. The church will close by 1:00 PM in the afternoon. Den checked his watch. Now, it was 12:20 PM, and nobody has turned up yet. This is a twin church complex. He crossed a bridge and took the stairs to come to the basement. Ten more minutes passed. All of a sudden, a local boy came and stuck two papers in front of a rock. The boy looked at Den, smiled and disappeared. There was a QR code. He scanned the QR through his handset barcode scanner. An embedded link and barcode is saved in his handset. This was his gate pass. He tore the code stamp and came outside. He confirmed to the Chief that the kit was collected safely.

While coming back, Den was passing by the Red Terror Martyrs' Memorial Museum. He stopped his car for a while. He sat in a nearby open-ground cafe. The museum has displays of torture instruments, skulls and bones, bloody clothes and photographs of victims. Few people who opposed the Derg communist government, were killed in a genocide. It was an Ethiopian civil war, and the Derg government planned political repression. In history, there were so many genocides across the world, either by government rule or by invaders. Modern days have changed. Now, carnage is planned secretly by business mafias and political law makers.

An attendant served liquor tea. Remi called with information. This morning, the US walked away from the 'Intermediate-Range Nuclear Forces Missile Treaty', blaming Russia for violating the terms to continue building missiles of mid-range, up to 5000 km. Russia blamed the US for building a military base with a high-range missile in Eastern Europe. Tension has further escalated. The UN Chief subsequently did a press conference and declared this as 'world loses brake in nuke war.' Mike retaliated in a press meeting. This affected the personal relationship between Mike and Chief with official escalation between the US and the UN.

Remi informed further, "By the way, **Vlad Medkev**- a senior Russian leader is on an unofficial tour to Djibouti. He may come to Ethiopia any day. This news is not public yet. Intelligence Officers are chasing him. Something is going on there. Be cautious."

"So I may see him in the meeting?"

"According to internal information, Russia is planning to withdraw from 'Opec Plus' and may back out from the production cut commitment. This may lead to a separate conflict and a new oil price war."

"Remi, don't you think there are so many critical political events at the same time and in recent days. This is piling up. It is difficult to find linkage among the events," Den said.

"There is no international politics without purpose. Try to connect the dots."

He finished his cup and paid the bill. Den had to check with Sir Jodman again. It was necessary to connect Sir Jodman and his friend- Mob before the meeting. At least he would be able to get some insider information from Mob in advance. He called, but Sir Jodman's mobile was switched off.

***

'Hilton Addis' is located in the heart of the Addis Abada city and within walking distance of the 'UNECA conference center' and the Ministry of Foreign Affairs. Nobody could imagine what was going on inside. The terrace banquet was booked for a private meeting. Delegates had reached the hotel the previous evening. There was a heavy security arrangement.

It was difficult to identify Den today. He's got good makeup on. He had a beard and was wearing a wig. He came in disguise as per the plan, but he did not know that other people were also masked. He was acting as Envoy of the European Union today. Although, he kept another set of clothes and wig ready in his briefcase as an alternative.

Participants were ready for the discreet 'Ethiopia meeting'. The attendees were senior officials in their domain. Den was equally thrilled and charged up. Everybody had to switch-off their handsets before the meeting started. This was a security protocol.

Ben Kong, senior investment officer at Calpers, is a scholar at the University of California. Prior to Calpers, he was a senior executive in the State Administration of Foreign Exchange. This Chinese state council governs the rules for foreign exchanges and manages the foreign reserves for the Government. This foreign reserve is held by the People's Bank of China. Mr Kong is one recruit in the 'Thousand Talents Program'. China recruits experienced professionals and scholars in the US and Western countries for double cross and espionage. Calpers had invested in 100 Chinese companies in diverse sectors like military equipment, surveillance systems, and AI in the last few years. Ben Kong spearheads this diversion of investment discreetly.

Wang Zing is a senior member of the Politburo standing committee and represents the state council for the 'One Belt One Road' Initiative. He is also a board member of the 'Asian Infrastructure Investment Bank'.

Nik Korchunov is a Senior Arctic Official of the Russian Federation to the Arctic Council and a key officer from Moscow for Polar strategy.

There were key executives from different Chinese conglomerates,

China's Communication & Construction Company is building a major portion of the One Belt One Road and artificial military islands in the South China Sea.

China Aerospace International Holding Ltd. is one of the largest aerospace contractors.

China Unicorn is an internet service provider in North Korea and instrumental supplier for 5G infrastructure.

Aviation Industry Corporation of China builds aircrafts and drones for the People's Liberation Army of China.

Hikvision is the video surveillance provider

Unicorn is a job contractor of telecom giant- Huawei.

A few Russian corporations were also representing their stake in today's meeting.

Novarik-the LNG giant, *Oboronlogistika*-the military shipping company in the Arctic and *Gazprom*- the state-owned multinational energy company who have large investments and assets across the Arctic, were present.

Two KGV Officers from the Directorate of external intelligence and the Commanding Chief of the Russian Northern Fleet- **Admiral Alexander Misokeev**, were also attending.

There was another gentleman, **Mr Igor Sechin**, who is a diplomat and a very old, loyal hand of the Russian President. He is the key role player in annexing Crimea from Ukraine and hence is under US sanction. He is a Senior Arctic Official of the Russian Federation to the Arctic Council.

The meeting was a full house. Den showed the QR code to the gate pass and entered the hall. An attendant guided him to take his fixed seat. The hall was on a terrace. The light was dim. There were security guards both on the ground floor and on the terrace outside the hall. Den looked around. Some seats were empty. Name plate of the Chairperson was written as **Vlad Medkev.** He was talking to his adjacent seat. Most non-Chinese people had beards. Den himself came with a false beard. Usually, a beard helps a person to be in disguise. Each member had a nameplate and a designation attached to the table in front of the respective seat. The Chairperson was also in a beard. Den tried to find out where Mob was, but there was no one named Mob. Den tried to identify the Interpol officer. He was not sure if the officer had already come in someone's disguise. Two new gentlemen entered and took their seats. Den knew one of them. He met this old gentleman at the Katowice climate conference. That nervous old man. He took his seat. His nameplate was 'David Taylor'. As per his nameplate, he was a senior Engineer in seabed construction and a senior Arctic Official. Den was surprised to see him here. Taylor also saw Den but had no facial expression.

The Chairperson Mr Medkev started addressing. He was speaking in English but with a Russian accent.

"We want to host our flag for the entire Arctic Circle, as it is already planted in the center of the North Pole seabed. It was a rust-proof titanium flag. The flag is secured. Similarly, we need to ensure the security and sustainability of our Arctic objective too. The 'Lomonosov Ridge', a 1,800 km underwater mountain range that extends under the Arctic to the pole, is a geological extension of Russian territory. Moscow is seeking UN approval for its claim that underwater ridges mean its continental shelf should be expanded, increasing its right to exploit the untapped reserves. We are ready to face off against anybody in this business, but we alone cannot create this supremacy. We need partnership. The Chinese Government is highly interested in this. There are a few critical exchange programs and business scopes that we are going to fix in today's meeting. Please cooperate," the chairman said.

Igor Sachin replied, "Kremlin has the top priority in four geographies. Europe, the Black Sea, the Baltic and the Arctic. Let me present the priorities and deals in the pipeline. Few of the stakeholders are present here who eventually would clarify their company's stand on the participation. We feed energy to Eastern Europe, but Ukraine is in the middle of the choke point and is creating problems.

Additionally, the US fueled the choke point by escalating the 'Three Sea Initiative' with the help of Romania and is creating a trade blockade. **Colonel Punakov** is given charge to create unrest with Russian-born local people in the Baltic States, Latvia, and Estonia." He introduced the KGB officer Colonel Punakov, sitting just adjacent.

Igor Sachin asked Admiral Misokeev to highlight some points on the task force. The Admiral replied, "Our special military task force, under my northern fleet command, has taken responsibility for the Suwalki passage. This narrow corridor in Poland's border between Belarus and Kaliningrad is strategically important for us. We want to cut the Baltic with military power through this corridor. Without the Baltic, our alternative route to Europe is choked. Washington is buying out Serbia with a 'Kosovo deal'. They will not raise the issue of Independence for at least the next few years. The US, in return, would provide a loan to build infrastructure for Serbia and Kosovo. A deal is made based on certain conditions. Huawei and any Chinese companies will be banned from participating in the 5G auction in the region, and both Nations will have to shift their embassy to Jerusalem. Washington is cleverly making the Baltic and Balkan complicated. For the Middle East, Washington's agent is Israel, and Beijing's agent is Iran. We are trying to develop Turkey in our favor. There are situations and plans. These ancillary problems need to be managed to safeguard our bigger investment and future ambition."

The Chairperson interrupted. "We have full trust in the capability of Admiral Misokeev and Igor Sachin. We need strategic warm water ports. Through the Black Sea and Istanbul, we get direct entry to the Mediterranean. We are not interested in the Middle East. We are interested in the Eurasian market. So we need Turkey in our favor."

"Thank you, Mr Medkev," the Admiral acknowledged his praise. That means Remi got the correct news that Russian leader Medkev came to Djibouti for a private visit, and he was around this region. Medkev is another right-hand man of the Russian President. All three musketeers Igor Sachin, Admiral Misokeev and Medkev were here.

Admiral resumed, "We speculate that the US may de-prioritize NATO for Southern and Eastern Europe and leave the region in the hands of others. The US would rather focus on the South China Sea with a strategic alliance with Taiwan, India, Japan and Australia. You must know that the US signed the 'Taipei Act' to support military aid and provide all sorts of security. We are not bothered about the fate of NATO, but it is high time that the Kremlin takes its position in Eurasia. On the other hand, the Red Dragon wants to cement its strong position in Europe as a major supplier over the US or any other cross-European captive players. Until Russia gets its position in Eastern Europe, it is difficult for China to win the race in Western and Southern Europe. When the interests of both parties coincide, this becomes an ideal partnership. We have Mr Wang Zing with us. He is a senior member of the Politburo standing committee of China. His vast experience in infrastructure projects would enrich us in ensuring our trade supremacy through the new channel and partnership.

Mr Jing was sitting in the corner chair next to the Chairperson. He nodded his head and smiled.

Mr Jing replied, "Gentlemen, together we should establish an alternative trade route as soon as possible other than the normal long route through the Horn of Africa-Red sea-Suez Canal. We identified two profitable and feasible options. One is the One Belt-One Road route through the traditional Silk Route of Central Asia and Southern Europe. Another one is in the Arctic through the Russian coastline, the North Sea Route (NSR). Operations are immensely complex. Multiple people are involved. Multiple tasks are being carried out to solve ongoing problems and choke points. There are several large-scale capital expenditures in terms of multiple constructions, drilling and underwater mining in the Arctic, military bases, icebreakers and commercial fleets etc. Naturally, multi-layer investments are required. This is not possible through a lateral straight route. Structured siphoning is required. Mr Kong is a master in investment structuring. He would support us furthermore. He has been routing billions of dollars of 'California pension funds' to Chinese companies. The US is happy to maintain an agreed return, yet still did not focus on decoupling investments in China. Their government still does not know that Mr Kong is committing espionage and is actually an approved agent," Mr Jing smiled cleverly, "What do you say, Mr Kong?"

"I am fortunate to serve my country", Ben Kong reciprocated, "I read through the proposal and can channel more funds if required. Let me elaborate on my blueprint. Russian energy trade with China is to be billed with the alternative currency of the Chinese Yuan, bypassing the value of the US dollar. Washington must be enjoying their tariff war. Let them enjoy themselves. We will gradually seize their leisure. China is selling dollar debt and buying gold heavily to be ready with an alternate foreign reserve. Washington will feel pain once this heavily affects the US Dollar as the world's reserve currency. Then we will enjoy ourselves. However, if we concentrate here, we will use a few sovereign fund houses to siphon some fat funds for us." Ben Kong is very clever.

Den was astonished to see what was going on. A government-sponsored conspiracy was being cooked with the help of corporations and Chinese & Russian leaders. It seemed to be a big game plan. He looked at Taylor. The old man was always an introvert. His facial expression was tense and annoyed, as usual.

The attendant came into the hall to serve tea. Representatives of the companies discussed some mutual points for a few minutes. Nik Korchunov helped them finalize the paperwork and agreement points. He is a lawmaker and knows this subject of paperwork very well. Russia has increased its military presence in the Arctic region multifold to protect its interests in the NSR with a squadron of SU-34 multi-purpose fighter jets. Additional military infrastructure, including radars, radio-electronic equipment and missile systems, are made available in NSR and the Baltic. Igor Sechin, Admiral Misokeev, and Nikolay Korchunov played instrumental roles here under the President's direction.

Den was watching each person across the table. This meeting was extremely important in terms of critical intelligence input. He thanked Chief for this opportunity. Chief really did a great job in getting the information about this meeting in time. He was very accurate.

Nobody knew the real identity of the Executive of Hikvision and the senior Engineer of China Unicorn. The senior Engineer of China Unicorn was actually a journalist, real name was **Walter Bart**, who came with a secret purpose. The Executive of Hikvision was **Oskar Schober**, the Interpol Officer himself, sent by Chief. Oskar did not get the opportunity to introduce himself to Den yet. Both were talking about the Chinese 5G bids and probable technical exchanges. Others were engaged in official conversation. Den also tried to talk with others. Nobody left his seats though.

After ten minutes, Medkev requested everyone's attention. "My dear friends and colleagues, now I request your kind attention to our blue-eyed baby, Greenland. China was recently betrayed by the Danish government, so we took a chance."

Den became conscious of hearing Denmark as a special mention.

Medkev said, "Even if CCCC was awarded the contract to build an airport and surrounding infrastructure in Nuuk, Denmark's government surprised us and blacklisted CCCC from the project. They took an investment from Nordic Investment Bank to carry on the project. They invoked high-value bank guarantees. Russia will back China to continue its strategic footprint in Greenland. Both countries formed a consortium and are buying a managerial stake in 'Greenland Mineral Energy'. It is high time to upgrade Kvanefjeld exploration. It is not only for uranium, but the seabed is rich with several other rare Earth metals. We will send you a white paper of a proposed investment spreadsheet in this regard. Each of the corporations may evaluate the strength of the proposal and make official investment decisions. We planned out sponsorship through cryptocurrency. This is an in-house cryptocurrency and will be tested as a pilot run towards our search for a Dollar alternative." Mr Kong also gave some suitable input on top of the Chairperson's speech. They discussed the investment scopes and Reserve Currency ambition in detail.

After a while, Medkev was back on the topic of Denmark, which Den was most interested in.

Medkev elaborated, "North Stream2' gas pipeline in the Baltic is a must for us. Denmark stuck their nose there as well and created a bottleneck effect. They are heavily influenced and sponsored by the US. They would eventually gift Greenland to the US PM. We cannot let it happen so easily. Arctic and Greenland Ambition is a top priority for us. We didn't mind taking drastic measures. So, their President had to die in the accident," a brutal laugh came from Mr Medkev.

The old man reacted for the first time. Taylor replied, "But the fact is just the opposite, gentlemen. Denmark's PM did not oppose North Stream2. Rather, he opposed Greenland's independence from Denmark."

"How are you so sure about this? Medkev asked."

"He was my friend, and we happened to be very close to each other. I know that he was killed."

The hall went dead silent.

Den watched the reactions. Almost everybody turned their heads to the Chairperson and waited for a few seconds for the Chairperson's reply. Only Oskar and Walter looked at Taylor. Den had heard Taylor's voice before. His voice was very similar to somebody, but Den couldn't guess.

It seems the entire room became abandoned for a while. The silence broke when Walter stood out of the chair to go to the washroom, but he fell over Medkev and fainted. It seems he had a sudden cardiac arrest. They had to take him inside for monitoring. Medkev called two of his attendants and asked to take Walter inside.

"Excuse me for some time. Let me go inside and help them. We are sorry for the mishap. You guys, please continue. I will come back within a few minutes," Medkev went inside. After five minutes, Oskar also went inside.

A lot of things happened within a short span. Den started reconciling. All mobile handsets were kept in a locker; otherwise, he would have noted all the facts and updated Remi and Chief by this time. The Interpol officer still didn't disclose his identity. Den was not even sure whether he was present. Even there was no attendee named 'Mob'. Den was interested in talking to Taylor in person. Taylor was a friend of Denmark's PM, but he could not just question Taylor in this forum. He had to wait for another time. He recollected, this old gentleman was seated just beside him in the Katowice conference and was sending a message to someone *that "it is also a hoax"*.

Attendants came to serve tea and cookies. It was just 8-10 minutes after Walter felt ill, and Medkev and Oskar were still inside. It seems that time came to a halt. A good tea might stimulate energy. Den was about to sip. He stopped for a moment. It was his unconscious decision. He saw something.

There was a small cross sign on the face of the cup of Taylor. Somebody has marked it with fluorescent color. And there was a similar mark in his own cup as well. His brain took nanoseconds to conclude that they were poisoned. Taylor was already having tea. He was still alive because of his presence of mind to hold the sip. He stood up, looked at the old man and rushed to the entrance without wasting time.

The others shouted, "Hey, what happened?"

"I shall just return from loo." Den did not have a single second to look back. He came out of the hall where there were two security personnel. He did not look up. He took the stairs. Security guards were unaware of what to do at that moment. The other people came out of the hall. The Admiral whispered to the security guard and instructed him to catch the guy. Den knew that he might not be able to make it. By the time he reached the ground floor, guards would have covered the entrance to catch him. The terrace was on the seventh floor. He reached the fourth floor. He heard footsteps from the top floor of the people chasing him. He reached the third floor. He was breathing heavily. He reached the second floor. A guard and a few attendants were still chasing him. The guards reached the ground floor. Den has just vanished.

***

Admiral and Nik came to the ground floor by lift. Medkev got the news, and he reached the reception. The reception manager came forward and enquired about the rush. There were other visitors in the lobby. So Mr Medkev did not want to make noise. He requested an ambulance.

"We have two patients. They suddenly got sick and needed to be hospitalized immediately!" Medkev yelled.

The news came out within a few hours. Medkev reported to C1, "We caught one fish, but another fish escaped".

C1 was extremely angry and ordered for the hunt, "Find him and eliminate him."

Oskar also found anomalies. He updated Chief that he missed the target.

Leads | Next Round

Escape to Alaska

Two weeks later

C3 was sitting in the first rear row of the Cab. He just came out of the mountain bunker of the defense center. He had C5- Ted Mateen, Instrumentation in charge of 'polar bear' in the cab. They had a joint meeting an hour back, along with the other key operatives C4- Dr. Bunn, C6- Eric Nichols and new recruit C8- Mac Metesky. Mac recently took charge from C7- David Taylor. The Authorities were not happy about the aged Taylor and wanted to give charge to Mac. This was the final movement.

The confirmation meeting was held three days back. It was an extremely secret meeting of key controlling committee members and working committee members, along with important stakeholders of corporations and political leaders who were funding the 'polar bear'. The location was neither Svalbard nor Ethiopia. The meeting took place in the **'Neom'** of Saudi Arabia at the bank of the Red Sea. The consortium agreed on a consensus for the final stage and gave permission to press the button. Now C3 and Ted Mateen were going to deliver the keys, which were in authorization envelopes, to two separate launch centers. Code words were L.2.0 and L.3.0. There was a third set of keys and a sealed envelope which they handed over to the concerned commander in the defense center itself, which was L.1.0.

Each sealed envelope had a code number inside. This is called 'key'. The respective commanders of three different launch centers will match to authenticate the order, and the key will unlock a new destiny of global order. These were top-secret deliveries. So C3 himself was taking charge of delivering the packets. He was wearing a long coat. In his left inner pocket, he kept the two locked leather packs. They will also visit two satellite centers for a final check on connectivity, integration and surveillance switch. Therefore, Ted was going along with C3. The cab was going to the airport. Each of the core operatives had their own false passport and identity.

Greenland

Launch control center L.3.0. | Extreme northwest pole of Greenland.

C3 and Ted Mateen showed their entrance pass, did a security check and entered the zone. The other delivery was done safely for L.2.0. Security personnel escorted them to the transport. They took motor sledge to reach their destination. The commanding officer and the other present crew welcomed them. Ted Mateen sat with the connectivity and technical team to cross-check the functionality of command integration and satellite communication. He signed the memo once everything was in order and satisfactory. C3 gave the badge to the commanding officer. The satellite will spot him through this badge. All three commanding officers of the three launch centers will be monitored by the Central Monitoring Team sitting remotely. C3 kept the key and sealed envelope in respective safes and locked the same with a passcode. These safes will now only be opened using a combination of codes as per the command. Nobody can open this safe anymore.

Before departure, C3 gave best wishes to the officer "Best of luck, commander. Wait for the final order. Be proud that you are part of a project which is going to create a new era in human history- an era of new global supremacy."

They also visited the scheduled satellite stations. Satellite imagery and monitoring data were funneled into the processing center. Only filtered data goes outside to collaborative agencies for further analysis and use. Sensitive data are classified and used only by specific people of the government or the organization. They checked the control system. They also checked the end-to-end signal communication with three launch centers and three shafts. Several underwater acoustic monitoring instruments surrounding the red zone and patrolling submarines were integrated. Those systems were also reviewed. The team was satisfied. Ted signed the memo. These were working perfectly. When the ambition was big, the plot was equally planned very meticulously so that there was no chance of missing the target or risk of information being leaked. C3 updated C1 that everything was ready. Only "Balls" were pending to be delivered.

Ethiopia

Den was able to escape with a storm in his mind. He got a chance to go inside the housekeeping room on the 2nd floor. There was an attached storage room with laundry stuff and housekeeping items where he hid himself for a few hours. There were a hundred questions, doubts and surprises that filled his thoughts. He had to escape now. He came prepared before the meeting and had a new set of clothes and wig. They might keep the entrance under observation, so he needed to change his appearance to escape. He wore the new wig and changed clothes. Nobody could identify him when he came down to the reception lobby. He had to take a chance. He swiftly went outside to blend into the crowd.

He could not contact Madam Mulu locally, nor Mike or Chief. He could only trust Remi at this moment. But he was sure his mobile was tapped. He had already switched off his handset, or else his location could be tracked. He failed to understand how he was dragged into this storm.

Den took a cab and went to Mercato. It didn't take more than ten minutes to reach the market area from Hilton Addis. It was a huge open-air market and immensely congested. Den boarded onto a nearby substandard lodge to avoid standard hotels or guest houses because they would ask for ID proof. His first job was to arrange a local SIM and a new mobile number. Without communication, he could not plan his escape. At present, it was his immediate priority to go out of Ethiopia and go underground. Medkev and their team might have put all the outgoing routes in the airport under surveillance. He was not able to keep faith in the local government, as they might be part of the nexus. Local administration might help them find Den.

He came to a local shop and bribed the guy to get four local SIM cards without proof of ID and bought four handsets. He would have to keep changing the phones to avoid location trackers.

Den came back to the lodge. He noted Remi's number before he switched off his original handset. He put a new SIM into a new handset and dialed Remi, "Hello, Remi. Please listen carefully. I am still in Ethiopia. I am calling you from a new number."

Remi screamed, "I was so worried! What happened?"

Den described the situation to Remi.

"I told you, Den, all roads lead to the Arctic. Now it seems their ambition to control the Arctic is only one side of the coin. They have a widespread blueprint. Chinese ambition for Europe is nothing new. China-Russian joint operation towards that goal is already public. It is interesting to see the investment siphoning racket of American money into Chinese companies and stocks. It seems they have many bigger plans. If Denmark and Greenland created a bottleneck, it was obvious that they had taken action already. It is very unfortunate. You did a brave job, my son."

"Think about Chief. I trusted that fellow, and he turned out to be a traitor! I made the mistake of booking my itinerary through the official admin. Chief has been tracking my movements to Nuuk. If they can assassinate a top leader, they can easily try to eliminate a small pig like me. They will not let go any chance of threats or leaks. He trapped me into the meeting and planned my killing along with Taylor. I just could not find any connection. The Interpol officer was a proxy. Either there was nobody present, or Chief specifically recruited his own agent to supervise the killing program in person. You see, Taylor was a common link from the UN Climate Conference. I remember Taylor got hints about hoax activities among the bureaucracy. I am sure Taylor found out who the mastermind was and hence he was killed! I could escape only by luck."

"Calm down, my son. Don't break down. This is all very surprising and equally frightening. Taylor was a senior Arctic official. I knew him for a long time, but we never suspected that he was involved in any global racket. He was a resident of Canada, but his home and family are in Nome, Alaska. He might have been recruited because of his engineering capacities."

Den thought for a while, "Get me there, Remi. I am sure that we will get a lot of information from Taylor's family. I have to do it. I cannot let it go. We have to blow their cover. I am afraid to imagine the scale of the probable conspiracy."

"Arrangements?"

"I need some basic stuff, money and a passport visa. I have a connection in Cairo. **Ibrahim Helmy** is a trustworthy guy for the job. When I was posted in Damascus and Jerusalem for field news coverage, he helped me with a lot of things. He is from Jerusalem and works in Alexandria Port. He has a freight forwarder and clearing agency. He will be able to escort me out of Ethiopia. I cannot switch on my handset now. Please find his number for me as soon as possible. One more thing, I need the number of **Madam Brown**. She is the Chief's executive assistant. I trust her."

"What is your plan?"
"Unmask the monster mastermind."

***

Remi arranged the number of Ibrahim within two days. Den contacted him and Ibrahim gave assurance to Den of his trip to Cairo. He was extremely glad to connect with Den after a long time. Ibrahim suggested a route via Gibraltar. He needed a couple of days to manage passports and visas to Cairo. Den is a US citizen, so he does not need a Visa to enter Gibraltar, but the people picking him up cannot receive Den from Ethiopia. It was too risky. Den first needed to leave Ethiopia immediately. Ibrahim planned the escape to Djibouti as a first pick up point, and they fixed a date.

Remi's phone was also tapped, but her name was not on the priority list. The monitoring officer missed the call log. It was delayed for a few days, which eventually saved Den. By the time they tracked his location, Den left Ethiopia and reached Djibouti. He checked into a hotel on the bank of Khor Ambado Beach near Port. Before he changed his SIM and handset again, he asked Remi to change her SIM and handset as well. Remi not only started using a different handset and number but kept calling some of her known persons in Ethiopia from the same old number to mislead the search party.

The search party kept looking for Den Smil in the wrong destinations. They were sure that Den was still in Ethiopia and must be planning to move out. The syndicate and the local government officers were also interconnected. Surveillance was made stronger. Ibrahim asked Den to stay underground in Djibouti for a couple of days. Although the plan changed slightly, it was decided that Den would travel further to Khartoum to bypass the disturbance in Tigray. Khartoum is the capital of Sudan and is on the border of Ethiopia. There, the Ethiopian police and administration have lesser control. Khartoum is located at the confluence of the White Nile, flowing north from Lake Victoria, and the Blue Nile, flowing west from Lake Tana in Ethiopia. This was going to be the start of the chase that Den will have to do to survive and ensure the Earth survives. It was now make or break.

Den was already tired of the continuous long journey. He first came to Khartoum via two-day road journey. Ibrahim's local person sent him two credit cards for personal use. He took a flight from Khartoum by showing another false passport and reached Cairo in the evening. He checked in at the 'Marriott Mena House' just adjacent to the Great Giza Pyramid. Ibrahim made sure it was a lavish arrangement for his friend.

Egypt

Ibrahim came to meet Den in the morning.

"Kayf halakum my friend," Ibrahim was so glad to meet Den in person. They sat in the open-air breakfast counter on the lawn. From here, they could easily see the Great Giza Pyramid. Den told his story. Ibrahim became spellbound.

"I am worried about you," Ibrahim said.

"How is it here?"

"The situation in Egypt is vulnerable as always. The US is not supporting Egypt. Israel is the new manager for the Mediterranean on behalf of the US. They together are backing Sinai causing local unrest and the western world blames us for the same. Egypt's agriculture cannot survive without 'Neil'. They played a game with the help of Ethiopia. Egypt gradually became dependent only on seaports and the Suez Canal. This is not in favor of the US. Instead, China is supporting us. They built the first foreign industrial zone and large scale manufacturing base in Egypt. Even Russia has come to support Egypt. They are building ports, nuclear energy plants and other infrastructure. Unfortunately, there is politics around Neil. Situations are not great here," Ibrahim exclaimed.

"The entire spider web is government-sponsored. I am caught in a planned vortex, but thank you so much, Ibrahim, for all that you did for me."

"I am glad to do this. Although, it was a difficult task for me. I often avoid traveling to Ethiopia and Sudan. First, I thought of planning your escape through Djibouti and then Duqm in Oman. Both are heavily guarded and covered by China. I work in the shipping industry and have some deep connections there with Chinese shipping lines and army officers. From Duqm you would have reached Dubai and it would have been an easier route. It would have been easier for me to manage as well, but that route would not be safe for you because of international surveillance. Gibraltar was a better choice in your situation."

"Thank you, man," Den said.

"Do not explore much in Cairo. It is better to confine yourself in the hotel as much as possible. You are not safe here. Take care," Ibrahim said before he left.

Den confined himself in the hotel for the next two days. Remi gave Den the number of Madam Brown. Madam loves Den like a son. She has been working in the UN for the last twenty years and will retire within the next three months. Den called Madam at midnight in Cairo.

***

Egypt is almost 6 hours ahead of New York, so madam had just come back home from the office. She is surprised to hear Den after such a long time.

"When will you complete your outdoor adventure? Chief has been sending you across the globe," she smiled. She maintains a travel roster of the staff because she is the key coordinator of the executive assistants of the senior officers in the UN, and rolls out the calendar to everybody. She knew that Den was in Hong Kong for deputation. Then, he went to Poland to attend the Katowice Climate Conference before he was sent to Ethiopia.

"Mam, I am in danger. I need your help," Den briefed madam on whatever happened. She was immensely surprised and afraid. "There is a mole in the system. I want to catch him red handed. Can you confirm whether Chief asked for my travel roster?" Den asked.

"Yes, the admin booked your trip to Nunavut. I handed over the roster to Chief, but in your calendar, it was scheduled for Svalbard! Chief changed your plan to Ethiopia."

That means his visit to Nunavut and Nuuk, along with Remi, has been tracked since the beginning.

Den requested Madam Brown, "I have two requests for you. Please support me in getting information about Chief's visitors for the last few days. Keep a tap on his movement and please ask your son to do a job for me. I need the call record of Chief and one other gentleman named Taylor."

Madam's son works in the CIA. He can help getting this information from Verizon and AT&T. Chief uses Verizon connection. Remi knew Taylor. She provided the mobile number of Taylor. Taylor used to use AT&T's connection.

"I am worried about you," Madam said.

"I am grateful to you. You won't be able to contact me using my original number. I am changing my number frequently, so I will call you. Thanks Mam."

***

There are mainly two routes from Cairo to Gibraltar. One is via Genova, Italy another one is via Tunisia. Egypt exports agricultural produce to western Europe through the Mediterranean while complementary pesticide and some preservative chemicals are supplied through air travel. China built chemical factories in Egypt. Ingredients come from China and they manufacture pesticides and preservatives in Egyptian factories. Genova won't be safe for Den. Ibrahim discussed and chose the second option. Ibrahim made all the arrangements and managed a cargo flight for Den to board as a crew member. Ibrahim came to see off his friend. Both said goodbye to each other.

It was a very long journey. From Gibraltar Den will go to Alaska. He had to first stop in Quebec, Canada and catch an interconnected flight to Anchorage, Alaska. From Anchorage, he took a small flight to Nome. Meeting Taylor's family was his immediate priority and he was determined. Remi arranged the logistics of the meeting through her source.

Nome, Alaska

Taylor used to stay in his daughter's house during his engagement in the Arctic Circle. Taylor's daughter is a nurse at 'Norton Sound Regional Hospital' where her husband is also a doctor. Although Taylor is resident in Canada, his son stays separate in their native home in Nome. There was tension between father and son. The son works at 'Trilogy Metal' as an operator in gold dredge. Remi fixed the appointment. Den came as a 'CSDP officer'. The Common Security Defence of the EU was taking charge of the investigation for the car accident case of Denmark's PM. The family members were still unaware of Taylor's death. It was very unfortunate.

'Nome' is another small town in the Arctic circle. It captivates with its pristine natural beauty, nestled between the Bering Sea and the majestic wilderness. Nome's history was marked by the 'Gold Rush' during 1898. Today it remains a haven for wildlife and a testament to Alaska's enduring allure along with its rich indigenous culture. Although time has changed. Today it anticipates a transformative development with the construction of a deep-water shipping port. This strategic endeavor from the Government promised economic growth, enhanced transportation capabilities, and increased connectivity for the remote region, positioning Nome as a pivotal hub for maritime activities and fostering prosperity for the community. Nome became the trade gateway of the Bering sea and Arctic all of a sudden. But People of Nome or Alaska do not know its consequences yet. They are unaware of the destiny that their land, life, culture and freedom will be taken over by the shipping mafias very soon. The tip of the conspiracy nears to their doorstep.

Den reached Taylor's home timely. Both sat in the drawing room. It was late morning.

They started the conversation. "Hi Sir, my full name is **Hazel Taylor**."

"I am Den Smil", he introduced himself as a CSDP investigative officer.

"Dad has gone to Norway for a meeting," Hazel said.

"Norway?" Den asked.

"Svalbard," Hazel replied.

That showed that the family was not updated on the change of venue from Svalbard to Ethiopia.

"What is his profession?" Den asked.

"He retired from IMO and is presently working as Senior Arctic Official in the Arctic Council. He was a civil engineer by profession, but he has some private engagements as well. I think he went to attend a private meeting."

"He is still enthusiastic and works at this age!"

Hazel smiled, "Dad is a workaholic."

"Does your father discuss everything with you?"

"Not really, but he keeps me posted from time to time. It is normal for him. We are very close."

"That is so nice, Ms Hazel. Why is your brother separated?"

Hazel hesitated for a few seconds but she replied, "Nothing specific. My dad prefers to stay with me."

"He is quite old. Why is it so important that he needs to be engaged with some private job at this old age?" Den inquired.

She thought for a few seconds and said, "We told him to stop work a lot of times, as I said, he is always workaholic. He doesn't care."

"What kind of private assignment is it? Can you please specify?"

"As far as I know, I mean what he told me so far, he has an assignment for some underwater construction. It must be related to seabed mining or an oil rig. He has been traveling throughout the polar region since last one year."

"Who is the employer?"

"I have no idea Mr Den, but how is it related to the 'car accident'?"

"Sorry that I am interrogating deep. Please appreciate that it is my duty. We know that Denmark's PM was close to him."

Hazel saw Den for one long minute, "Yes, he was." She took her mobile from the shelf. She showed some old pics of the Denmark PM and Taylor. "They have known each other for the last 30 to 40 years." She showed some recent pics. The last pic was of the funeral of Denmark's PM. Then she started crying all of a sudden.

"I understand. It is unfortunate. I am just doing my duty of interviewing you. Please cooperate, Ms Hazel." Den knew at the back of his mind that he came here with an urgent purpose and he had to get maximum possible information. Den equally felt sorry that he could not disclose the fact about Taylor and Ethiopia meeting to Hazel. This was not the correct moment.

Hazel still had tears. She looked at Den for two long minutes, silently. Her face changed. She first closed the window of the drawing room. She was morose.

"I know that their venue was changed to Ethiopia."

Den was silent for a while. He wondered, "Your dad told you?"

"No."

Den was surprised. She again opened her handset and showed another pic of the funeral. It was a bombshell. Den was shocked to see Sir Jodman in the frame.

"Uncle Jid told me. Uncle Jid, dad and the Denmark PM were common friends. And I know who you are."

Den raised his eyebrows. Another bombshell was waiting though.

She offered 'labrador tea'. This is a local speciality and made of rhododendron leaf.

She explained that her father was not happy with his private employer for the last few months for some reason. "The employer was not happy with him either. He was taking a longer time to finish the job. The employer was impatient and might punish dad for so many wrong tasks. He was present in Nuuk a couple of weeks back. He was in the middle of his trip in a submarine."

"Submarine?" Den asked.

"This was their transport heartline for going to different sites."

"The private employer took the submarines on rent?"

"Who assured you that the employer is private?" Den asked sarcastically.

"What do you mean?"

"Sometimes the government has private operations."

"You sound very complicated." Den replied with curiosity.

"Even I am not sure. Dad never told me anything about their employer, but whatever he indicated, and the scale on which they were working, it has to be a government partnered project. I do not know which government it is. I will try to show you something later."

She continued, "The employer asked him to go to Nuuk. There was an oil spill. Dad doubted that the employer bypassed him and intentionally damaged an oil rig, but the oil rig was under his supervision. Their submarine, while returning from the job, was floating on water for some hours. They collided with a fish boat and they opened fire on fishermen."

Temperature of the conversation was raised. This started opening up a lot of things. "I know the case. I was present in Nuuk during that time", Den admitted.

"Uncle Jid told my father about you. He mentioned you were a United Nations staff. Dad recognized you once Uncle Jid shared your pic to him. Dad acknowledged that you were present at the 'Katowice Climate Conference'. Do you know why my brother is not staying with our Dad? There is a lot of tension between them. I also do not support dad at this point. He is racist. He hates Russians. My brother's wife is a Russian. He only has pride for Canada, the United States and other developed nations. It is his peculiar habit."

Den smiled, "It may not be only his habit. Post World War II, Russia is a common enemy in all the US films, video games, literature and political agendas. This is methodical propaganda. It even continued after the Cold War. Nobody wins in this race though."

"I do not know the government group Dad is working with. I also do not know who his employer is! Most peculiar is that Dad's boss is Russian. All of us tried to convince dad to change. He was changing. One day, Uncle Jid called me. Perhaps you went to Uncle Jid's house, as you had some information about the 'syndicate'. Uncle was convinced that there was a common root between Dad's employer and the syndicate. Either they are the same or have common interests. Both of them are on a mission to ruin the Arctic Belt. We together convinced Dad to call you to come for the Svalbard meeting, but the venue was changed later."

Den looked at her eyes. He was not in a situation to let her know what exactly happened in Ethiopia. He needed more information.

"Let me show you something now." Hazel brought a small diary that had a map inside. "Dad was carrying his laptop, but he left this diary in the drawer this time. He said he would come back soon after the meeting.

"Can I borrow this diary for a day? Can you trust me?" Den asked, "I can help your dad to come out of this mess," Den bluffed.

She thought for a few minutes. Both completed the last sips of tea. She handed over the diary to Den.

She replied, "For security reasons, dad couldn't connect with you. Uncle was supposed to talk to you."

"But I didn't receive any call from Sir Jodman. I tried him several times!"

"He has been suffering from a fever and was recently detected with Covid virus", she halted for a moment and then began crying, "He passed away."

Den was left with another shock. He was breathing faster. He asked, "What's your dad's nickname?"

"Mob."

***

Everything was mixed up. It was not an easy puzzle to solve. Den returned to the hotel and took a shower. It was 1pm now, so he decided to get some lunch. He finished his lunch in the room quickly.

After eating, he took a cigarette and opened the diary. He was sure Taylor might have written some crucial information in his daily roster notes. In most of the pages Taylor wrote technical specifications. There were drawings of oil exploration rigs, seabed mining, canister-shafts setup. There were to-do lists pertaining to mechanical installation, etc. There were dates and meeting venues. This was going with his profession and present engagement. There was no issue with this. These were of pure engineering. This did not interest Den. He was looking for vital leads. There were two specific things that caught Den's attention. On one page, there was a map with six marking and on another page, there was a list of six codes-

S_1.0 - 634736785939pb

S_2.0 - 741931772520pb

S_3.0 - 7417401152614pb

PR_I.0 - 7018511481139pb

PR_II.0 - 781428152100pb

PR_III.0 - 310508921011pb

Den now knew his single point agenda. He had to totally devote himself to the investigation. Madam Brown managed to arrange CCTV footage of Chief's visitors and his mobile log. She also arranged Taylor's mobile logs. Her son arranged the mobile logs for her. File size was huge so she shared it in the cloud drive. Madam Brown informed that Chief had enquired about Den to Madam Brown because Chief knew that Den was close to Madam Brown. Chief informed Madam Brown that he was desperately looking for Den but Den's mobile was not traceable.

Den searched and studied the call logs and CCTV footage the whole night. By the time he finished, it was dawn. There was heavy snow falling outside. Taylor had no call log to Chief's mobile number. Nowadays, people carry two numbers and one of them is used only for a special purpose and among a close circle. If frequent calls to a specific number are not identified, it does not mean that one person has no connection to that specific number. Chief might have connected through a different number altogether. It was difficult to conclude. Although Den did not know if Chief carried any alternate number. There were a few interesting text messages from Taylor. One of them was known to Den.

"It is also a hoax"

Taylor had texted this to Sir. Jodman. Den could only see half of the massage that day in the conference, but the full massage said:

"It is also a hoax. We are playing a false game in the UN climate program. The main plan is different"

Taylor had other interesting texts to Sir Jodman as well where he had written:

"Why do we obey C3? He is Russian and may mislead us"

This really proved that Taylor had the same racist hate mentality that Alaskan American's had for the Russians. C3 might be Taylor's supervisor. Den was not sure if C3 was actually Mr Medkev, or someone else. If that was true, then why did Taylor choose to work in a Russia-China nexus? This confused Den the most. Although, he remembered conversations between Taylor and Jodman in

Jodman's house. Taylor was quite annoyed with the employer and was perhaps losing trust.

On the map, there were six marks. Den is almost sure that these were related to the six codes written in the diary. Five marks mostly surrounded the Northwest Passage of the Canadian coast and northern slope of Alaska. There was one separate marking in the Gulf of Mexico. Den could make out that there were three spots located in a series which were in the northwest territory. One was in the crossing of the triangular points of Cape Dorset, Coral Harbour and Ivujivik in Hudson Strait. Another one was near Dundas Harbour and between the T-point of Lancaster sound and Baffin Bay. The third one was at the entry point of Northwestern Passage and spotted between Blank Island & Melville island, where the northwestern passage connects from Beaufort Sea to Baffin Bay. The other three spots were not in any series but rather scattered. One was in Prudhoe Bay of North Slope in the middle of Sag river. Another one was marked near Svalbard Satellite station. The other one was in Bayou Choctaw of Baton Rouge-Louisiana near Oklahoma and the Gulf of Mexico. The first three spots were on water whereas the other three spots were on land.

This compelled Den to think whether this map indicate any sabotage or military attack in the marked territories of the Canadian Arctic, Svalbard and the American coast in the Gulf of Mexico. But, Taylor was an engineer and expert on site installations related to oil rigs or seabed construction. Den tried to imagine the possible ways that Taylor was linked to this.

Den's eyes were blown after seeing some CCTV footage of the Chief's visitors. Using the footage that was of the corridor, Den was able to identify the gentleman who entered into Chief's cabin. He was Oskar of Hikvision. This person was present in the Ethiopia meeting. Footage was dated just one week back from the meeting.

Just then, Remi called. She collected a very important lead from her friend Juha. Juha is a senior intelligence officer in 'IceEye' surveillance. She had few classified files and imagery of the Polar Region. During the conversation Juha disclosed the same to Remi. Both of them are good friends. Juha often helps Remi with her research regarding critical information. One lead was about underwater shafts, the patrolling submarine and poseidon to specific locations of the Northwest Passage. The file reported three locations. Surprisingly, in Taylor's map, there were marks around the Polar Circle. Also, there were three codes of similar category in his diary. Den told Remi the findings. The other lead had a very surprising angle. Imagery covered a ship traffic movement from the Kvnefield-Narsaq area of Southern Greenland to the Port of Hope in Canada.

"Why is it uncommon?" Den asked Remi.

"It still does not close the loop, Den. Kvnefield is a large-scale mining area with the second largest deposit of rare Earth elements in the world. Do you know where the ship started? It started from the nearby uranium block," Remi explained.

"Greenland Minerals Energy!"

"Correct. Presently Denmark and Greenland filed an arbitration on change of management in GME. Contract mining was awarded to this company when major shareholdings belonged to Australia, but China later took over as a major stake in GME; hence the arbitration. Politics in Denmark is changing so fast."

"Greenland is supplying uranium to Canada?" Den said, surprised.

"Exactly. Canada itself exports uranium and caters almost 22% of world output. Cameco has a large facility for uranium conversion in Port of Hope, Ontario."

"Yellowcake"

"Correct, Den."

"Is there any forward supply from Ontario to the Arctic?" Den asked further.

"Nobody knows. Although Juha was reassigned to another job. She took these leads out for me."

"The final supply of the Uranium billet needs further processing. The closest enrichment facility is in Portsmouth, Ohio-USA. 'Centrus Energy Corporation' runs this facility. Cameco and Centrus have been trading and complementing each other for a long time. There is no special mention for this. I guess if the final cargo is getting ready in Ohio, it has to go via Labrador to reach the Arctic, if they are involved. This is all really surprising", Den wondered. "Remi, get help from Juha. We need confirmation and proof of this consignment as soon as some movement is visible from Cameco Or Centrus to the Northwest Passage. If final grade uranium was supplied and that connects the dot with the other leads and marked areas in the map, this concludes only one possible fact, a brutal fact."

Remi asked with fear, "What?"

Den took a long breath, "They built nuclear toys."

"You mean they planted nuclear bombs in those marked locations?" Remi asked.

"Not really. There are a total of six marks on the map. If we analyze the marks along with the context, except the Gulf of Mexico, all other locations have very low population density. In fact, there are specific four spots in the middle of NWP that have no inhabitants. The two rest areas in Purau Bay and Svalbard have small populations. Neither of the six locations have a military or naval base. If the agenda is to destroy a port or other construction, this would have been easily achieved by ICBM or ballistic missiles, but the nukes are placed underwater. Either the bomb is planted, or it will be hit by the drone submarine, Poseidon. I cannot even say that these are testing sites. Usually, underground testing sites are far from the mainland, but these marks are close to the continental shelf of the mainland. So, the motive may not just be a bombing."

"This is very peculiar indeed."

"Please share the details, Remi. I have to cross check the locations of satellite findings with the map. If they do not match, we have to start from scratch."

"Are you sure?"

"It is a hunch, but I have no choice. Whether the guess is right or wrong, I am sure of the fact that a political syndicate has planned a conspiracy plot. The UN Chief probably leads the syndicate, along with other key personnel who are under Chief's command. Taylor was an earlier trustworthy member and was in their close circle but might have opposed some orders recently or failed in some tasks. He might not have been in good standing with the syndicate anymore. They killed him. I am sure that Denmark's PM was assassinated. It was a political murder. Sir. Jodman would have given some important leads. Now I doubt the reason for his death too. It is not difficult to believe Sir Jodman was on the killing list."

"You are saying that Sir Jodman was a collateral kill?"

"Most probably it was. It proves that it is a very vast syndicate, and they are ruthless in their mission."

"Take care, Den. Be safe."

Den went back to the hotel. He should not move much in public places. 'Hotel Nugget Inn' is on the bank of the Bering Sea. Now it was a polar night. In two months, a local annual festival 'Iditarod Sled Dog Race' will start from Anchorage. The race takes a thousand-mile-long journey from Anchorage to Nome and it usually takes fifteen days to reach the final destination. A few small-scale races of dog sledding and snowmobiling are also arranged in the surrounding area during this annual event. Two consecutive festivals, 'Fur Rendezvous' in Anchorage and 'Iditarod Sled Dog Race' in Nome, mark the beginning of the end of a long polar winter and signal for the spring. The resident people of the polar circle hope for better lively weather for the rest of the year under the midnight sun. But there was no hope for Den. He knew that his immediate destination was very uncertain. He already realized that he was trapped into an unknown destiny.

Consolidate

Georgia

The locations of satellite interceptions and the marked spots on Taylor's map matched. Den conducted a thorough background check on David Taylor as well. Taylor, in his early days, was part of Operation 'Long Shaft'—an underground nuclear test project by the Atomic Energy Commission of the US. The Island of Amchitka was initially selected for the tests, but the site was later deemed unsuitable, and the tests were moved to the Nevada Test Site. He was part of the site installation team of several underwater nuclear tests for Operation 'Wigwam' near Southwest San Diego, Operation 'Hardtack' and Operation 'Swordfish'. Taylor was then engaged in the offshore installation of oil rig platforms and gained rich experience by working in the difficult and extreme geography of the Arctic. The syndicate recruited the old man because of his extensive experience in underwater site construction and used him to build the six sites marked on the map. Den started going over all of the facts and leads he had. His mind now concluded that the US was in danger. The syndicate already planted their nuclear toys, and they were now just waiting to pull the trigger.

***

The coronavirus started spreading rapidly. After China, Iran and Italy, WHO announced Europe as the new epicenter of the pandemic.

The next day, an explosion happened. 'Times' Magazine wrote an article on the fire. An ambiguous journalist released an article named "The Covert Political Meeting". The article depicted the inside narrative of the Ethiopia meeting almost verbatim. This set a fire and detonated the political rivalry between three superpowers, the US, China and Russia. Mike went to the press conference in the morning, where they aggressively criticized the nexus of China and Russia for their Arctic plans. The article fuelled the relationship crisis when the US PM accused China of leaking the Coronavirus from the Wuhan Lab. A Chinese spokesperson retaliated in a formal press conference. The Russian Foreign Minister also supported China in their retaliation. The situation reached a new boiling point, and diplomatic relationships between these countries came to an all-time low.

The Ethiopia meeting was a covert meeting among business and political stakeholders. They discussed critical political strategies and the collaboration of business houses towards Arctic supremacy. However, there was no discussion on any military or nuclear movement. Rather, they fixed fund siphoning, other projects and ongoing diplomatic routes to confront the US. This is the new Cold War. Den was able to connect the dots of the UN's climate hoax of proxy policies for false climate investments. He also realized that the plan was something else. Very few people were aware of the secret Ethiopia meeting. Still, the whole secret, along with a detailed description of the conversation, came out. The article changed only the names of the characters and the companies. The killing was not mentioned, but the descriptions of the other activities were accurate. The writer did not disclose the name of the Chairperson directly as Medkev, but he was described as a Russian commander. Den speculated that there might be an agent in disguise inside the hall who was spying and then sold the insider information to a journalist.

***

Den came out of the hotel room. He lit a cigarette. The surroundings were dominated by a pristine blanket of blue snow. His breath was coming out as a puff of dense white vapor. But The icy terrain was dark and blue. The town of Nome itself is completely quiet during this time of year because of the extreme winter conditions as if it is uninhabited and life is hopeless. But the sky has hope. The sky was green. The sky was adorned with a breathtaking display of the 'aurora borealis'. Den lit his second cigarette. The green northern light was dancing and probably sprinkled light of hope for Den. The complexity of the conspiracy was ice frozen beyond imagination. But Den was still hopeful to consolidate and find a way out.

The temperature of global relations went beyond the boiling point. Ben Kong, Senior Investment Officer in Calpers, was arrested because he was exposed in the article. Washington started taking action against all similar American companies for their unauthorized investments in Chinese companies and charged them with illegal siphoning. The matter escalated to the Senate to try and find out any espionage that might have occurred. The US government ordered a thorough background check of a Chinese-born recruit who was in a high official position across bureaucracy and the congress. The US PM even ordered a bill to be drafted towards the restriction of Chinese companies in the American stock exchange. Washington would probably plan more stringent sanctions on Russia. Strategies for the Baltic and Balkan regions would be reframed. The US Govt will soon mobilize the forces from Poland to Belarus and the Baltic. The Government drafted an official complaint to the UN Security Council against Russia for creating unrest in Latvia and an illegal invasion in the territory.

***

A single article came out and changed a lot of political directions in the US and fast tracked a few critical pending actionable. The government's decision to take action against the odds was pending for some time. They were waiting for enough justification and the right moment. Now they can take the necessary legislative steps. The US National Defense Bill was already made into an Act, i.e. 'National Defense Authorization Act' (NDAA), in recent times. This emphasized more analytics and intelligence surveillance on Russian military activity and Chinese economic progress in the Arctic region. This had two major recommendations, which were pending final sign-offs due to a lawsuit filed by the local Alaskan organization "Kawerak Inc". One recommendation was to build an 'Arctic Development Bank', which was a proposed financing arm for civil and marine construction surrounding the US-Canada-Arctic coastline. Another recommendation was to build a new strategic deepwater port and the expansion of existing ports to the polar territory. "Kawerak Inc." is a consortium of regional tribal governments. They filed a lawsuit a year back for potential threats to local natural resources and probable damage to Indigenous people. Natural resources and inhabitants are getting ruined by heavy construction and business traffic. The Kawerak presented recommendations for improvement on disaster management for oil-spill, air pollution, potential interference with subsistence hunters and the vulnerability of cultural resources. The matter was escalated in the UN forum. Hence there was a hold order for quite some time. Even expansion and buildup plans for a few Arctic ports were on hold by the US Army Corp of Engineers (USACE). But the recent outbreak of Russia-China aggression through the article for the polar circuit will help the US to advocate their stand and clean up pending bills actionable in their favor. At the outset, they would be able to push the agenda for final clearance.

***

Remi called. She read the article. It was not only the Coronavirus outbreak on the front page of all media houses, the article "Covert Political Meeting" also created curiosity and chaos. Critics wrote that this was a significant cover story of covert politics. With what Den described to Remi earlier, Remi could easily make out that the article was all about the Ethiopia meeting.

"Every day there is a shock as if we are on a time machine," Remi said.

"Imagine the aftershock of the nuclear toys, Remi. We are riding on a time bomb."

"How do you stop it? In the last few days whatever you are able to consolidate, it is not heading to any kind of breakthrough. Everything is heading towards ruin," Remi sounded like she had no hope.

"Yes, indeed. The present outbreak fueled the stereotypes of political rivalry and conversations between the governments. This does not carry any proof or roadmap to reach out to the original undercover agenda. The present escalation will concentrate on strategy dispute and policy vulnerability. They will not realize that we will still be far from the fact of the upcoming disaster. Toys are timed. Time is running out. We cannot stop them. There is no way to catch the monster. They will also find me sooner or later. We perhaps lost the battle, Remi."

"Den, I urge you. You should go underground immediately. Make an escape plan asap and be invisible. Evil has already made its destiny. Better you survive first. Leave all of this and get out of it."

"Chief is clever and the syndicate is uncompromising. Do you think they will leave me alone?" Den said with frustration.

"But there is no other choice at this moment. They are too big. You won't survive it."

"God knows."

"It seems to be a very serious game," Remi said.

"What do you mean?"

"The 'International Maritime Organization' is getting restructured. Polar Code failed. Climate actions are null and void. What else is left out there? Arctic officers are nothing but proxy business agents. What do you expect from them? Taylor was a simple collateral kill because he didn't follow the hard rules. Do not be surprised if one day they dismantle the Arctic Council. Business is a greater priority than the environment. War and business never care for nature. So, plotting a nuke is not a surprise. It is very much part of the game plan."

Den endorsed Remi's views by nodding his head.

Remi asked, "By the way, in the article the journalist described one senior arctic official. He was named 'Dimirik'. This must be a false name. What was the original name? Do I know him?"

"He seemed to be a very influential envoy. He was Igor Sechen."

"Sechen? That is impossible, Den! I know Sechen very well. He broke his leg a few weeks back and was absent in our last Arctic Council Meeting in Reykjavik, Iceland. He would need at least another two months to recover. What are you saying?"

Den was surprised, "Are you sure?"

"There is no doubt about this."

"Can you share his pic so I can cross-reference it?" Den asked.

Remi sent a screenshot from LinkedIn to Den's new number. Both were now using different numbers.

Den was immensely surprised. Igor Sechen was a completely different man. But he didn't understand the requirements of this fake character.

"I am puzzled, Remi. Thank you so much for this."

***

Remi requested Den to collect a parcel from her person. Remi was collecting a few samples of Arctic plants, needle leaves of conifer trees, mosses and lichens of boreal forest which typically grow in this part of the globe. She would collect this on behalf of Dr. Thomson This was required for their research.

Since Den was present in Nome, he would collect the parcel in person. He went to Anvil City Square. It was a fifteen-minute drive through the ice-covered roads. Ice breakers clear the passage every day. He saw the statues of 'Three Lucky Swedes'. He could imagine the spurt of fortune that happened suddenly in the life of these three Scandinavian gentlemen who found gold here, mainly in the region of 'Anvil Creek'. Thereafter thousands of migrants rushed to the area and established camps beside the bank of the 'Snake River' with the ambition to mine gold. It was madness. He went inside of Old St. Joe's Hall. It is listed on the National Register of Historic Places. He met the Manager. She was a local Yupik woman. Her family and generations have been surviving here since the Russian-British colony. Den introduced himself, and she handed over the box. It was lightweight.

A very old man was sitting next to the reception. He was also a local Inupiat. He comes to the hall every day and spends some time. He was smoking. One third of the Arctic population has a smoking habit. He saw Den and smiled. Then he said something in his native language.

The lady translated and smiled, "He is asking whether you are trying your luck! All that glitters is not gold. He thought that you work in a gold mine and have come here to collect gold sands. He is mad. Please ignore him".

***

Den came out with his parcel. Suddenly one point struck his mind, "all that glitters is not gold". He followed the news of Ben Kong's arrest, although he had not gone into depth with the news. He was not using the internet much because of security and probable surveillance. He searched and discovered a new shock. Ben Kong was also a different person. This was another discovery where the person carrying the same designation and name was actually a proxy. It was not the original Ben Kong who was in the meeting.

He did not have video footage so he could not recheck the background of the other attendees, so Den started searching by name and designation as far as he could remember. As usual Admiral Misokeev was a different person from the one who was actually present in the meeting. Den then did a background check on Oskar who was found to have a connection with Chief. Oskar acted as a senior engineer in Hikvision in the meeting. Den had his video footage given to him by Madam Brown, so he could investigate further.

Interpol Officer Oskar was currently posted in Mexico. Den was now doubly sure that Chief sent Oskar to monitor Den intentionally. It was a well-thought-out plan. Everybody came out to be a proxy. Some characters were completely false. Some exist but used a fake appearance at the meeting.

There was a person called Walter who fell down due to a sudden illness and was taken inside. He was representing China's Unicorn. Den still did not know what happened to him.

Den whispered to himself, "Something is wrong. It seems to be faux."

Meanwhile, Remi reconfirmed the fact about Igor Sechen. She had called the original Igor Sechen and was sure that he was still bedridden. It was confirmed that a false meeting was planned, and that it was very dramatic and misleading.

Den made a plan to narrow all of the information down to find the root of everything. He had a relevant connection in Russia, **Dr. Alexander Schalnev**. Dr. Schlnev was the lead scientist on Project Status-6. Russia launched this project a few years back to build torpedo-shaped robotic mini-submarines, called 'poseidon'. It is an autonomous, nuclear-powered and nuclear-armed unmanned underwater vehicle. This is being built by the 'Rubin Design Bureau', capable of delivering both conventional and nuclear payloads. NATO was also investigating and has been trying to trap Dr. Schalnev. Poseidon acts either as a robotic carrier or a drone missile. This has seabed or mobile launch site options. In the seabed option, known as Skif, poseidon can wait on the sea floor before hit time. A ship or carrier submarine can also be used as the platform for deploying the drone. The seabed launch option was designed and patented by Dr. Alexander Schalnev. He was now the senior scientist working with the Rubin Design Bureau in Russia and for the government. He was very knowledgeable about the nuclear technology fraternity. Den had a good relationship with Dr. Schalnev. He would not sabotage Den. So Den can take help from him.

***

Dr Schalnev heard the events from Den and agreed to help.

"Den, I am not sure about our government's involvement in all you said and experienced. I acknowledge that Status-6 is a government project, and we are serious about it as part of our northern fleet control and our polar militarization. But I am surprised that I have not been in loop for any nuclear deployment so far, at least in the context of what you said. I suggest that you meet **Dr. Hrant Ohanyan** in Georgia. You cannot use me as a reference, obviously. You have to approach him independently. He may have sensitive leads and information related to what you are looking for. He is the godfather in illegal nuke trafficking and knows a lot."

***

Georgia is party to the 'Non-Proliferation of Nuclear Weapons Treaty' (NPT) and the 'Comprehensive Nuclear Test Ban Treaty' (CTBT). They also follow additional protocol in the 'International Atomic Energy Agency' (IAEA). Georgia is a founding member of the 'Organization for the Prohibition of Chemical Weapons' (OPCW) and a party to the 'Chemical Weapons Convention' (CWC) as well as 'Biological and Toxin Weapons Convention' (BTWC). In the past, they were accused of dual use of biological weapon production capabilities. Tbilisi's 'Central Public Reference Laboratory' had a repository of dangerous pathogens and viruses. Officially Georgia is a neutral country in nuclear, chemical and biological weapons. Even after all these protocols, Georgia has been a key middleman in Eurasian high ticket smuggling of commodities and arms.

Georgia is one key regional player in central Asia's choke point of the Caspian Sea and the Black Sea along with Belarus, Armenia, Azerbaijan, Moldova and Ukraine of the Eurasian Customs Union. No customs are levied on goods traveling within the customs union and unlike a free-trade area, members of the customs union impose a common external tariff on all goods entering the union. One of the consequences of the customs union is that the Eurasian Union negotiates as a single entity in international trade deals, such as the World Trade Organization, instead of individual member states negotiating for themselves. 'Eurasian Economic Union' (EAEU) has created a single market in eastern Europe, Central Asia and Western Asia. After US sanction on Russia, it is an alternative plan of Russia to re-collaborate earlier Soviet states into a single market where Russia is mostly benefited by being a major supplier of energy, infrastructure, agriculture and military support. Belarus, Kazakhstan, Armenia and Kyrgyzstan are already under Russian influence. Russia is struggling to capture the Caspian coastline because of Georgia. Georgia keeps a balance between the West and Russia.

Georgia's long Black Sea coastline is demarcated as Abkhazia and is not monitored by Georgian authorities because of its autonomous status. Moreso, this has easy marine access through the Caspian Sea to large uranium deposits in Kazakhstan. This became a key transit point for various legal and illegal nuclear and radiological materials due to its geography, unsecured borders, internal conflict and corruption which run as a parallel supplementary industry in itself, beyond all proliferation efforts. Historically, this region is a strategically crucial region of the ancient silk route occupying a narrow neck of land between two bodies of water and is one of only two ways to reach the Middle East from Europe by land. Merchants used to have a choice of three routes—either travel by sea, take the route across the Balkans and Turkey, or go through the Caucasus Mountains. In modern days, invasions stopped but unrest continues in the Caspian gate.

***

Dr. Hrant is a professor at the Andronikashvili Institute of Physics on the outskirts of Tbilisi. Den prepared a plan. He only had to indicate that he is interested in 'cake'.

Den reached out to Dr. Hrant. Dr Hrant asked him in their conversation, "What is your favorite color?"

Den replied "Yellow."

Dr Hrant asked him again, "What would you prefer to eat?"

Den replied promptly, "Cake."

Dr Hrant understood the indication that Den was a party. The appointment was fixed.

Den knew that this smuggling syndicate was dangerous and if he had to buy secret information, he needed deep pockets and security. He alone could not handle this game plan. He consulted with Remi and decided to reach out to Mike. Mike may be a safe bet and a helpful avenue at this moment. He was powerful and had machinery to support the situation. It was a long and risky chase. Government backing would help. Time was very short.

Den first collected information from Madam Brown on the present schedule of Mike. It became easy for Den, as Mike was present in Canada at that time. Huawei's CFO, who was the daughter of the promoter, was arrested under a bank fraud charge, routed their business through an Iranian subsidiary. This had made Us-China bilateral affair worse. Mike was meeting foreign minister of China in Vancouver.

***

Mike received a short message from an unknown number, *"Please arrange my transport from Nome. Need to meet. Top urgent and confidential. - Den"*

Den was missing from Ethiopia. Mike got the sense of urgency and importance. He quickly made the arrangement within the next evening.

Vancouver, Canada

Security picked up Den from the Airport. He checked into the 'Pan Pacific' hotel at the 'Waterfront Convention Centre'. This is situated on the bank of the harbor. This has cruise ship terminals. The meeting with Mike was arranged privately inside one cruise line. Den briefed Mike as both of them finished two rounds of black tea. Mike kept asking his questions in between the conversation, and Den clarified. Den covered most of the events from Katowice, Taylor, his visit to Nuuk, Ethiopia meeting, his escape, the fact findings and Chief. Mike was stunned. He rubbed his finger on his chin for sixty silent seconds.

"Den, you don't know what a great job you have done. I appreciate your bravery. I am equally sorry to hear about the kill attempt on you. Thank God you could escape, but I fail to believe the facts on Chief. He is wearing a mask of a gentleman!"

"I also was in shock at first. Once I connected all the dots, all these point to one single Devil."

"Chief arranged your gate pass for the Ethiopia meeting!"

"Yes, and it was made up," Den said.

"So, you are saying that the article could describe the meeting perfectly? As you know, we started taking action on ground and pushing our cases to the UN security council."

"Could you find the columnist?" Den asked.

"Not yet. The magazine kept this anonymous and published it as a proprietary copyright article. They will not disclose anything since this must meet their non-disclosure policy."

"Sir, let me try. I alone cannot fight this battle."

"It is not your battle anymore, Den. This is a concern for American security. I am thinking of involving the CIA. I have to discuss this with the US PM," Mike replied with kind support.

"No, no, no, not at all. There may be a mole. Let us keep it discreet for now."

"Please understand, we alone cannot handle this. Coverage from the CIA will help. Do not worry. They are our loyal agency. I will manage them. What is your plan?"

"If the nukes are deployed, I am sure that their governments are not using the common predicted route. Supply and transit might have taken place through an alternate channel. It is my hunch that Georgia may be the best alternative. At least we will be able to find out a link and I will try to pull out relevant information. I have some connections there."

"What do you want from me?" Mike was curious.

"Please increase surveillance in the spotted area immediately but keep it a classified task. And make my security arrangement." Den requested Mike. Mike realized the seriousness of the situation.

"This is not enough. I will discuss this immediately with our National Security Advisor and put Northern Command and NORAD on alert. I am sure that there is no silo underwater, or else our security surveillance would have caught the target spots. They must be patrolling with their submarine in the region and decide to hit through a ballistic missile or poseidon drone. NATO has strong intercepts on Status-6. This seems to be serious. Do not worry Den. You have gone through great trouble for this. My team will extend all possible support and security to you. We need solid evidence to build up pressure on Chief, so that he either automatically resigns or is sacked from his post. It will be a shameful affair in the history of the United Nations, but we have to catch the mole at any cost."

"Thank you, Sir."

"One more thing, put on a skin sticker so we can track you. I will deploy guards to cover you, so you don't need to worry. This is necessary for your security. You are entering into the lion's cave. We will have to pull you out immediately when it becomes necessary. The Georgia gang are into uranium smuggling, so they are not easy people. Be very, very cautious, Den. Do not get caught. How are you sure that they will sell business information? Buying such leads has a fat cost."

"I will not buy. I will blackmail", Den smiled.

***

Mike made all the arrangements for Den. Den will now stay in Vancouver Kitsilano beach for a couple of days. He will first go to the US military base in Thule, Greenland. Then he will fly to the intermediary station in Poznan, the Polish US consulate. From there, the Air Force will take him to Tbilisi, Georgia.

***

Den made sure to study the global supply chain of nuclear weapons and resources before appearing to the scholarly scientist.

There are two types of nuclear weapons, and they make use of the strong nuclear force by either splitting very large atoms apart or by squeezing very small atoms together. Highly Enriched Uranium (HEU) is a critical component for both civil nuclear power generation and military nuclear weapons. A high proportion of the world's supply of radioisotopes is also used in medical diagnosis and cancer therapy. The International Atomic Energy Agency (IAEA) attempts to monitor and control enriched uranium supplies and processes in its efforts to ensure nuclear power generation safety and curb nuclear weapons proliferation.

Kazakhstan has twelve percent of the world's uranium resources and is the World's leading uranium producer. The government is committed to increasing uranium exports and is considering future options for nuclear power. Australia is the world's third-ranking producer, behind Kazakhstan and Canada.

Fifteen percent of Canada's electricity comes from nuclear power. For many years Canada has been a leader in nuclear research and technology. Canada's production comes mainly from the McArthur River and Cigar Lake Mines in northern Saskatchewan, which are the largest and highest-grade in the world.

The US is reviving its uranium mining, though almost all the uranium used in the US commercial reactors is imported. The US has ninety-five nuclear reactors providing about twenty percent of its electricity, which makes the US the largest producer of nuclear power.

Eighty percent of uranium is mined in just five countries, only one of which (Canada) uses uranium for nuclear power. The major producing countries only sell the fuel. The processing and supply chain is diverse. Transportation is an integral part of the fuel cycle. Countries having capacity and technology in the fuel cycle has allowed them to build nuclear weapons.

Uranium as it is taken directly from the Earth is not suitable as fuel for most nuclear reactors and requires additional processes to make it usable. Uranium is mined either underground or in an open pit depending on the depth at which it is found. After the uranium ore is mined, it must go through a milling process to extract the uranium from the ore. The next process is complex. This is ac-complished by a combination of chemical processes with the end product being concentrated uranium oxide, which is known as '*yellowcake*'. It contains roughly sixty percent uranium whereas the ore typically contains less than one percent uranium. The last leg is 'enrichment'. Yellowcake is processed into a gas, uranium hexafluoride. Hexafluoride can be fed into centrifuges which separate out the most fissile uranium isotope U-235. Low enriched uranium for civilian reactors has a three to four percent concentration of U-235. Weapons-Grade uranium is ninety percent enriched, which is called HEU (highly enriched uranium). Through Fuel fabrication, the uranium hexafluoride can be converted back to uranium oxide, which is pressed and baked into '*pellets*'. The pellets are put in metal rods, which are used in a reactor.

As the value chain itself has a complex process, it requires multiple stake-holders. Some countries have expertise in yellowcake conversion whereas some countries have better technology in enrichment processing. Each stage has to complement each other. The market is equally complex and highly regulated. Naturally, there is a black market and its smuggling route is equally complex.

Georgia

Den arrived in Georgia. Its converging borders of Eastern Europe and Western Asia in the South Caucasus region between the Black Sea to the west and the Caspian Sea to the east made its landscape politically significant and complex. Relations among the neighboring countries and economic ties are equally conflicting.

Dr. Hrant and **Mr Sumbat Tonoyan** reside in Batumi. This is a popular beach city on the eastern coast of the Black Sea. Mike made all the arrangements for Den. The appointment was held at the 'Sphere Beach Resort'. The place was suggested by Dr. Hrant.

A beachside corner table was reserved for them. Their meals and drinks were pre-ordered so that nobody would disturb them. The resort is designed with a tropical aesthetic, with palm trees swaying gently in the breeze and colorful umbrellas providing shade for the guests. Now it was 4:00 in the afternoon. By the time Den reached the destination, the twin musketeers were already waiting. Den could guess from a distance that the gentlemen sitting at the corner table must be his men. Den walked over to get closer to them.

One gentleman stood up and asked Den, "Are you looking for Dr. Hrant?" Den smiled and reached out to shake his hand, "I am Den Smil".

"I am Dr. Hrant," the gentleman said. "Let me introduce you. He is Mr Sumbat Tonoyan, who will decide our deal and fix all the arrangements. I have given your brief to Sir," Dr. Hrant pointed to the other gentleman.

Mr Sumbat seemed to be older than Dr. Hrant, but he still maintained his young physic.

Mr Sumbat greeted Den. "I was working in the 'Eurasian Economic Union' earlier. Unfortunately, after Uzbekistan was suspended in 2008, I became jobless," Mr Sumbat smiled. "Officially, I am now a broker."

"I support Sir in technology and technical collaboration. You could call it a partnership," Dr. Hrant replied, smiling.

Dr Hrant prepared drinks for all. They also verified the passport of Den. There was no time for leisure cheering. Den sipped the first peg and got straight to the point, "I am working at the UN. I would have hidden my identity, but I thought you guys could find me anyway. I didn't come for a peace deal. I came to you for a serious request."

Mr Sumbat lit a cigar and started, "My dear friend, I appreciate that you are being straightforward with us, but which government do you represent? The UN cannot buy our material. In smuggling, the buyer and seller always change their face and formation when their intermediary agent makes a deal. But this trading is peculiar because it is legal. Do you know why? Because in this trade, the ultimate party is always the government irrespective of how the goods are procured or sold."

Den was a chain smoker. He could not resist but lit his cigarette at the same time.

Dr. Hrant asked, "You must know that we only deal in yellowcake. We are not in the whole fuel cycle of enriched pellets. But if you want, we can connect you to the relevant parties. Do you want any specific material grade?"

"I don't want any material. I want information," Den said while putting more ice cubes into his glass.

Dr. Hrant looked at Mr Sumbat, and they both began laughing.

"My dear friend, you must know that information is more expensive than material," Mr Sumbat stated.

"No problem. I want to make a fat deal."

"Oh! That's nice. We love to deal with deep pockets. If you want a great juice, you have to care for delicacy and pour fruits & sugar. What do you say, Mr Den?"

Den didn't waste time. He again went straight to the agenda. "There is a nuke deployment in the Arctic, and they received some unauthorized supplies that came from here recently. I want to confirm the source." Den exploded this bomb of information at the heart of the conversation.

Mr Sumbat now looked at Dr. Hrant.

Dr. Hrant started, "We trade across the globe. There is no specific restriction or negative list as such that there cannot be any supply to the Arctic. Whoever pays the price, and we sense that the business is classified, we make the deal. We do not have any prejudice against a specific government or caste. As we already said, the party is always the government. It is only a private hand that acts as an intermediary who delivers or takes delivery on behalf of the government clients, but we do not work for any government."

"I should be very specific. Sites are across the northwest passage in Northern Canada, Baffin Bay and Greenland," Den said.

"We reiterate, Mr Den, we only deal in material trafficking. We are not interested in the final deployment. We are not aware of any such supply to the Canadian Arctic that happened recently," Mr Sumbat replied.

"We all know it is the integrated value chain. One stage complements the other. You may be dealing in the core isotopes, yellowcake and supply to an enrichment facility or reactor, but please do not make me believe that you are not aware of the final stage. We have your background. You are well connected to this smuggling fraternity. I gave you specifics. I hoped you would open up. Tell me your price, Mr Sumbat."

Mr Sumbat did not want to be excited. He completed his first peg gently and then replied, "My dear friend. First of all, let me tell you that this is called trafficking, not smuggling. Let me again tell you, gentleman, the government authorizes the formal consignment as per their policy. There is still something left out of the total wallet which they cannot authorize officially. So, they come to us. You guys call this unauthorized," he calmly replied.

"I understand this. And I agree with you on this pattern and route, Mr Sumbat. But I can't believe that any authorized or unauthorized nuke trade through the secondary market happens without your awareness!"

"Thank you, Mr Den, for your kind words. Yes, we do hold some control and capacity in this business. But trust me, this is not diversified. There are two nuclear highways in this unauthorized supply chain. One route runs from Russia through the Caucasus Mountains to feed the Muslim Brotherhood in Iran, Turkey, Syria and Iraq. The other route is linear. That is the ancient Amber Trade Route via Poland or the Volga River through Russia. We move material via the Moldova-Ukrain border and through the Dniester River to Poland and then to the Baltic region. Hope this information satisfies you. We do not know beyond this."

"Ok, then, please hear me out. Let me explain my deal. Then you can confirm your decision," Den said.

"What do you want?" Dr Hrant asked.

Den took out some documents and kept them on the table. "This is the contract of 'Urenco' with 'Tradewill', a subsidiary of Tenex, which is the overseas trade company of Rosatom-Russia's state atomic energy corporation. Under the contract, uranium waste tails are sent to the 'Ural Electrochemical Combine' in

Novouralsk, Russia for further processing. The enriched uranium product then returns to Urenco," Den said.

"What's new in it? Depleted uranium, also known as DU, contains a reduced proportion of Uranium-235, which is an isotope used as fuel in nuclear power stations. Reprocessing can allow fresh fuel to be produced. Germany, along with other European countries, is energy-dependent and procures energy from diverse routes, whether it is in the form of fossil fuel, gas or nuclear power. By the way, we describe DU in this context as 'recyclable material', not 'nuclear waste'," Dr Hrant argued.

Den replied wisely, "I know that you guys make good deals in this pocket of business, but your fate can be changed anytime."

"What do you mean?" Mr Sumbat asked.

"Have you thought of the situation when Germany decides to close all its nuclear reactors and move completely to hydrogen? How much business would you lose? We have the next climate conference scheduled in London. Presently, this is deferred because of the Coronavirus and lockdown. The UN is trying to pressure all developed nations to fulfill a reduction in carbon emissions quota. We all know this was done with the right intention, but execution is a big hoax. No significant changes are going to happen. The fossil fuel lobbyists continue to grow their business and explore even more in fossil fuels. The debate started cropping up to choose between nuclear energy and hydrogen. Although both are carbon-free, the radioactive spill and nuclear waste are negatively impacting nuclear energy. There is pressure being built up to pursue the closure of nuclear reactors. We do not want to stop the nuclear energy business suddenly, but this can be deferred if you want. The more it gets deferred, the more you have residual time to survive in your business, at least for European clients."

Mr Sumbat lit a cigar. He stood up and started walking around. He understood the gravity of the proposal.

"Pay us five million dollars or equivalent. And we will do this business against the advance," Mr Sumbat replied after a long silence. His reply was abrupt.

"I came prepared, Mr Sumbat. You tell me the channels, and the money will be transferred. But I cannot pay you upfront without collateral. You have to agree on my deal first before you get any money. Please think once more. Even if you do not make a deal, I do not lose anything. You lose. I will depart. Better take a risk and get me in there. We can grant at least a five-year moratorium from the

European Union. You would be able to continue with your European clientele for the supply of radioactive raw materials."

"You are extremely clever, Mr Den," Mr Sumbat replied after two long puffs. "Who is not!"

After Den departed, both Mr Sumbat and Dr, Hrant debated among themselves on the subject. They were not able to come to a conclusion easily. They had a third partner, Dr. Bunn, who was recruited for a special mission by somebody the last few years and earned Dr. Bunn earned fat. He was underground somewhere in the extreme North. His accurate location was not known, though. He recently came back and applied for political asylum in Abkhazia, a nearby sovereign state. He betrayed these two partners and grabbed the full payout. The relationship between Dr. Bunn with Mr Sumbat and Dr. Hrant has not been in good shape since then, now that they got the scope of a revenge. Additionally, they had more time to adjust the business loss due to the German and European decision to close down their nuclear energy. It would be wise for them to agree to the proposal from Den Smil. Revenge is better than revenue at some points. They realized that Dr. Bunn would be the best trade-off at this moment. However, they were still unaware, it was a sheer coincidence that Dr. Bunn was the fourth key person (C4) in 'polar bear'.

***

Once the job is done, the conspirator usually eliminates the team and any threats. Sometimes, they decide early. C1 had to eliminate C3 and C4 in due course. C3 spearheaded the operation, so it was necessary for C1 to eliminate him once the final job would be completed. The same reason was applied for C4- Dr. Bunn. He was the technology in charge and designed the core warheads for 'polar bear'. Both C3 & C4 were put on the first list of death contracts.

The position of the second man, C2, was the most interesting. He was the defense supervisor, but he had never participated in any meetings. His job was always to advise and execute the orders from the backend in terms of defense support, security, machinery and mobilization. He was aware of all the decisions behind the tasks, but he never came in front. He was a shadow. C3 was the only supervisory face of the execution team. The main conspirator was C1.

The relationship took a turn between C1 and C2. A few days back, there was an extreme fight, disconnect and blame game between C1 and C2 on a few subjects. C2 was not an outsider. Both work in the same cabinet. So it was difficult for C1 to put C2 on the assassination list. C2 was also PM's man, and so is C1. However, the situation deteriorated and put these two master planners in a state of rivalry. C2 was pissed off. The breakdown of this relationship and ego war would soon push the 'polar bear' to a dangerous corner.

***

Den was on his way to Sokhumi. Dr. Hrant called him and agreed on the proposal. Dr. Hrant disclosed the background of Dr. Bunn and his recent assignment at the North Pole. Although he did not know the exact address of Dr. Bunn's new residence in Sokhumi. It was decided that their man Scot will help Den to find Dr. Bunn. Mr Sumbat and Dr. Hrant had connections in the territory, they knew some activities and probable locations where Dr. Bunn had been around the city. Scot was driving the car. His job was to spot Dr. Bunn, and thereafter, Den would take charge of catching him. The fund transfer arrangement was made by Mike through a laundering route. They will release one million in their first tranche. Mike was also mobilizing his men from Batumi to Sokhumi for the defense. Mike asked Den only to identify the mouse but not to touch it. His men will catch Dr. Bunn and place him in custody at the right time. They cannot do this operation publicly. Catching Dr. Bunn will be a breakthrough to the US government as well so Mike took utmost interest and mobilized full support.

Sokhumi is another beach destination on the east coast of the Black Sea. Sokhumi is the capital city of Abkhazia and is known for its old botanical garden and several beautiful sand beaches. Den arrived at his destination in the evening. The car came inside the courtyard of the 'Leon Hotel', which was 10 minutes away from the sea.

Scot would first try to get information from local sources. Mike's men have already reached and will join the search operation. They will have to wait to find the mouse. Mike and Den will have to catch Dr. Bunn at any cost. Dr. Bunn might be a key witness to the conspiracy. They were very close, but Den was still unaware that their mousetrap was not going to work well because a final order was already released to eliminate the mouse.

Scot has confirmed information from a source that Dr. Bunn recently returned from Baku from a business trip. There was an ongoing ethnic and territorial conflict in Nagorno-Karabakh between Azerbaijan and Armenia. Earlier, it was purely political conflict since Christian Armenian people were never ready to be part of the Muslim-concentrated Ottoman culture of Azerbaijan. It became more complicated when the business-economical allies fueled the conflict in respective interests.

Azerbaijan is a big energy exporter to its close ally Turkey and a key buyer of arms from Russia. If the trade route between the Black Sea and Caspian Sea under the South Caucasus region needs to be stable, relationships between Georgia, Armenia and Azerbaijan are essential. Russia and Turkey built labs and factories in Baku for medical isotopes and nuclear reactors. Dr. Bunn, after his assignment in the Arctic, now took a new job as a linkman in this energy project in Azerbaijan. Dr. Bunn was traveling to Baku frequently.

Central Market, Lighthouse and the Granada Cathedral were some of the places where Dr. Bunn usually visited. He sometimes goes to Beach Delmar Club in Sochi Harbour at the Russia-Georgia border for business. Novorossiysk Sea Port was another area that Dr. Bunn visited for trade and the shipment of goods. After he came back from the Arctic, he was completely cut off from his old partners. He was also absconding from team 'polar bear'. He earned enough capital and was trying to build his own business. He paid a fat fee to the government administration for his safe asylum. Den's search party tried to hook up some government officials to reach out to Dr. Bunn.

Scot was trying hard and in the field all day and night to find him. There was a strict order from his boss. Mike and his men were also waiting with the mousetrap. As the days passed, Den also walked around the city and tried to find the target by his own means. Georgia was completely new to him, so he did not have any assets here. He had to depend on Scot and Mike's men for this.

Den was sitting on Promenade Beach. He was looking at the sunset. As he gazed into the distance at the shimmering orange sunlight dancing on the sea surface, he realized that uncertainty was an intrinsic part of the human experience. No one had all the answers, and life often unfolded in unexpected ways. He was engrossed in the watercolor of the Black Sea. His next life was uncertain. He could not join back to his job in the UN until the real demon was uprooted. He couldn't imagine that Chief was the mastermind of such a big-scale conspiracy. He was almost close to catching the first fish, but the water was very deep. Through this lead, he would need to dive deep to catch the entire nexus. The future was elusive, but he was ready to face the uncertain twists and dangers. He had to stop the devil.

Four days passed without any result. Dr. Bunn seemed to have vanished.

Dr. Bunn was one partner of the notorious smuggling gang. The gang was earlier charged with uranium trafficking and illegal trade, but police could not establish proof against the three musketeers. The racket has been active in this smuggling business for a decade, but the big fishes were never caught.

Ultimately, they caught the big fish after two days. Den got the call from Allen. Allen was one member of the security team sent by Mike.

Mike called Den, "We got him! Please immediately return to Thule Base. We cannot waste time, so a flight has been arranged for you. The local admin of Georgia will start investigating very soon once they find Dr. Bunn missing. Our men already got him in safe custody and will take him back to Thule. We want to interrogate him right in the center of the target zone in the Arctic. We must thank you for reaching out to that bastard. I am sure he knows a lot of secrets. He is a vital operative. He will lead us to the main syndrome!" Mike exclaimed.

Den was already in the middle of this crisis. He was dragged into this conflict by chance. He then escaped a murder attempt. The syndicate was still hunting him. The arrest of Dr. Bunn gave him a lifeline. He was probably headed to this climax without much time. It was an immense relief to Den. He informed Remi of the progress, and she was equally excited about the news.

He was not sure whether this was the end or the beginning of the climax. The conspiracy needed to be blown out by any means with immediate priority. Perhaps Den was close to succeeding.

This area has a humid, semi tropical climate. Den was not able to cope with the constantly changing weather. Moreso, he had been running the last few months like a globetrotter from one corner to another. Extensive travel, change of frequent extreme weather, anxiety and uncertainty choked his health. He seemed to have some skin infection and influenza. Now Den feared that he might be detected with Coronavirus, but he did not have time to quarantine for two weeks. He had to rush, so he didn't get a test. He got Paracetamol tablets and decided to go ahead. It was a gamble by putting one's own health at risk, but at this time, he was not able to think of anything else. He had a single-point agenda to stop the nuclear threat.

***

The threat of a world war always lies beneath the reason for stockpiled conflicts of the world order. World War I did not just start because of unrest in central power. History only depicts that Archduke Franz Ferdinand, heir to the Austro-Hungarian Empire, was shot to death along with his wife by the Serbian nationalist Gavrilo Princip in 1914. Russia used Serbia to eliminate the central power. Germany unconditionally supported the victim and went against the assassination. War started and then escalated, but there was a prelude. It was actually the '*Triple Entente*', a counterweight treaty of France, United Kingdom and Russia, against the '*Triple Alliance*' of Germany, Austria-Hungary and Italy, which formed the stage to fuel the prospect of war on a larger scale. More precisely, the global powers were already divided into two rival sides whose principal objective was to retain and capture the economic supremacy of the world's busiest trade route in the Mediterranean. The situation was ready to head towards the global war. World War I was the first event, and World War II was an inevitable second event after a short interval. Similarly, World War II also had a prelude. The second war was an obvious punitive impact of the '*Versailles Treaty*'. The threat of another World war, what a new generation may call 'World War III' in chronology, prevails and piles up with the recent geopolitical complexities. The reasons and nature also remain the same. It is an extreme political rivalry and a competition for economic supremacy.

After Brexit, Germany and France are leading the EU and trying to stabilize the presently fragmented Europe. Chancellor Markel's determination to diversify and supplement international ties with Russia has created a new cold war between the US and Germany. The Russian 'Nord Stream Two Gas Pipeline' project is of equal priority to both Germany, Europe, and Russia. Nord Stream Two starts from the Ust-Luga area of the Leningrad Region of Russia. Then, the pipeline stretches across the Baltic Sea. Its exit point in Germany is in Greifswald.

The project was halted in December as a pipe-laying company, Swiss-Dutch Allseas, suspended operations due to US sanctions. The US had put restrictions on the involvement of any European pipe-laying company or specialized ships or supplies. The House of Representatives of the US Congress adopted the

'National Defence Authorization Act' (NDAA) for the next fiscal year, which obliged the administration to toughen sanctions against Russia's Nord Stream Two and Turk Stream pipeline projects. Germany opposed that this was a direct assault on the legal system and sovereignty of Germany and other EU nations.

Russia did not stop. After the US sanctions on European ships, which were engaged in Nord Stream Two, Moscow arranged their own transport. The pipe-laying ship, 'Academic Cherskiy', had reached Germany's Mukran port in the Baltic. This was the staging area for the pipeline's construction and only eighty kilometers away from the land exit point of the pipeline in Greifswald. Germany made it perfectly clear at the highest level that it could introduce sanctions against the US and could even persuade its EU and NATO partners to act as a united front against Washington DC. The US PM openly threatened to withdraw the US from NATO because Germany and its allies were implementing the Nord Stream Two project. According to their logic, since the US pays Europeans for their safety, Europeans, in return, must buy American liquefied natural gas, even at a higher price. The proposal was peculiar and complex.

It was a mystery that Denmark granted unexpectedly swift approval for resuming construction of the pipeline in Danish waters, potentially clearing one of the last hurdles for completing the project at the center of a geopolitical tussle. An accident to Denmark's PM happened subsequently. Den remembered the statement of Taylor in the Ethiopia meeting, Denmark's PM already granted the Nord Stream Two construction. If that was true, then the CIA could have eliminated him for revenge or to stop him from making the decision, even though the decision ultimately happened. But there was another school of thought that the Danish PM was not granting permission for the pipeline, so he was killed. Then, this fuelled the second probability of Russian involvement and that the KGB had executed the assassination plan.

US lawmakers and officials feared that Nord Stream Two would give Moscow greater political leverage across Europe. Construction of the 1230 kilometer pipeline was nearly finished, but it needed to complete a final stretch of roughly 120 kilometers in Danish waters. Five European energy companies had provided long-term financing for fifty per cent of the total cost of the Nord Stream Two project. This was in addition to the existing successfully running gas supply through 'Nord Stream One'. Europe's gas production was reducing and would eventually increase their energy imports. Russia already established a track in the blue stream gas supply directly to Turkey via the Black Sea. This supplemented the traditional land corridor via Ukraine, Moldova, Romania and Bulgaria. Both the Baltic and the Balkan remain a top priority for Russia because they can establish significant achievements in that ambition through these gas pipeline projects and access to European consumers.

There was a deal. In the Gulf, there was a huge stockpile of chemical weapon waste from World War II. Denmark wanted to easily rehabilitate the toxic waste to Russia in exchange for an agreement on the pipeline. It was decided that Russia would buy the recycling energy material at a higher rate. Sometimes, even beyond fixing the deal, one party consciously keeps a provision and tight knots so that there is scope in the future for further negotiation in favor of themselves. This is a trick of the business.

Iceland

A two-member team was sent to sabotage the MOU, Agreement and Technical document of the North Stream Two Pipeline. One person was given the task of managing alterations in legal contracts. He was **Mr Jeffrey Pence**. He was a senior engineer in Gazporn and was an instrumental founding person in the first Nord Stream. He was an automatic choice for this 2nd project and was in the team of deal negotiation and approval. He was a close ally of Denmark and German officials.

Another person, **Kelvin Floyd**, was given the task to malfunction a government portal and circulate the revised duplicate soft copy into the system. He will also manipulate the core operative machine of Nord Stream Two and spoil the pipeline. Floyd was the same person who was the system and networking officer in 'polar bear'. He worked on the launch code protocol and codes for 'polar bear'.

Jeffrey already knew the relevant bureaucrats of Nord Stream Two project, so it was easier for him to manage and manipulate the contract papers. He managed access to the secretariat department of Copenhagen. It took almost a week. Some licensing clauses were supposed to be amended so that even after the work was completed, the gas supply would ultimately cause a halt due to the requirement of additional certification and a few critical licenses.

Floyd boarded Hotel Utkiek. The task must be foolproof. Floyd was not using the stereotype route of hijacking an IP through an open-source internet bug. He would have done this sitting in another part of the globe. He has come closer to the target system and hence took his station in Greifswald itself, which is 150 kilometers away from Copenhagen. He was waiting for an important delivery. The courier, 'Rubber Ducky Pendrive', reached Floyd after three days. This special pen drive is a device that works as a programmed keyboard in the shape of a USB drive. When this is plugged into a computer, it starts writing automatically to launch proxy programs and tools, which may either be available on the victim's computer or loaded onto the server in order to extract information. Floyd couriered the device further to Jeffrey in Copenhagen. Jeffrey managed to load the device into the Copenhagen governmental data center. Along with this, Lan Turtle was connected to the server switch for stealthy remote access. Floyd was controlling the access remotely from Iceland. He easily established spoofing and pushed the duplicate files into the system. The documents were replaced as per plan. Floyd also set a timer into the core operative machine to spoil the pressure valves of the pipeline. A stretch of the pipeline will explode in time intervals. Nord Stream Two will be destroyed as per plan.

Floyd executed another crucial espionage. He knew the date and time range of the car accident. He needed crucial data about the accident of Denmark's PM. Floyd pressed the range and downloaded the CCTV footage from inside the tunnel, which was earlier classified and encrypted. Floyd was an expert in breaking private keys and encrypted files.

But Floyd actually did a double cross. He stole the secret information without any permission and previous plan. Floyd got a call at night. He confirmed to the caller that the job was done. It was C2.

***

Dr. Bunn opened up everything. His witness and version hold invaluable intelligence that can break the conspiracy. Den was able to consolidate the important facts so far. After the arrest of Dr. Bunn, he would now reconcile the whole event, actually all of the events. Dr. Bunn confessed that 'Chief' launched a dual mission- 'polar bear'. On one side, they partnered with the Russian and Chinese governments to build supremacy in the North Pole by seabed mining and illegal underwater drilling for fossil fuels. There are five such areas across the Arctic, including Svalbard. The sixth spot is in the Gulf of Mexico. They planted 'nukes' to spoil Oklahoma, the largest 'Strategic Petroleum Reserve' (SPR), of the US.

Oklahoma is a vital transshipment point with many intersecting pipelines, huge storage facilities and easy access to refiners and suppliers. Damage at Oklahoma's petrol reserve will cause lethal destruction on trade routes on a global scale. This will severely impact not only the captive fuel supply to America but also disrupt leased committed storage of other Latin American and a few European countries. The plan was devastating.

On the other hand, the virus breakout was man-made. This was also part of the dual mission. Oil price, commodity trade, global commerce and the economy are all closely interlinked. There was a conscious business and political plan to disrupt the order. Humanity was compromised.

The confession revealed further that Dr. Bunn and Taylor were hired professionals. Management was not happy with Taylor for his slowness and integrity issues. Management was losing trust on Taylor, so a new person replaced Taylor and took charge and fast-tracked the job. Dr. Bunn was hired specifically for the Oklahoma bombing. Mike's person informed Den of this in detail.

Thule Airbase, Greenland

Den still had a mild fever and skin infection. He was on medicine. The attendant came inside Den's room and gave him some protein soup. He was now in army custody of Thule. A video call was projected on the mounted TV. Call was from Mike.

Mike began his brief, "We are trying hard to interrogate. First, the immediate priority is Oklahoma. The US Navy has been deployed to spot the location. We are keeping this discreet in case the planner is monitoring us through a satellite. There is a risk they could detonate anytime remotely. The team is trying to catch hold of the probable system which can defuse the nukes. For illegal underwater mining and drilling, we deployed a separate team to spot the locations and gather proof. Thereafter, legal action will be taken against this, and we will pursue this case to the International Court of Justice."

"The arrest of Dr. Bunn is a huge success for us," Den said.

"Yeah. It is extremely important to us. He is kept in a heavily guarded security zone."

"That is great, Sir."

"Do not be in shock if I tell you that while interrogating him, we got a lead on who the other mole in our system is. He has double-crossed us and must be the right hand of Chief and the other mastermind of this conspiracy."

"Who is that mole?"

"National Security Advisor of US- **Joseph Bolton**. His code name is C2. Bolton is a traitor."

"The spiderweb is spread wide."

"It gets wider. Coronavirus is a man-made breakout. Texas University used to fund the Wuhan Virological Lab for its research. We are withdrawing the collaboration. We sent our scientist audit team, but they are not cooperating. We even engaged our investigation team and the CIA for the death of Dr. Lee. He was a whistleblower. We suspect that it was a coverup."

"A biological weapon?" Den asked.

"It broke out from Wuhan. We will need to scale up our investigation. The entire world came to a standstill because of this pandemic. Industrial and economic activities are at a complete halt. The world is moving towards a depression, which China wants to leverage. They infused supply to compensate for the lag and global demand in their ambition for economic supremacy. They planned to change the global order overnight. We cannot let it happen. It is high time that we should punish the fox and wolf."

"Both are clever animals.

"Bolton was a US ambassador to the UN before he became the National Security Advisor. I hope you can understand the link of his relationship with Chief," Mike said.

"I know about him. Mr Bolton is reputed for his war affection. But a conspiracy of this scale from him is very unusual!"

"It is he who always has been pushing our policy and PM to advocate for military intervention in Iran, Syria, Libya, Venezuela, Cuba, Yemen and North Korea. The list is long. Now he activated a different war, but this time he sabotaged it."

"Cleaning up this web will not be easy, I guess. We need proof and facts to establish everything," Den said, amazed.

Mike replied after a long pause, "I have a plan. The climax is near. Bolton is in Michigan, and Chief is in New York. We can catch both the fox and the wolf in New York itself."

New York

Den came back to New York. This was as per plan. He already compromised his health. But the World was under threat. The demon needs to be stopped at any cost. Probability was very low. There was neither any support system and allies nor a visible fate in the rogue future. He had to rise one last time and find ways to resolve the crisis. He would be ready to confront Chief shortly, but the plan got put on hold. Mike was detected with COVID-19 and had to be admitted to a hospital. There was hardly a household or office floor that was still out of the viral influenza. Den completely locked himself in his home for safety. The usual busy picture of New York had already changed to an abandoned city as if no civilization existed. Everybody was inside. The city 'that never sleeps' was completely silent as if it was uninhabited.

Unrest was picking up, which broke the silence of New York from time to time. The 'Black Lives matter movement' resumed in Chicago after another brutal murder of a black African American- George Floyd, by an American Police. One police officer kneeled on his neck for at least seven minutes despite the forty-six-year-old George Floyed gasping for breath and repeatedly saying, "I can't breathe."

There were several similar racist, brutal incidents in America, but this time, the people could not resist themselves and came onto the road to protest. Unrest spreaded in different parts of the US, including in California, Ohio, Colorado and New York. The movement scaled up to another kind of unrest. An unrest of toppling colonial statues of white supremacy occurred in the US, Britain and different parts of the world . In Britain, a statue of the seventeenth-century slave trader- Edward Colston was toppled by protesters and dumped into the very same waters of the Bristol Harbor that launched slave ships centuries ago. Protesters have also made threats against statues of former prime minister Winston Churchill, who was an extreme racist and architect of colonial policies that led to mass starvation and the torture of people in several colonised countries. The movement escalated further and targeted statues of Roosevelt and several other old Presidents and Kings.

It was true that many records of colonial crimes were destroyed long ago. Governments want to avoid embarrassing information going out to the public. Stockpiles of a few sensitive and classified files still remain in secret custody. Historians have not been able to trace any of them yet. Recently, those secret files were made digital and transformed into film tapes for preservation. The original copies were burned. There is a secret chamber in Svalbard called the '*Arctic World Archive*' where some governments keep classified encrypted files in a repository. This is similar to the '*Global Seed Vault*'.

This is managed by a Norwegian data storage company, "Piql" and the state-owned coal-mining company, "Store Norske". Piql follows Swiss banks' non-disclosure policy for their clients and works for both private and government parties. Kelvin Floyd works in Piql, which is why he was hired by 'polar bear' for the specific job of designing and program launch codes. Presently, he was in Iceland to finish his recent assignment of file spoofing for Nord Stream Two. George Floyd was his elder brother.

Floyd and his mother, **Mrs Loretta Bullard**, came to New York. They were attending George Floyd's funeral. His body was released after four days. The funeral happened, and because of the restrictions, there were very few people. Social gatherings were restricted due to the lockdown. Police had to take pain to manage the protesters on the road. With the days going by, the intensity of the protests was increasing and getting violent in some areas.

Mrs Bullard is President of "Kawerak Inc.", a nonprofit consortium of regional tribal governments in Alaska. She was an ex-commissioner of the Denali Commission and an executive board member of the 'Alaska Federation of Natives Board'. She was also a representative member of the '*Sustainable Blue Economy Conference*', which was recently held in Nairobi in collaboration with Canada and Japan. Through that network, she was connected to IMO and the Arctic Council, so she knew Remi very well.

Remi called Den and asked him to meet Mrs. Bullard. Nome is emerging as a strategically important point in the Arctic and Alaska. The rule of development is to bring in big, new things at the cost of old, small things. Industries always destroy natural resources and turn native cultures vulnerable. There was a plan to expand Nome, the Alaskan port, into a larger deepwater facility. The expansion plan proposed extending the harbor much farther into Norton Sound and dredging the outer area so that it is deep enough to accommodate big vessels like fuel tankers and large cruise ships. This was a federal funded expansion, and the bill was approved by the Congress. The 'America's Water Infrastructure Act' was pushing several other port expansion and Greenfield Port projects across the Arctic.

Kawerak and local tribes have protested against this industrial expansion as it posed potential threats to local natural resources and, therefore, to the Indigenous people who depend on those resources. Mrs Bullard was planning to meet Chief to discuss this vulnerability in the official forum of the UN. She will meet Chief of the UN HO on Friday. Today was Tuesday.

Den will be meeting Mrs Bullard and Kelvin Floyd in the afternoon. The appointment was scheduled by Remi.

***

They assembled in lower Manhattan. They came to the third floor of 'Fraunces Tavern'. It is one of the oldest and historical buildings in New York City. Although the museum and restaurant were closed, Den managed to get in through his sources. He was able to use the gallery room for a couple of hours. It was not very safe to meet them in public or at a hotel.

Den first showed condolence for Floyd. Mrs Bullard was morose for her son's death. Floyd was sitting in a chair and listening. He was quiet. Den and Floyd did not know each other yet.

"Are you American or European?" Mrs. Bullard asked a peculiar question to Den.

"No, mam, I work here at the UN. The recent incident was very unfortunate. It is more unfortunate that people have to identify themselves by virtue of citizenship or caste."

"Extreme polarization of the human mind and social divide is inevitable. Hatred and violence in racism never changes with time," Mrs Bullard said, sadly.

"Very unfortunate that no generation is able to change it."

Mrs. Bullard said, "Change is not possible. Indigenous people, minorities, poor, simple and less intelligent people have always been used as a commodity exchange or garbage. The method of colonization only changed to sophistication. You cannot understand. The Western world thinks that their supremacy over the human race will continue, and they are the lawmakers of the Globe. But the problem is deeper. If Nature and natural resources collapse, ruin will happen faster for all of mankind. The government is not bothered to protect its biodiversity. You cannot solve this with fake propaganda."

Den was listening patiently. Mrs Bullard continued, "Do you know about the 'Northern Bering Sea Climate Change Resilience'? This restricts oil and gas exploration in the Arctic, Chukchi, and Beaufort Seas. But the present government passed an executive order to roll back this and ordered it to revoke it. The executive order titled '*Implementing an America-First Offshore Energy Strategy*' sets forth a policy that has the goal of maintaining global leadership in energy innovation, exploration, and production."

Den acknowledged the fact, "the indigenous people are now at the mercy of federal decisions."

Mrs Bullard also agreed with Den, "the developed world perceives this as development. The fact is just the opposite. These are serious lies. Since there are lies in societies, it is eventual that there are lies in policy making," Mrs. Bullard said angrily.

"I agree that it is policymakers whose business agenda is to spoil the pole. I mean both the poles. The North Pole has immediate business value, so there are industrial activities that can take place. The South Pole and Antarctica are still virgin but this would face the same outcome once we exhaust the resources in the North Pole," Den said.

The attendant served the coffee. Den ordered black coffee. Den took a cookie and resumed talking. "Foreign policy and geopolitics frame the fate. The government sometimes goes beyond the official agenda and conspires in a specific operation to achieve the bigger goal. Official machinery is used for unofficial missions. I know some of those. But I do not know whether the spoiler is sponsored by one government or a consortium of governments."

Floyd raised his eyebrows and looked at Den. He didn't say anything yet. Instead, he was sipping his coffee during the conversation.

"What do you mean?" Mrs Bullard asked.

"You must know that Remi is going to publish her new research paper. Her topic is *Arctic Business*. Her work is very extensive. She collected a lot of information. Some information is classified, but for now, she would only restrict her paper for climate. She is not covering the industrial side of the Arctic, or else she would have to publish a lot more volumes at a time," Den smiled.

"Yeah, I am aware. I admire her. She requested our help with information. Kawerak supported her work. She could not be present at the 'Blue Economy conference' in Kenya, but she collaborated with us. The conference identified the potential of the blue economy to create employment and combat poverty and hunger. It brought countries together to learn how economic development and healthy waters go hand in hand. The impacts of climate change and plastic pollution in oceans and waters have increased the need to develop an inclusive and sustainable blue economy. This builds on the momentum of the UN's 2030 agenda of 'Call to Action for global warming'. This was the first conference."

"Do you trust this?" Den asked.

Mrs Bullard looked at the far sky. She was silent for a while. She replied, "Let me tell you, Mr Den, there is an agenda behind the iron curtain to shut down IMO, the Arctic Council and the 'Conference of Parties'. It is being tried out to consolidate this new idea and the organization of the Blue Economy conference as an alternative to it. There is a lot of budget for climate and the environment will be made to seize. They would rather pursue their economic agenda in the frame of environment-friendly masks and faux setups. They will forego the earlier pledge and resume from scratch. Buying time is easier and it is nothing but a trick. This is business. Hence, this is complex."

"I am working with Remi. Rather, I picked up a task not for her but for myself. We all know that the Arctic is melting fast, but we are concerned that the Arctic has made the ice melt faster."

"Yes, the polar region is getting more traction all of a sudden. Industrial and shipping activities have increased multifold in the region, whether it is the frequency of cargo ships or military patrolling for fossil fuel exploration. Rather, our native profession of fishing and prospect of more scientific expeditions have drastically either come down or diversified."

"Exactly. Have you thought about the reason for this sudden shift to Arctic importance?"

"I told you, Mr Den, tribal people are now at the mercy of federal decisions. Perhaps we are losing our land. I do not know much."

"I know it exactly."

Mrs. Bullard grabbed Den's hand with both of her hands and exchanged warm gratitude, "It is really nice that we met, Mr Den. I am concerned that we are losing our soil to another's hand. I lost my one child here. Perhaps this country never included him in its soil because of his skin color."

Den apologized to Mrs. Bullard and expressed condolences for Floyd one more time.

Floyd was completely quiet the entire time. He was in a storm of realization. His mind was changing. And it changed forever. A turning point in life is always God's gift, and it always happens suddenly.

***

On the very next day, Den got a guest at his apartment. The security room informed him that the guest's name was Kelvin Floyd.

Final Plan and Final Command

Svalbard Satellite Station

A submarine heading towards Finnafjord, Iceland, contains the pickup. This was the final lap. Nuclear balls were getting transported to the sites. The heavily guarded convoy started from Portsmouth, Ohio. The material was enriched at the 'Centrus Energy Corporation' in Ohio. The convoy passed through the US-Canada Peace Bridge over Lake Erie. After it crossed Peace Bridge, it took Queen Elizabeth's route and passed through Niagara Falls. Then, it reached Port Hope via Toronto. Before enrichment, the early stage of the fuel was prepared at the yellowcake conversion facility of 'Cameco' in Ontario, Canada. The ore isotope was smuggled from Greenland Mineral Energy's uranium mine in Kvanefjeld. From Port Hope, the cargo will move by sea. The Skjold class high-speed vessel of the Royal Norwegian Navy picked up the cargo and shipped it to Iceland via the St. Lawrence River and Labrador Sea. The 'Greenland-Iceland-UK' gap is a key choke point for naval forces to protect one of the busiest sea routes, the English Channel, which is why it always got support from NATO. Even though this area was heavily guarded by NATO, the secret shipment somehow took place successfully. This was managed very delicately.

From Finnafjord, the parcel was handed over to the submarine. The '30B UF6' containers were carrying highly enriched uranium material. The Chief of Boats signed the receipt and gave it to the master of the ship. This was a transhipment, so there were exchanges of vessels and transport modes. Finally, the submarine will deliver the parcel to the sites. One installation engineer and one instrumentation engineer will accompany it and enter the shaft. Three top executives, the Sub-Captain, the Chief of Boat and the Executive Officer, will unanimously acknowledge the parcel and authorize the final delivery. This is the protocol of the submarine.

The first site was near Dundas Harbour, which was beneath the T-point of Lancaster Sound and Baffin Bay on the way from the east coast of Greenland to the North slope of Alaska. This is a key entry point of the Northwest Passage. The submarine reached Dundas Harbour and came closer to the shaft. Two crew divers came out of the submarine. There was complete darkness in the 4500 feet below the water's surface. The only source of light was the mounted helmet on their special diving suit. The suit was designed to withstand the extreme water pressure and temperature of such depths. One crew pressed the passkey to open the lockgate. They entered the shaft and installed the uranium ball into the canister. The instrumentation guy rechecked the connection. After successful installation and checking, they both came back to the sub.

The second site was at the crossing of Cape Dorset, Coral Harbour and Ivujivik in the Hudson Strait on the way to Churchill Port, Canada. This was an important gateway for the US-Canada shipping route via the Hudson Bay.

The third site was also on a similar route. It was at the entry point of North-western Passage and between Blank Island & Melville island, where the north-western passage connects the Beaufort Sea and Baffin Bay. This is another key choke point for the future container port in Moosonee, Churchill Port, for future Canadian trans-Arctic navigation. The railway distance from Moosonee to Chicago, Toronto and the Great Lakes is much shorter than the railway distance from the Pacific Coast container ports. Site locations were researched and chosen specifically for a big purpose.

The warheads were ready.

Taylor, if alive, would have supervised and received the update of the final installation, but now Mac was taking the charge. Updates were passed on to C3. All critical updates ultimately go to the main commander and mastermind C2 and C1. But there has been a relationship issue among C2 and C1. C1 did not want to take a chance and had instructed the key operatives to bypass C2 for all future tasks in 'polar bear'. The instrumentation in charge, Ted Mateen, was also hospitalized for COVID. So, the responsibility moved to the second in command for instrumentation, Kelvin Floyd.

***

Den collected updates about the health of Mike from his secretary. The secretary informed that Mike's condition was stable, but he needed hospitalization for more days. Mike was put in the ICU for better care due to his acute oxygen deficit.

Den had no time to wait and waste. He will go to Michigan. It was urgent. It would take at least 8-9 hours by car, so he started early in the morning from New York. He was carrying the file where he kept all the leads, intercepts and findings. In the file, the six spots were expanded upon. The file was locked by a number code. As per Dr. Bunn's confession, there were five spots across the Arctic Circle where seabed mining and illegal underwater drilling of fossil fuel were being carried out. The sixth spot in the Gulf of Mexico near Oklahoma was plotted with a hydrogen bomb. Dr. Bunn might be lying because some of the information was not correct.

Den knew the fact by this time that the sixth spot was not plotted with a nuke. They constructed a large SPR underwater with vast undisclosed capacity to reserve fossil fuels. It was an advanced preparation to stock the fuel at dirt cheap price to arbitrage and sell it at a very high price in the future. This was Baton Rouge in Louisiana and was very close to Oklahoma. The largest commodity trader was backing the deal in coordination with the government. The syndicate built two similar large petrol reservoirs in the other two spots. One was in Pudau Bay in North Slope, another one was in Bear Island of Svalbard. The other three spots across the NWP were plotted with nukes.

On Den's drive, he was thinking about how the COVID pandemic and an inherent global lockdown made the world's trade stop. The virus grabbed the full globe with its devastating community spread. After Europe, it was the US's turn, which gradually turned it into a graveyard. The way it harmed people's lungs, it also stopped all industrial activities, shipping, production, consumption and human movement. It changed everything. People were speculating if the world was headed to the graveyard of unemployment and an economic depression. This also created another issue by way of a crash in the price of oil. The pricing index became negative for the first time ever. This was exactly the situation for which those special petro reserves were built. This was made up to create an artificial future price for fat profit. Things were on target as per the plan.

Den got what he wanted in Michigan, but by playing a risky game. The next course will not be a mere adventure but a high-risk gamble for him. He was already under surveillance, his life was put on line. This will probably be the single chance but he will take the final risk.

***

There has always been a marriage of convenience between powers at the UN. At present, five countries, the US, the UK, France, Russia and China, have the special status of permanent member states at the 'Security Council', along with a special voting power known as the "right to veto". If any one of the five permanent members casts a negative vote on the 15-member Security Council, the decision will not be approved. Any resolution needs to be recommended by the Security Council with at least nine affirmative votes. That means other than five confirmed votes from permanent members, at least four more affirmative votes out of ten non-permanent members are required to pursue the recommendation to the 'General Assembly'. Then, a 2/3rd majority vote of the General Assembly would decide and approve the final resolution. Presently, the UN General Assembly has a total of 193 member countries.

The UN has six main wings: General Assembly, Security Council, Economic and Social Council, Trusteeship Council, International Court of Justice and 'Secretariat'.

The General Assembly is a universal representation with 193 member countries deciding policy. The Security Council, with fifteen member states, has primary responsibility, under the UN Charter, for the maintenance of international peace and security. The Secretariat is the working body of the organ that executes the mandate. The Secretary-General is the Chief Administrative Officer of the organization, appointed by the General Assembly based on the recommendation of the Security Council for a five-year, renewable term. UN staff members are recruited internationally and locally and work in duty stations and on peacekeeping missions all around the world. The Secretary-General chairs the Senior Management group, which is responsible for planning, policy drafting, information sharing, budgeting and programming with respect to emerging global challenges and issues.

The Security Council decides the peacekeeping program and when and where a UN peace operation should be deployed. The Security Council establishes a peace operation by adopting a Security Council resolution. The resolution sets out the mission's mandate and size. Presently, there are thirteen peacekeeping deployments across the globe. The Head of Mission reports to the Under-Secretary-General for Peace Operations at UN Headquarters. The Secretary-General also appoints a Peace Operation Force Commander, a Police Commissioner, and senior civilian staff. The Department of Peace Operations (DPO) and the Department of Operational Support (DOS) are then responsible for staffing the civilian components of a peace operation. The UN has no standing army or police force of its own, and membering states are asked to contribute military and police personnel required for each operation. Peacekeepers wear their countries' uniforms and are identified as UN peacekeepers by a UN 'blue helmet' or beret and a badge. Civilian staff of peace operations are international civil servants recruited and deployed by the UN Secretariat.

Other than its main positions, the UN also has several other bodies, entities, and specialized agencies. IMF, World Bank, Human Rights Council, UNESCO, UNICEF, Framework Convention on Climate Change and IMO are a few of them.

Remi is a senior executive of the IMO Council. IMO is the UN's specialized agency, responsible for the safety and security of shipping and the prevention of marine pollution by ships. IMO consists of an Assembly, a Council and five main Committees. The assembly is the highest governing body responsible for approving the work programme, voting on the budget and determining the organization's financial arrangements. The Assembly also elects the Council. The Council is the Executive Organ of IMO and is responsible, under the Assembly, for supervising the work of the Organization.

The United Nations Framework Convention on Climate Change (UNFCCC) was an international environmental treaty adopted in 1992 and opened for signature at the Earth Summit in Rio de Janeiro in 1992. The objective of UNFCCC is to stabilize greenhouse gas concentrations in the atmosphere at a level that would prevent dangerous anthropogenic interference with the climate system. The framework sets non-binding limits on greenhouse gas emissions for individual countries. The convention started in 1995. 'Conferences of the Parties' (COP) monitor progress in dealing with climate change. In 1997, the Kyoto Protocol was concluded, and legally binding obligations were established for developed countries to reduce their greenhouse gas emissions in the period 2008–2012. The 2010 United Nations Climate Change Conference produced an agreement stating that future global warming should be limited to below 2.0 °C relative to the pre-industrial level. In 2015, the Paris Agreement was adopted, governing emission reductions from 2020 on through commitments of countries in Nationally Determined Contributions (NDCs), with a view of lowering the target to 1.5 °C. The Paris Agreement entered into force on the fourth of November in 2016.

***

Other than the climate agenda, a lot was going on in the UN. All of a sudden, the calendar was marked for several immediate priority meetings in the General Assembly. Surprisingly, most were interlinked and made for the Arctic,

- Greenland and Taiwan applied for sovereign statehood and independence.

- Inclusion of new States for permanent status. Canada, Germany, India, and Japan were in the race.

- To start a Peacekeeping program for the Egypt-Sinai conflict.

- Restructuring of some Organs/ Agencies. IMO was one of them.

- Situation of oil price crash and OPEC+

The meetings were prioritized in order and will be discussed before the other pre-scheduled meetings for the situation in Libya and the Balkans, COVID-19, China's law enforcement in Hong Kong, etc.

Fixing policy decisions or geopolitical conflicts of this stature is not easy. A country buys votes from another country in return for an alternate price. Negotiating these deals follows a common protocol. This means they get compensated for compromising. If a country opposes something, the other has to find ways to compensate them with alternative benefits. Otherwise, political equilibrium is not possible. It is a complex process.

Canada was already ramping up for UN permanent membership. They were currently in the US lobby. Canada started a bigger engagement in African investment and aid. The 'USMCA', the US-Mexico-Canada Free Trade Arrangement, was upgraded from the earlier North American Free Trade Agreement, or 'NAFTA'. The Arctic Cooperation Agreement between the US and Canada on the northwest passage about bilateral cooperation has also been upgraded with a mutual agreement on a few new terms. The US has already declared its priority on the Arctic. The Canadian north coast is the gateway in the high north. Both the US and Canada already complement and depend on each other economically on specific industry segments and resource mobilization. Canada was the best and safest bet for the US on the subject of North Pole politics. Free trade and a huge investment in ports were just a few steps to cement the mutual relationship. It was in the US's interest that they convinced Canada to be a partner and a part of the Arctic ambition. In return, the US would back Canada in getting their permanent UN member status.

The US knew that China would veto on Canada, Taiwan and India for being contenders in the race for permanent membership. Instead, Germany might win confidence from across the states atleast with Russia in condition of supplying gas to Germany through the Nord Stream Two Gas Pipeline without any break or other influence. This was a win-win for both Germany and Russia. Germany-Russia-China emerged as a natural ally in the UN Security Council voting. So China will never veto Germany at this moment. China also will not oppose Germany because of being able to secure a 5G telecom contract. With rising tension between the US and Germany, the United States would put a veto on Germany. It was a simple political trade-off. Clearance of Canada was a higher priority for the US than vetoing Germany. The US would like to earn clearance of Canada with a condition to pass Germany on another hand.

Naturally, the complex equation was solved easily. Permanent seats in the UN Security Council for Canada and Germany were conceptually finalized. On the other hand, in the question of application for sovereignty, Taiwan was opted out, but the chance for Greenland was high. Keeping Greenland separate from Denmark was in the interest of the brigade of China and Russia. In every project or investment, China had to solve the equations of Greenland together with Denmark bureaucrats. Naturally, China preferred to simply use the negotiation matrix. Russia was viewing the connection from a different perspective to push Greenland out of the Nordic Region. Russia has never been interested in Greenland because Greenland's territory was close to the Canadian coastline and 'NWP'. Russia did not get business benefits or political coverage from Greenland.

Rather, it was easier to influence Denmark alone and strengthen the 'Arctic silk route' through 'NSR'.

Russia can focus its NSR and Baltic ambition on the Nordic region with the help of Denmark and Norway. Russia has triangle coverage with three of its northernmost military-naval-air bases surrounding NSR and the Baltic. HO of Northern Command, Kola peninsula, a new base in Alexandra Land and Kotelny Island, made the Russian coastal defense powerful and aggressive. Location advances two major Russian objectives in the Arctic. It enhances Russian territorial defense and improves monitoring and control over maritime activity across the Northern Sea Route.

As its northernmost military installation, Alexandra Land pushes Russia's military and the forward line of defense further north into the Arctic Ocean, making it a key outpost to observe NATO activity and capabilities. Russia always prefers to get additional support from Nordic states. Naturally, Russia would play neutral on the subject of Greenland's independence from Denmark. Hence, recommendations for the independence of Greenland were also final. In world politics, these deals and decisions often happen in the backdoor. Pursuing a forum and completing a resolution is a mere formality in the front gate.

There were other potboilers in the South China Sea, such as Iran coming closer to China, the China-Russia pact for commerce and currency, the moral decoupling of the Germany-US relationship and the boiling tension of Turkey with Greece and Mediterranean coastal countries. All these were war situations. It was difficult to predict a particular event or situation that would eventually lead to a more dangerous global war. One significant race can definitely be made responsible for such future World Wars, if at all, with the complexity of the 5G contract and value chain of rare Earth elements combined with a semiconductor chipset, which were going to dictate terms and define the law of future geopolitics. The world stage was set to go all out for war. This was multi-dimensional since there were multiple parties, problems and geographies.

Tensions escalated, and the situation became more intense. World War has already silently started. The powerhouses were already polarized with different combinations and conditions among allied-axis forces. There was complexity among rivals, but there was equal complexity within the same group.

Tromso, Norway

As per the plan, Floyd and Den landed at the Tromso airport. They were guests of **Mr Buljo Gaup**, the ex-minister from the ruling Labour Party and ex-chairperson of the Bar Association. He is a retired parliamentarian and was recently reappointed as a jury member of the 'Nobel Committee'. He was also a Judge in the Supreme Court of Norway before joining as Minister in Parliament. Now, he is spending most of his old age working for indigenous people.

Den didn't know Mr Gaup directly but knew he could use his influence to arrange entry passes in the Svalbard Satellite Centre. After the recent Michigan meeting, it was decided that Den would meet Mr Gaup in-person. For this, Den needed to travel 450 km from Tromso to a tribal village- Karasjok. Mr Gaup often stays in his native family house in the far north. Without help from Mr Gaup, it might be difficult to arrange a final entrypass for Svalbard Satellite Station. Although Floyd had access since he was instrumental in developing 'launch codes' but he had to go to Svalbard this time with disguise.

The taxi left the Tromso airport and took Storgata's main street and then took the Tromsobrua bridge. They will cross the bridge to come to the Arctic Cathedral. Floyd bought biscuits, bread and dry fruits for the long journey. It would take at least seven hours to reach Karasjok. This was a small village of the indigenous tribe 'Sami' near Floya mountain.

Mr Gaup graciously welcomed Den and Floyd into his native tribal home, immersing himself in the traditional ways of the Sami people. In the evening, a heartwarming tradition unfolded as they were invited to a communal gathering inside a 'lavvu tent', where he mingled with the villagers. They shared local music known as 'joik', a hauntingly beautiful art form, and indulged in a feast of Nordic cuisine. Here in Karasjok, Den witnessed the untouched authenticity of a tribal community, living their lives in a manner far removed from the bustling modern world, offering a fascinating glimpse into the remnants of an Earth where such remote and unconventional places still exist in today's time.

"Sir, I heard about your work on indigenous rights. We appreciate your involvement and the stands you take," Den praised Mr Gaup.

"But I am not Minister anymore," Mr Gaup laughed. "It is unfortunate that I was compelled and dragged into this. It still affects my health at this old age. It would have been a peaceful space if I was aloof from this world politics. It ruins."

Den endorsed, "It has changed for the worse. Lawmakers and beneficial owners are changing this faster."

Mr Gaup replied, "Wrong. It is a misconception that it is changing now. It was always there. There was no single time or generation, where humans had lived their lives without politics or war."

Mr Gaup arranged the local delicacy for today's dinner. He requested the guests to participate and pick up the dish. There were potato flatbread rolls, called 'Lefse' and thick reindeer stew, called 'Bidos'. The guests were delighted.

"These are wonderful, Sir", They continued the conversation while having dinner.

Den was curious about Mr Gaup since he was on the jury for selecting the Nobel Peace Prize nomination & winner. Den showed his curiosity and asked Mr Gaup.

Mr Gaup bluntly replied, "Do you really think that few retired politicians can judge and select the Scientists or Authors in their respective academia? Obviously, it is not. Selecting a single contributor among so many genius efforts around the globe in that respective field is not enough. Selection is often an influencing process. I was a criminal judge and then a retired parliamentarian. I don't have the talent to choose or vote for the Nobel Laureate. My present role is worse. I am a council member for the Nobel Peace Prize. This is peculiar. Throughout the time, this selection is a political process. Please don't quote me outside of here. The council members have no power. Decisions often come from other powerhouses, and the decisions are mostly interlinked with political deals. I hope that you guys can understand," Mr Gaup shyly smiled.

"Yeah, there were some controversies," Den said, "It is still a mystery and equally embarrassing that most of the time, the Nobel Peace Prize was given to those politicians who were named for wars. From the backdoor, the lawmaker fuels the war, and the same lawmaker causes a ceasefire at the front gate. Vietnamese revolutionary, diplomat and politician Le Duc Tho turned down the prize when his name was announced along with then US Secretary of State Henry Kissinger in 1973. Mr Kissinger pulled American troops out of South Vietnam while the South Vietnamese government and the Viet Cong were to agree to a coalition government. But within a year, South Vietnam had fallen into the hands of North Vietnam. Mikhail Gorbachev won the prize in 1990, just a year before the collapse of the Soviet Union. There are so many peculiar examples."

"I was never a jury in the selection process of 'peace award' to Presidential candidates, but I know the influence chain," Mr Gaup smiled. "Even the recent winner got massive backing from specific government investors. It happened in the past and it will happen more frequently in the coming years."

"I met Mr Abiy Ahmed recently. I hope you mean him."

"Please be patient. Peace will be broken very soon. There are multiple stakeholders and multiple dealings going on surrounding that Red Sea corridor."

"I already experienced it in Ethiopia," Den recalled.

They completed the dinner. It was going to be a unique experience for both Floyd and Den while spending the night in the Lavvu tent.

***

There are other similar traditions in the polar circle. Inuit people stay in small snow huts called 'Igloo' across Greenland and the Canadian Arctic. The region is home to different culturally distinct groups of indigenous people. The 'Inupiaq' reside on the Seward Peninsula as well as the King and Diomede Islands between Siberia and Alaska. 'Yupik' tribes primarily reside in the Siberian Arctic and are closely related culturally and linguistically to the Chukotka people of the Russian Far East. 'Inuit', whom we commonly call 'Eskimo', stay mostly in Greenland, Alaska and the Canadian coast. Tribes of the Polar Circle were mostly limited to their respective territory because of the scarcity of economic prosperity in extreme weather conditions and lack of exploration. Still, some of their earlier generations could manage to cross the geography and explore other lands. Even the modern North American land never belonged to the Dutch-Spanish-English invaders. 'Lenape' were key indigenous people of modern-day New York much before Dutch settlement. They used to speak Norse and had origins from Greenland. There are plenty of such examples. The population of all these old tribes are reducing. Their traditions and social existence also faded with time. Because the World does not need them. If an abandoned territory suddenly gets commercial traction for future opportunities, at first, the investors invite migrant workers of both white and blue collar. The native locals compromise by handing over their land and hence lose the right. Eventually, they either become laborers or join in grey jobs to service the new migrant guests.

***

Den was a migrant to the USA. It was his second year in New York City. Although the entire North America is inhabited by migrants. The city is dense with a working and business population and never sleeps. New York could retain its position as the notional capital of the World for a long period. It happened post-World War. It was not Spanish, Dutch, French, or English rule anymore. The busiest town emerged as the economic nucleus of 'capitalist politics'. It's skyscrapers, neon-lit Times Square. Wall Street symbolizes the monolith of modern-day superpowers. Washington-New York is the present lawmaker of the World. And they execute it either by natural commercial-political progression or by artificial means. There are several complicated tools, tricks and diplomacy available to ensure this. The world order keeps changing and shifting the hegemony between states. However, during medieval-modern times, this was mostly concentrated in the West. The future order tends to shift towards a new geography, the East for the first time. The emerging powers of China and Russia of the East threaten to displace the existing great Western powers as regional or international hegemons. This myth of the 'Thucydides Trap' compelled Washington and New York to go after the competition and enemy aggressively. They needed immediate strategic action.

***

The next morning, they were served with the local coffee. It is hardly a day without coffee for a Norwegian. Mr Gaup arranged everything from the local traditions to satisfy his guests. Although Den doesn't drink coffee at all, he will manage.

Mr Gaup asked Den, "So, gentlemen, what is your exact purpose in Svalbard? Bolton briefed me about you."

"I am sorry, Sir. I cannot disclose my mission. We will go to Svalbard Satellite Station to access some covert information. There is a conspiracy plan, and there is a global threat, so this visit is discreet and very critical for us. We must thank you for helping us in this journey. Mr Bolton might have told you the conditions."

"Are you working for the American government?"

Den didn't say much on this, "We are not government staff. We work for the government."

"I agreed to help based on my deep relationship with Bolton. I am taking high risks, though." Mr Gaup halted for a moment and continued, "Nordic states are lazy. I mean, they don't hold aggression for a long time just to sustain in competition. It always happened while Danish Vikings captured Britannica or they adventured on marine trips. They never ever accomplished good commerce. The time is changing, though. Nordic states have another global opportunity where they may play a key role. This time, commercial judgment should be the priority. However, bilateral and group relationships are complex. Norway is divided between the West and Russia. Denmark and Germany came closer gradually. But after the unfortunate death of Denmark's PM, nobody knows their future." Mr Gaup completed his coffee.

Mr Gaup continued, "Denmark, after approving NS2, also approved long-pending tunnel proposals to connect Hamburg to Copenhagen and Puttgarden to Rodbyhavn. These are some of the world's longest roads and rail tunnels. The Scandinavian to Mediterranean Corridor is another billion-dollar investment for trans-European commerce. This is one ambitious project for the EU, with the support of Germany and Denmark, to establish the tunnel from Helsinki in Finland to Valletta in Malta with the Alps in the middle. Germany is pushing the EU for consolidation to become a dependent European flatland. There are vulnerable neighbors. England, France and Poland are the closest competitors in this European flatland, and you guys wanted help from me at this fragmented time? The Arctic is linked to this geopolitical plethora and Svalbard is no exception to this! The risk of information leaking to Denmark, Russia or the US is high. In either of the scenarios, I am at huge risk."

"Risk is lower, though," Den replied. "The fracking revolution transformed the US from an importer of energy to an exporter almost overnight. Political lawmaking is almost a systematic process. Negotiation and tricks play a significant role in this process. The US government often uses two master tricks in global competition. Either they use a sanction embargo or start tariff wars. After the ongoing tariff war between the US and China, the latest additions are the US and EU. Washington started imposing tariffs on the EU, and ultimately, the

EU had to buy LNG in exchange. The future LNG market does not belong to Japan because of slowness. Rather, China emerged as the biggest importer. Russia was the natural choice for their supplier. Russia has a geographical edge in transporting LNG either through a pipeline or vessels into East or Central Asia and Europe at a lesser cost and hence gained supremacy. The US is left with only one market, Europe. The US applied the same trick of a tariff war with China. China also agreed to import a portion of LNG from the US again. So, Washington is able to retain some upper hand on this at the negotiation table. You would get legitimate backing, so please don't be afraid, Mr Gaup."

Mr Gaup took two days and used his influence to make an arrangement for entering into the Satellite station. But the condition was that both Den and Floyd had to take disguise and false identity.

Longyearbyen, Svalbard

Den and Floyd landed at Longyearbyen airport. It was a private chartered flight that started from Oslo and came via Tromso. Arctic World Archive is just five kilometers away from the airport. The Svalbard Global Seed Vault is almost adjacent to it. Svalbard is one of the northernmost inhabited lands in the world and is in between Norway's mainland and the North Pole. Its main settlement is in Longyearbyen.

Floyd has taken an ePass for the Archive. His company, Piql, manages this data storage archive along with a mining company, Store Norske. Floyd managed to get permission for Den to join as an electro-optics technician. They will first go to the Archive since they were not staying in a hotel. They had official assignments and will stay inside. The Archive is under an abandoned coal mine where there is a separate portion for staff accommodations underground. The main destination was Svalsat- Svalbard Satellite Station, which was within walking distance.

This satellite station is owned by a Norway-based company called "Ksat Kongsberg". Kongsberg Satellite Services, or KSAT, is a joint venture between Kongsberg Defence & Aerospace, the Norwegian Space Centre and the US Aerospace & Defence equipment manufacturer Lockheed Martin. KSAT provides telemetry-tracking-command, or TTC, services for LEO satellites. Its ground stations in Svalbard, Inuvik and Nuuk scale its northern hemisphere capacity with global network coverage. The robust TTC communication, along with its expertise in the Launch and Early Orbit Phase, or LEOP, makes KSAT strong and dependable in its segment.

This ground station, along with another similar station, the 'Inuvik Satellite Station' of Canada, collaborated with the launch code infrastructure. The network was integrated with three launch code centers of 'polar bear'. Floyd knew the functioning of these stations because he was given access to the core network system of the station while working on the launch code design. He never visited here in person, so the staff of the stations did not know him. Mr Gaup, through his close contacts, arranged proxy permission for them. They were going as radio engineers.

Den would have experienced midnight sun had he come in the summer. Now the time was for polar night all through the day. Very soon the local people will witness the transition to spring before going to midnight sun. The temperature was now -15 degrees. Only the staff quarter underground was maintained with pleasant temperatures through the use of equipment.

After the 'George Floyd incident' and the 'Black Lives Matter' movement, Floyd had a realization. He confessed his assignment of a nuclear weapon plot with his mother. Before the meeting with the UN Chief, he went to meet Den in his apartment and broke down. He was crying and desperate. Den gave him an opportunity for revenge. Once a person breaks down in a crisis and wants genuine atonement, he can be trusted because he is changing for good. Floyd knew the exact spots and the plot. The picture was clear. All the leads endorsed and coincided with the fact-finding and analysis already done by Den. Immediate action was to stop the detonation. So they made a plan. Hence it was critical to come to Svalbard first.

Next day in Svalbard

Floyd was elaborating to Den. He had to disrupt the whole machines and logic system through multiple Floyds & malfunctioning. This was not easy. Moreover, Den had to physically hook some devices up while avoiding eyes and the CCTV. They were taking a huge risk, and most importantly, there was no PlanB. Nobody could afford a single mistake. They would get no second chances.

Floyd invested a full day to catch hold of the system. He eventually penetrated the system, established an artificial cage to insulate the launch architecture and jammed all transmission alerts to the destination. Earlier, any alteration in the launch architecture was supposed to trigger an alert to the three Launch Control Centre, or LCC. Alert Files were copied and kept in a virtual middleware vault. Floyd hijacked the trigger points and replaced the destination with a proxy for a temporary period.

Now, the Launch Control Centre will not get any warning bells. The next action was to go inside SvalSat and install two discrete devices. After the devices will be installed, the third step will be to access the launch code string to stop detonation communication.

Den was ready. He came to the satellite station as scheduled. The weather was cloudy, and there was heavy snowfall. The station was on top of high plain land. The main operation hall, power station, mobile research unit and radomes were spread over a vast area across the tundra. His authorization card had false information to match his disguise as a radio signal engineer. He had to pass through the gates and do a security check. He collected the work order badge from the workshop reception. He took a ski bike and went to dome number 7. Floyd was monitoring everything remotely. As per design, the Transponder of this antenna transmits the uplink radio signal to the satellite. Then, the transponder of the satellite amplifies the signal and re-transmits the same thing on a different set of downlink frequencies to the recipient transponder in a weapon warhead. These are electromagnetic radio spectrums at dedicated frequencies. The communication message string was encrypted by a private key, and the completion of the communication will be only successful if the decryption will be matched with the public key.

The bombs in the silo launch tubes were connected to the electronic racks along with their transponder and detonation switch.

The launch code was communicated and validated through Radio Frequency Identification, or RFID. They planned to install a Software-Defined Radio system, or SDR, to clone the original signals and replace them with duplicate signals. Emergency action message was supposed to be authenticated by a multi-factor key match. Then, only the launch command will be successful and can detonate a bomb. Their ultimate mission was to make the matching fail.

Den had a valid admit card to work in dome7. He opened the control box of the antenna and plugged an SDR token. It will take at least ten hours to clone the radio signal before the malfunction will start. Replacement of the signal of the device will happen after the main control panel is hijacked. This will be done with a second device called the 'Rubber Ducky'. This device is a programmed keyboard that automatically writes to launch malware in the system's brain. Once the first task was complete, Den came out of the dome7. He will have to come on the next day to install the second device. This device needed to be launched in the main server room. Avoiding people will be difficult, so the next task was riskier.

***

Launch order of an encrypted 'Emergency Action Message' is initiated in a private 'Permissive Action Link', or PAL, which triggers a ten-digit code to launch Commander. This launch code, *L-code*, is to be validated with a combination of authentication code, *A-code*, given in sealed envelopes in pairs that are kept in two different safes. The Commanding officer opens the vault with his own password and the last three digits of the *L-code*. The Executive officer opens the vault with his password and the first three digits of the L-code. Each envelope has several eight-digit *A-code* according to the option of sites or targets.

The first six digits of one *A-code* has to match the first six digits of the Commander's *L-code*. The exercise should be successful for both the Commanding officer and Executive officer in each launch control center. This is then a match order, and it is a valid launch order. The Commanding officer confirms the match order to the PAL. The PAL then automatically triggers the second *OTP*. The next final step is a match-key. There are key-safes for this part. The Commanding officer opens the key safe with a combination of his password followed by the last three digits of the A-code and the *dynamic OTP* thrown by the PAL system to the Commanding officer's individual recipient system.

Sometimes, this *OTP* generation is maintained in a separate physical unclonable function, or PUF, an analogue device for an added security layer. Similarly, the Executive officer also opens his key safe with a combination of his password followed by the last three digits of *A-code* and *OTP*. Two officers pick up the keys and push them into the '*butterfly lock*'. Both officers have to agree to the launch and punch the final combination of their own password, *OTP*, full *L-code* and the two middle digits of *A-code* (fourth and fifth). Butterfly lock opens and then, they press the final '*red button*'. This launch command communication is carried out through one LCC, either a land station or a mobile submarine. Often, they carry out this through multiple LCCs as well in case agreement of multiple officers is required before the final press. In 'polar bear', the syndicate was using three LCCs. Each LCC was assigned to one nuke site. There were three nuke sites.

***

Both Floyd and Den will go to the station this time on the 2nd day. As per plan, Floyd will engage with the crew while Den will enter the server room to plug-in the 'Rubber Ducky'.

Floyd took a false name as '***Anderson***' and Den's new name was '***Frederick***'. Floyd and Den passed the security check. It was just half an hour before lunchtime. Everything was as planned. The ground station master asked Floyd to submit the authorization letter. After approval, both came inside the operating hall. A network engineer was assigned to Floyd. The engineer guided him in the signaling architecture. Floyd started discussing the task thoroughly. The previous day's installed device started its first level malfunctioning. The signal of the ground station was disabled. The engineer was helping Floyd to decode the error files. Floyd instructed Den to check in the server room. This was now lunchtime, so the hall had a very small number of staff.

Den went inside the server room. He took ten long minutes before coming out of the room and updated Floyd, "Jacks are working fine. There should not be an issue in the network or connectivity."

Floyd instructed Den, "Then there is a bug in the radio frequency spectrum and machine communication. Please go to radome7 again and reconfirm the plug-in".

"Do I send someone along with you, Mr Frederick, for assistance?" The engineer asked Den.

"Ohh, no, thank you. I was working there yesterday. I know the way. I can manage."

Den took a ski bike and went towards his destination dome7. Floyd told the engineer that Den might take some time to fix and better he would come back after lunch. The engineer requested Floyd that lunch be arranged here itself.

"Thank you for offering lunch, but my colleagues are waiting in the Archive. Let me come back after an hour. Den should also finish by that time. I will inform him. Please carry on with your lunch," Floyd said.

He came back to the base in a hurry. There was not a single minute to be wasted now. He had to escape from Svalbard as soon as possible. Transport was pre-booked. He took his bag, got into the lift and came upstairs. Once Floyd was ready, a pickup car was waiting outside.

***

The accident happened after an hour. Den, while installing something in the control panel, was caught red-handed. It was a small device. It seemed to those who caught him, that Den came with bad intentions. They called the police.

It was a serious charge to be caught spying and stealing data. The local administration got a sense of seriousness, and it was escalated to the Governor of Svalbard. They were also searching for a second colleague, but Floyd already boarded the flight. Floyd managed to escape just in time.

***

Everything was in vain. This happened all of a sudden. Den took a risk but he failed. The interrogation started. After a while Den confessed that he knew about the conspiracy project 'polar bear'. However, he was not a party to it and was limited in his role. He came to the ground station to disrupt the communication frequency. He also disclosed about the syndicate and its main mastermind, Chief. The syndicate, with the help of Russia and China, had developed several illegal strategic petroleum reserves and underwater drilling rigs across the Arctic. Surprisingly he did not confess the whole fact. He disclosed the version of Dr. Bunn that the syndicate also plotted a nuclear bomb in the Gulf of Mexico to destroy Oklahoma.

A few days back, a hit wave thawed the Siberian tundra and set the area on fire. The news of the conspiracy broke out in a similar fashion. TV channels and news reported with breaking headlines "Conspiracy Mastermind Secretary General of United Nations" and "A Secretariat Espionage". The global stage experienced a sudden surge in excitement and intensity as the breaking news unfolded.

***

The very next day, Den was transferred to Norway's mainland. Heavily guarded helicopter fleet took him to 'Horten Naval Base' of the Norwegian Royal Navy.

Remi was worried. Den last updated her on the progress of the investigation, and he was going to Svalbard along with Floyd. Remi also got the news. Police reported that Den was caught red handed, but his team leader, Anderson (originally he was Kelvin Floyd), was still missing. Floyd was in disguise. Nobody identified the original identity of Floyd.

The international community will not easily believe Den, and the investigation will unnecessarily torture him in search of more answers. The syndicate would surely put the detonation plan on the back burner for some time, but this may be a simple speculation. It is not sure, even after all of this, if the plan would be deferred or executed on schedule.

Lieutenant General Morten Lunde was head of the Norway Intelligence Service. He himself came to Horten along with two other officers. The seriousness of the case led the matter to Interpol and the International Court of Justice. One Interpol officer also joined in the interrogation marathon. This was the same Interpol officer who was present in the Ethiopia meeting dressed in a fake character as Hikvision staff. He was also found in the UN Chief's office.

The FBA also submitted their interest in interrogating Den. This will be an international espionage case, but the Norwegian Intelligence Service did not want to rush it. They wanted to handle it in a legitimate way.

Den seemed to be trapped in a tough cage this time. The local and international police have accused him of a serious charge. Moreover, the syndicate was monitoring him. His entire effort and plan were at stake. Floyd escaped in a double cross. Again, time took a U-turn for the worse for Den.

***

Four officers were sitting in the chairs and surrounding Den. General Morten first opened the discussion.

"I myself came to meet you, Mr Den. It is not relevant if states and nations are united or not. Actually, they are not, but this is a matter where the Secretary General of the United Nations himself is convicted. Naturally, multiple nations are dragged for this breakout. Some nations are party to the crime, some are targets, some are sponsors, and some are beneficiaries. The rules are common. You were caught red-handed. We have CCTV footage, so we will not waste time by asking you to confess whether you attempted any sabotage. We all know this." Den didn't react to anything.

General Morten again asked,-"what is this device?" The other officer kept the device that Den was caught with on the table while trying to install it on the motherboard. It was sealed in a packet now.

"I was tasked with installing a hack. The ground station is used as part of the nuke launch ecosystem. I was not doing any sabotage. Rather, I was on my way to stop it," Den said.

"Do you think people will believe in your story? Your other colleague had escaped. Have you realized that?"

"It is unfortunate. Anderson is not my recruit. Rather, he was part of the launch code design team. He changed his mind for some reason and wanted to help me in getting there. It was a coincidence that we met in New York very recently. He decided to join me in spoiling the detonation. He knew how to break the path. We agreed and came to Svalbard to malfunction the satellite system first. It is really unfortunate that Floyd did a double-cross. Otherwise, we were very close to success."

"I reiterate, Mr Den, you were caught on the spot. It is you who has to plead and prove your innocence."

"Please engage with Mr Mike Power. He will be able to publish background in my defense and elaborate on my assignment to stop this business. I am not guilty. I am saving the North Pole."

"You mean the Secretary of State? Are you serious? Think twice. Do not rush with lies. You may skid."

"Please try it out," Den said in a calm tone.

"This is an international crime, and we have urgency to resolve it. You should cooperate. Mr Den, you are a secretarial chap. You may have diplomatic backing. I promise you that my police will not torture you, but this guarantee is limited only to the first level of interrogation. We want this case to be solved fast. Otherwise, I cannot guarantee the same courtesy at the next level." Morten Lunde said. He was cold-blooded.

"I know the exact locations," Den said loudly. Den realized that he was seriously trapped. He had to use tricks and took a chance to survive.

General Morten was an experienced intelligence officer. He raised his eyebrows and smelled the opportunity.

Oskar has not asked any questions yet. He was only looking at Den and doing his job as a surveillance agent. His eyes were stone cold.

Permission from Canada was taken discreetly within two days. A seven-member team was formed by the Norway Intelligence Service and Canada Security Intelligence Service. Den would escort the team to the heart of a few sites. However, the probability of leaking the information to the syndicate or the mastermind was very high. There was a threat of preponing nuke detonation.

After a long debate, the team made the decision to cover two specific locations. Den described the spots as per the version of Dr. Bunn. Ideally, they would have engaged Dr. Bunn in this expedition, but Dr. Bunn was no more, he was eliminated.

Svalbard

The helicopters landed on Svalbard. Destination was the newly built SPR.

This underwater oil reservoir was being operated with the help of the SvalSat ground station. The arrangement was fully automated. A crude tanker comes to a nearby halting spot. An automatic pump pours the defined quantity of crude into the Poseidon waiting underwater. The loaded sub goes to the reservoir and unloads the crude into the chamber. The sub acts as a transit voyage from the deep sea to the reservoir.

Oil consumption dried during the global lockdown, so crude oil was being stored for the future. Trading companies and Governments will have to wait for a revamp in demand and price so that they do not lose any margin. Until such time, the fuel was kept in storage. This storage was unreported and illegal. Commodity traders, along with sponsor lawmakers, invest heavily in building artificial situations to inflate or deflate the price as per the rule of the speculation business. Commodity business cannot survive without this trick of arbitrage.

However, it was still not certain whether the global pandemic happened as an accident or it was created artificially.

***

They will now head for the next stop. This particular expedition was risky because they were now heading to the 'nuke shaft'. A nuke could be detonated at any time.

***

C1 heard the news about the arrest of Den and his attempt in Svalsat. It was under investigation. He was immensely surprised and angry that someone could figure out their system trail. He doubted C2 and guessed that he was the mole in the system. The relationship between C1 and C2 has not been smooth and trustworthy for the last couple of months. However, most of the core operatives- Taylor and Dr. Bunn were killed. The decision for Ted Mateen, Eric Nichols and Joseph Bolton were deferred. They were also in the kill list but this will be executed only after a successful detonation and the 'polar bear' is accomplished. His immediate target was Den Smil.

C1 was in his room. He ordered his secretary and maid not to disturb him for the next few hours. He would sleep.

He dialed a number from a private line.

"Sir, Bolton is the leak."

He might be the boss of C1. The recipient's voice showed he was in utter distress. Boss replied from the other side of the call, "Bolton would soon take voluntary retirement from his position. Do not worry about him, but stop the other chap immediately! You should have done this before, but now it is too late. Do not experiment much. Do the first thing and do it now!"

"OK, Sir. I will manage him."

"You don't get it. You are stupid. Do not waste time running behind the moles that you would catch anyway. Finish the priority! We cannot let it be exposed to intelligence or investigation. Blow it. This is the first and most immediate thing to do. Finish the task!"

C1 replied, "Sir, I am a bit skeptical. We should hold it for some time. There is a risk of slippage. There are eyes all around, and international agencies will investigate in depth."

"You are a stupid pig!" Boss was loud and angry, "None of you could manage it well. The more you delay, the more you pile up the probability of getting exposed. Investors of the Neom Meet will ask questions about the timeline and demand returns. There are crucial commitments that I cannot change. A lot of other stuff will be at stake. The entire string of the game plan will be spoiled,"

C1 was silent and feeling immense anxiety and confusion.

"What are you thinking? We have to remain in business. I do not care about the slippage. We will engage this separately. Calculate the future benefits. We cannot hold back. Initiate the command now! This is necessary. Do it now!"

"Of course, Sir," C1 said meekly.

The boss was upset with C1. It was quite obvious that the boss didn't take it lightly that 'polar bear' was almost exposed just before the critical stage of final execution.

C1 dialed C3, "**Navani**, initiate the command tomorrow. It is urgent. I got the green signal from Chief."

C3 was not Vlad Medkev. He was **Alex Navani**. He is an active non-communist political leader in Russia. He was hired by the syndicate for fat money to spearhead the 'polar bear'.

***

The sub reached the nuke site. The navigation crew was alarmed that the object was detected. The sub was on standby while the two naval divers, two investigative officers got ready to dive. They came out from the hyperbaric chambers, and the shaft was visible. They were trained divers for the deep sea. The underwater condition beneath such depth is always extreme with very high pressure and cold temperature. The cylinder shaft was not very wide. A maximum of 3-4 persons could get inside for work. The technical team used to work at the time of installation and instrument connection. There were three hyperbaric lock gates similar to submarines. One was used for the supply gate. An unmanned vehicle may plug into the gate. The lock gate may open and pull the necessary cargo inside the shaft. There were channels where a robotic lift may fix the material at respective points. The technical crew used to visit frequently for final fixation. Taylor was the installation supervisor. He visited all the three nuke sites. Dr. Bunn also visited quite a number of times. He was a nuclear warhead expert, after all.

Den knew the passcode from the diary of Taylor. The Investigation officers had taken the pass code from Den. The other two lock gates were used for human entry and exit. They pressed the code in the mounted panel on the gate, and the team entered the shaft.

The entire operation was being monitored by General Morten and Den remotely from Norway. Den only accumulated leads and analyzed information to guess that there was a global conspiracy and a nuclear threat. After today, he witnessed the official death warhead.

The nuclear shaft was 1000 feet under the sea. He speculated that some commanders in some parts of the globe may now press the button to start the nuclear war. This could explode at any time, and they were in the epicenter.

The officers checked the canister. They wanted to be doubly sure. But there was no launch pad, so the warhead was not going to be launched from here to strike. The bomb will explode here itself. This was planted. Actually, this was a nuclear 'test site'.

The team registered the relevant pics and clips as very important pieces of evidence. The team returned to the sub. The helicopters were waiting and saw the dorsal fin of the sub. It reached the Labrador Sea and was rising to the surface. The helicopters will pick up the naval team and fly straight to Oslo.

***

General Morten wanted another round of interrogation with Den, so they assembled in the wardroom.

Officer **Jaron** started first, "We are lucky that the toy didn't explode in the middle of our search." Jaron was an intelligence officer in the E14 unit of NIS.

Den didn't say anything.

"You misguided us! You said there are six SPR across the Arctic. But we found 'nuke test site'." Jaron said.

Den replied, "I spoke the truth to the extent whatever was known to me."

Another officer, **Catholic**, asked a direct question, "Your device is a radio signal copy machine. We found out the manufacturer. It is difficult to believe that your boss sent you there to spoil. It is still a mystery to us. You didn't open up much on this!" Catholic was the Security Liaison Officer.

"I went to copy the backup log. My task was only to plug the device to take the backup signal and detonation log, but it failed. However, the system will continue to function." Den was sounding like a syndicate member. He had something on his mind. He was clever.

Catholic was firm, "I hope you would have acknowledged by this time that you are in deep trouble. We caught you red-handed. There may not be a short-term conclusion or easy escape. Tell us the bigger plot."

"Then I must say that it is a complete failure by your agency that it was not brought to your notice that the last few years of underwater construction and supply were going on. It is really surprising. Or are you compelling me to guess that the Canadian and Norwegian governments have the same vested interest of some form. I am only the scapegoat!" Den smiled.

"This Northwest passage is Canadian land. Our unit will find out the root cause very soon," Catholic said.

"Let the ice melt, and this may not be your own territory anymore. You would realize that this would become a sovereign shipping route for global trade. Very soon, territorial claims with coverage of the continental shelf may get stuck in the upcoming traffic jam there. Be prepared." Den replied firmly.

The officers realized that Den was a tough nut. They would probably have to try and break him in prison or private custody. They needed a court order. So they didn't bother him anymore.

One guard remained with Den in front of the jail. The guard went to the washroom for a few minutes. Nobody could escape from here. Oskar came suddenly. He was holding two coffee mugs. He offered a mug to Den.

"This time, the mug has no poison," Oskar said.

Den recollected the Ethiopia meeting. Taylor and Den were given poison, but Den escaped.

Oskar whispered, "They cross-checked Dr. Bunn. It was good news that he was already arrested, but the bad news is that he is dead." He thought that this information would shock Den.

Den replied quietly and more shockingly to Oskar, "I already know this. He was killed."

Oskar departed within a minute before the guard came. Den finished the coffee gradually. There was a piece of paper pasted at the bottom of the mug. Den grabbed it and read it.

***

The judgment day came. As per the plan, there will be a series of three explosions in the Arctic belt. These were zero-yield bombings, but this was planned in such a way that even the minimum radioactive spread and the hit wave would devastate the ecology forever. The ice walls and marine life will vanish. And a new economical trade route and few new global equations will emerge at the cost of nature.

PM's order was punched in his PAL. Usually, the nuke launch order is triggered from the PM's system directly. C1 was an intermediary commander. C1 pressed the final button in his PAL. This generated *L-codes* within a second for the respective Commanding officer, or CO, and Executive officer, or EO, of all three launch code centers. They opened the envelope-vault and validated it with an *A-code* as per protocol. It was a match-order.

Within a minute, the crew realized that something had gone wrong. The *second OTP* didn't come. It should have come within a second. Without this, they could not open the key-safe. Without the key, a launch was not possible. The system waited two minutes and then automatically enabled the key-safe combination without the second OTP. Officers tried after two minutes accordingly. This attempt also failed. Key-safe did not unlock. This was reported to C3- Navani. A similar incident happened for the other two launches as well. Navani was present in the 'Cheyenne Mountain Complex', where they spearheaded the control panel and channels.

The technical team was desperate and working frantically to fix the issue. Half of the team was virtually connected because of the present pandemic. The key

Engineer of the launch code project was Kelvin Floyd, but he sabotaged the mission. They were not able to resolve the challenge without Floyd.

The command centers had an exhaustive satellite connectivity network and robust surveillance system over the North Pole and Arctic Circle. It was identified that the entire launch code-communication string was compromised. A complex spider malware had gained access to the channel and manipulated the whole system. Navani was immensely afraid of this mess because he knew the consequences it could cause.

***

The news exploded in the room of C1. The launch failed on all three sites. His anger erupted like lava from a volcano. He fumed like a mushroom cloud post-nuclear bombing. He was sitting in his study with a bunch of printouts. One file was a draft charter and revised chapters of newly proposed '*The League of States*'. A group of influential policymakers and political leaders conspired to dilute the United Nations and wish to form a parallel organization with similar stature of sovereign authority, rulebook and global recognition. They would name this "The League of States".

Another file was the draft text of the revised 'NA**A**TO' Articles, which, after the inclusion of the Arctic, will now be called the 'North Atlantic and Arctic Treaty Organisation'. The direction and territory of coverage were being reviewed. Moreover, the new age security provision and priority for the Western nations changed. So, the legislature will be used to form another similar body to support the Indo-Pacific region. They would name this 'Indo-Pacific Treaty Organisation', or IPTO.

***

Commander Navani left the mountain complex command station immediately after the mess. He will abscond to some place. He will go to Belarus. He had connections there and will arrange his escape.

Navani was already on C1's kill list, but C1 was waiting to finish the mission first. C1 guessed correctly that Navani would run off. Two kill warrants were issued with immediate priority Alex Navani and Den Smil.

***

Den was shifted to the custody of Norway Intelligence Service's new headquarter situated at Lutvann Lake near Oslo. He was under trial, and the investigation report was being prepared.

General Morten did his job as per plan. He will now call Remi. Both knew each other and were already connected.

"We owe it to you, Morten. Thank you very much for trusting me and deciding so quickly", Remi thanked Morten on call.

"Hey, Remi, please do not put me in shame. I am glad that I volunteered for your mission."

"Counter mission," Remi smiled.

Although she kept traveling for her work and stayed less at home, presently she was in her house in Oslo. She was coming to Lutvann on the very next day to see Den in custody and meet her close friend General Morten.

***

C1 could sense the upcoming outrage. C1 had to face the consequences. Consortium investors, such as Corporations, who invested in the 'polar bear' for business prospects, would ask for a return or refund. Politics and business always complement each other. At times, they jointly build the offense. There was no single party to the conspiracy. C1 had to manage the government as well. After all, this was a government-sponsored mission. His job, reputation and position were at stake. He was in deep trouble because he will be questioned by the senior authority and senior stakeholders. He will get a call anytime from his mastermind and might get suspended.

He got a call in the evening. It was Remi. She wanted a deal.

Final Meet

New York

United Nations headquarter in New York, along with all its global offices, agency offices and affiliated centers, were preparing for the big event. This was the 75th anniversary of the UN Charter. Although the UN officially came into existence in October 1945. Just after Germany's unconditional surrender in May, it was evident that the end of the war was just a matter of time. However, the Manhattan project of the Atomic Bomb was still live and in its final conclusion. The peace destroyers planned for peace-making initiatives. In June 1945, delegates from 50 nations came together to sign the United Nations Charter, a historic moment for global peace and progress that set the context for a new way to control nations. It was a very significant and clever move by the superpowers. The charter gave supreme authority and veto power to only the allied nations and victors of World War II. The victorious military powers were still controlling the same monopoly in terms of authority and could decline any procedural resolution regardless of its popularity across the globe and necessity in the region.

The 'veto' is the most undemocratic power in the frame of democracy. The controlling Nations often impose their own will on others for vested interest. This could be seen in the 'Yalta Conference' of President Roosevelt, Prime Minister Churchill and Premier Stalin in San Francisco. The victors wanted to keep veto power in the hands of the controlling powers.

Just after the end of World War I, the first predecessor- 'League of Nations' was formed at the 'Paris Peace Conference' in January 1920 to prevent another global conflict and maintain world peace. In other words, this was the 100th anniversary of the so-called peacekeeping organization. Although the US cleverly opted out of formally joining as a member of the League of Nations, they still ratified the 'Versailles treaty'. The US didn't want to be the target of any future breakout in

Germany or European conflict but rather wanted to control Europe from behind. President Wilson was incentivized with a Nobel Peace Award. However, the fact was they failed to maintain world peace. World War II was inevitable.

Over the last 75 years of post-World War II, the controlling powerhouses painted the world with a brush of false propaganda. It was narrated that humanity has thrived towards global peace, prosperity, and harmony. Several alliances have been formed to build cooperation in the fields of security, economy and sustainable development. Though some of the early alliances, such as NATO and the Warsaw Pact, focused on military cooperation, soon the world witnessed economically driven collaborations such as the 'Group of Seventy Seven', known as G-77, 'Organisation for Economic Cooperation and Development', or OECD, and 'Group of Seven', known as G7. The end of the Cold War around 1990 added even more meaningful dimensions to the world order, driven by aspirations of free trade, such as the 'World Trade Organisation', political integration like the 'European Union', and economic cooperation like the 'G20' and 'BRICS'. Finally, the last decade witnessed the noble aspiration to leave no one behind. The world got together to commit to the 2030 Agenda for Sustainable Development, a blueprint of peace and prosperity for people and the planet. The agenda of sustainable development urgently called for a global partnership to end poverty, improve health and reduce inequality while spurring economic growth and tackling climate change. These were diplomatic spheres of hoaxes. Actually they wanted a stable global market.

A consensus was formed where Western troops were allowed to raise military aggression and expansion by foreign invasion and establishment in the name of peacekeeping. The legality of some of these military actions was questionable, but with no court to appeal to and the undemocratic concentrated Western legislature in the UN charter, this question has never been examined. China didn't use veto for these military actions in the last two decades and, in exchange, got all-out policy support to be included in the global supply chain of trade. The undeniable consensus was very simple and full circle. Without conflict, there are no military actions. Without military actions, there are no arms sales and oil demand. Without arm sales or a petrodollar, there is no churning of world currency and fat foreign reserves. Without this, there is no supremacy. Till 1971, the 'Republic of China' was the only odd man out in the five-member Victor panel. Post 1971, the seat was replaced with revised recognition to the 'People's Republic of China' and China was included with a strategic share of the pie.

It was a marriage of convenience, but the romantic diplomacy is now broken because the partner became the competitor. Protectionism and isolationism are replacing globalism. A probable change in competition of world order is coming.

New York

Den was released from Norway. Most surprisingly, he was dropped from all extradition charges and prosecution all of a sudden, but he was released with some conditions and restrictions on his movement. He came back to his apartment in New York, and he was back to his earlier mobile number. He had to use some temporary numbers for the last couple of months due to being underground.

Today was a sunny Saturday. Den would now go to the 'Manhattan Mansion' to end the climax. The planned final meet and the judgment day. 3 Sutton Place, Manhattan Mansion, is the official residence of the UN Secretary-General. UN headquarter was just ten minutes away from this residence. Den had come here a couple of times. All were official. This time, the visit will be unofficial.

Den didn't take his car today. He first walked down to Pearl Street. The first destination was Fraunces Tavern. He came inside the cafe. Floyd was waiting. Den took an antidote injection of the n-nerve agent. Both departed for different destinations. Eventually, they would meet again in another place after some time on a cruise.

Den booked an Uber. From his flat in Stone Street, he would hardly take ten minutes to reach the Manhattan Mansion. Although he is a UN staff, he does not stay in Waterside Plaza, where most of the foreign staff and their families stay. He stays in a separate rented accommodation from the office in old Stone Street.

....

The Uber took the FRR driveway. With the Brooklyn Bridge on the left and the Manhattan Bridge on the right, the car moved onwards. He was going through the coast of the East River. There might be just five more minutes by which he will reach his destiny. He did not know his fate. He was going to face off the conspirator within the next few minutes. Den knew that he was under surveillance. He was being tracked. His cover was blown. The risk was immense, and he was not sure if he could make it. He will soon confront the mighty syndicate and its monster mastermind. The syndicate of the conspiracy was powerful. Today's plan was full of risks, and his stance will be even riskier.

He reached Manhattan Mansion, and an attendant took him to the personal waiting lounge on the first floor. Den knew there would be some guests of surprise that would join gradually.

***

Chief was holding a curved stem-blend billiard pipe today, which was one of his personal pipes. The bowl of the pipe was packed with Virginia gold-class sweet tobacco. The bore was made out of copper and briar wood, and the mouthpiece was gold-plated. Chief had a personal hobby of collecting different pipes, tobacco leaves and smoking utensils. He had quite a rare collection of that stuff. Once upon a time, he was an avid smoker, but he left long back. Hobby continued. Now, he only smokes on special occasions.

A Spanish doctor, Nicolas Monardes, wrote a book in the late 16th century about the history of medicinal plants in the New World. In this, he claimed that tobacco could cure thirty-six health problems. Tobacco and cigarette companies created a myth by presenting tobacco as a healthy tool. It was a well-thought-out plan for business. During the 1600s, tobacco was so popular that it was as good as gold.

Similarly, the tobacco and oil businesses go hand in hand. Both industries knew of the fatal consequences but still purposefully misled the public with the wrong information and continued boosting demand. Tobacco gave enormous to North America. On the other hand, the US established its currency as the world's reserve currency through their newly created Fiat Money, the petrodollar, in exchange for oil contracts.

Den started first, "In the office, I did not see you smoking, Sir."

"As you know, I left smoking several times," Chief smiled, "You are coming to my residence. This time, it is your personal visit, making this a special moment. So, I took out this pipe. I would love to smoke for a moment. This pipe is one of my favorites. This is a similar prototype of the very ancient pipe found in the Egyptian mummy. However, I am alive," Chief laughed loudly.

"I have three guests. Two are already here and are waiting on the boat. We have to go to a nearby place," Chief said, blowing out a puff of smoke.

"You should have told me before, Sir. I would have fixed it for some other convenient time," Den said.

"This meeting is highly required. You also know this. We will talk about 'polar bear'." Chief replied firmly.

Both were cold-blooded.

Den has brought a leather bag. It was number-locked. He was carrying a secret file and important proofs.

"Let's go. We will not waste time here. Carry your file. I have mine. We have few deals to make or break." Chief brought a zipped envelope.

***

Chief asked the securities not to accompany but to follow. He himself will drive along with Den. It was only a five minute drive to reach the jetty. The chartered boat was waiting on the East river. The meeting was arranged in privacy. The boat will not go towards the Brooklyn bridge and rather move closer to Roosevelt Island. Before the Dutch & English colony, this was inhabited by the 'Lenape tribe' and at that time, Manhattan used to have hospitals, asylums and jails. And now it is surrounded by Manhattan skylines and tech parks. Time changed. This private meeting will either probably resolve the 'polar bear' Or change the future course to much more conflicting and riskier. This was the climax of the plot.

This was a medium sized two storied yacht. Security personnel needed to wait outside on the river bank. Only the captain and one attendant crew were allowed inside the boat other than the guests. Everybody came here with a purpose. Den knew that the situation was on the line and he had to make or break. Chief entered first. Then Den stepped inside the boat.

Mr Bolton- ex-national security advisor of the US, and Walter were sitting on wooden benches. Guests were sitting at a distance and everybody was masked. This was the new normal after the present COVID pandemic. They exchanged warm courtesies with everyone. The cabin temperature was not just warm but was waiting to boil. This was the calm before the storm.

Chief sat on a nearby chair, and Den took a stool. Here inside the cabin, only Walter was the odd one out who was not known to Den and Chief. He was invited by Bolton, but the other three knew each other. Den recently met Bolton at his residence in Michigan.

Chief opened the zipped folder and kept a fat bunch of papers. "This is the tentative final draft for the revised charter."

"It is good then. Geopolitical statehood and the situation evolved a lot. The UN charter definitely needs a structural upgrade," Den replied.

"This is not for the UN. A new body is being formed. Eventually, the new body, 'The League of States', will replace our UN. The revised charter is made on new and own terms."

"Who is owning it?" asked Den.

"It is an open secret that America has been spearheading the World Bank and West Europe runs the IMF. Over the period, the UN has become more democratic, and hence, it is necessary to dilute and diversify its sovereignty. Obviously, it is the White House who will own the new league. This is a virtue of the order of power," Chief stated.

"Are you blaming the US?"

"Den, the United Nations is facing a severe budget deficit. Do you know why? This is due to delayed payments from member countries and, mainly, from permanent seat holders," Chief said.

"Yeah, it is very unfortunate. The US's withdrawal from some committed and required initiatives will not only boost the problems but also it would damage the trust and balance," Den replied.

"Likewise, you are losing trust in me!" Chief smiled.

Den didn't say anything.

Chief continued, "The National Oceanic and Atmospheric Administration, or NOAA, predicts that by 2050, the polar circle will be almost ice-free by the summer. The Arctic states are excited about this new scope of business. Whoever establishes supremacy on the roof of the earth would rule everything. This is a race for a new world order. The North Sea route through the Russian coast is already easing. So, for Russia and Nordic nations, no extra effort is needed. But, the North West Passage is still challenging. Naturally, the US and Canada cannot wait so long to leverage the ice melting. They have to fast-track it, or else they may lose the entire game to Russia."

"Then who formed the 'polar bear'?" Den asked abruptly to Chief. Nobody else was talking. There has been no discussion on this topic yet. Den started the topic without any prelude. Mr Bolton rubbed his finger in his chin while he finished his last ship from the coffee mug. Walter was completely silent as of now.

"Governments planned the 'polar bear', who are the beneficial owners of the game plan," Chief replied.

"You are diverting, Sir."

"Believe me, I did not form it." Chief looked at everybody in the room and continued smoking.

It was noon when the attendant rang the bell. He came inside the cabin and informed that Mike came, but his security personnel wanted to come for a check first.

The security officers came inside the boat. They first ensured that there was no hidden camera, microphone or recorder inside it. Den and Walter were thoroughly searched. They didn't even spare Bolton and Chief. Once they were satisfied, they returned to Mike.

There was pin-drop silence in the room for a few minutes before Mike entered. Den was surprised because he observed no knee-jerk reaction in the faces of either Mike, Bolton or Walter. As if all were aware of today's agenda. Den was alone. If they were all together and associated, they might not take a chance for any violence here, but the human brain is revengeful and ferocious.

***

Mike was okay with the arrangement and asked his men to leave. It was his personal meeting with friends. His car and guards will be waiting on the jetty.

There was another round of courtesy exchanges. Everybody asked Mike about his health because he had just been discharged from the hospital after being cured of coronavirus. He was better now.

Mike was upset about Den, "Where were you? I was looking for you."

"I tried to contact you, but you were in hospital, and your mobile was switched off for some time, Sir. I spoke to your Secretary." Den replied.

"I was expecting a callback," Mike said, annoyed. "Anyway, we are here for something else. I will speak to you later."

Mike turned to Chief. "I was expecting a private place. Since we will discuss sensitive topics, is Den required to be here?"

Chief replied, "I asked him to come. He is required because he has a file. He also has a deal."

***

Chief kept his pipe in the case for a cooling time. He will relight it shortly.

He stood up and said, "Gentlemen, we all know each other in some way or another, and few pairs have had their respective dealings in the past. In short, we all know each other. We have one critical thing in common between us, we know about the 'polar bear'.

The cabin was quiet and waiting for the storm. For now, there was a light cold breeze from the East river.

Mike replied first after a while, "We know, but I doubt that all are involved!"

"Certainly not. Somebody is accusing. Someone is convicted, someone has a secret to sell, someone is investigating, somebody is party to it and somebody is not party to the conspiracy task but is aware of it. This is pretty complex, isn't it!"

"Someone is speculating, too, but the truth remains in its place", Den interrupted.

"Naturally, each one of us may have an accusation or counter-accusation against someone or anybody. It is obvious that this is creating multiple issues. No one would benefit from this dog fight. International lobbies and intelligence agencies are super active in this situation. So, we urge you all to patch things up. We assembled here not to discuss 'polar bear'. The project has already failed, but it has still not been caught. Let's not stretch it. It is to everybody's benefit if we settle it amicably among us. Each of us in this room has a deal." Chief completed with a silver line.

Atmosphere started warming up. Each person might be experiencing a rough wind in brain cells.

Walter opened his briefcase, took out a file and pushed it toward Mike.

"Sir, it is a copy for your proofreading. I have written my price on the cover," Walter said.

Mike found that it was written as *one million+one million US dollars.*

"It is a very heavy file, Walter," Mike remarked.

"You know the content, but I will break it up. The first one million is to forget what happened in the Ethiopia meeting. It was plotted, as we all know, but I can forget it completely at this price," Walter smirked. "Another one million is for the anti-virus. This is still misrepresented, but I know your government would like to continue the confusion for a longer period. This file may break the tune, so please decide with care. Washington cannot afford to lose this deal. I worked hard on it. Please appreciate and pay a good price. I will not lose. You and your Government will lose." Walter was sounding very mysterious and clever.

The US, through its secret military base at Dugway, Utah, funded Canada to develop bioweapons. This was a collaboration to test bio and chemical weapons. A dangerous virus was being prepared to deploy in Europe and Asia with the goal of pausing the human race for a while. Killing mass for the sake of politics is called genocide, but the same massacre is called collateral damage if this is for the sake of business. The COVID-19 conspiracy was planned with multiple agendas. One was to drag the oil price to a historical low and disrupt world trade. Once the virus was ready, an anti-virus was obviously being made by some pharmaceutical corporations. The capsule was transported safely from Texas to Canada. It was on the schedule, but it broke out much earlier than scheduled. Two scientists sabotaged. One was Dr Sheen- the biochemical scientist of 'Texas Medical laboratory'. Another one was Dr Xiangguo Qiu- working in National Microbiology Lab in Winnipeg, Canada. Both masterminded in stealing the research and brought SARS-CoV2 virus to the 'Wuhan Institute of Virology' in China. While transporting few samples were mishandled by the smugglers. The sample capsules leaked from the Wuhan wet market. Thereafter, Wuhan lab sold the secret to Russia for vaccine development. The proposed biochemical-weapon became a boomerang. It was a double cross. The US did not manage to create the antivirus formula themselves, nor could the US escape from the damage caused by COVID-19. Millions of people have died in North America and Europe so far due to this Coronavirus. The secret research was smuggled into another country. Dr Kin was another fellow scientist in the Texas lab and co-assistant to Dr Sheen, who knew this secret. Dr Kin tried to be a whistleblower and was later killed by the CIA.

If this information comes to the public, Washington will be in deep trouble and embarrassment before the election. So, Mike will buy this at any price. Walter even went further in the file and elaborated in the next chapter. China, by selling the virus formula to Russia, which they stole from a Canadian lab, wanted to achieve two immediate agendas. One was a cross-holding investment for future vaccine sales and, hence, fat revenue. Russia and China jointly created the healthcare silk route to supply and export COVID-19 vaccines to take the first moving advantage globally.

Another one was Russia's unconditional support for the South China Sea. Moscow's recognition of the 'Nine Dash Line' in the South China Sea, which Beijing will use to demarcate its claims on the waters, shielded a deal in return for Chinese economic support for Russia's outer continental shelf claims in the Central Arctic. Already, the two sides have collaborated financially in the Arctic. When Russia struggled to secure funding from Western banks for its Yamal liquefied natural gas project in the Arctic due to sanctions following the annexation of Crimea, it partnered with China.

Two Chinese banks, the Export-Import Bank of China and the China Development Bank Corporation and China's Silk Road Fund, supported the agenda with billions of equivalent dollars for prospects in the Polar Circle. As a result, Chinese companies gained a combined 30% stake in one of the largest LNG projects in the world. Last year, Russia and China entered a deal that saw state-owned companies from both countries team up to ship LNG from the Arctic. Russia's major LNG producer Novatek and state-owned shipping company Sovcomflot partnered with two of China's state-owned enterprises, COSCO Shipping and Silk Road Fund, to manage a fleet of dozens of ice-breakers to transport the fuel from Novatek's plants, including Yamal LNG. The roadmap was clear, but geopolitics is complex. Walter's research and investigation were masterpieces.

Chief took a long breath, "You are putting your life at risk, Walter. Government has the machinery to kill or destroy you immediately."

"I know, but who wants to kill a golden goose? Hope you all acknowledge that I have other official secrets about the China-Russia marriage in the context of future politics. It is a honeymoon pack. Realize my value and then decide. You can buy your life from me. Pay the price." Walter was confident in his reply but he sounded shrewd.

"You played very clever, Walter." Mike whispered. Although Mike at the back of his mind, decided to agree to the manuscript even at a high price. This file needed to be destroyed with immediate effect.

The job of Walter was over. He has poured eye opening secrets in everybody's mind. Now he will depart. He had submitted his deal and now would wait for the buyer. The next half of the meeting was going to be extremely confidential and restricted to a closed group only. Walter was not required. He departed.

Now, this was the turn of Mr Bolton and Mike to face off. As soon as Walter left the boat, Mike started shouting at Bolton.

"I wish Jesus could save you, Bolton. You are a traitor!" Mike shouted with anger.

Chief predicted the stink. "Hey, Gentlemen, again, I am requesting that we assemble here for a solution. Make a deal. Do not resume the blame game. This will not benefit anybody."

"Let me put up a straight demand then. Bolton, we need an edit on a few pages."

"What do you mean?"

"Your Book, where you lied", Mike replied.

"How do you judge, Mike? Do not have prejudice. Let me speak the truth, and I will speak loudly this time."

"Then you should be loud with your confession as well. What do you think?"

"This is not my autobiography. I will complete the paper and stick to the topic. This is my book. Do not intervene."

"You are writing rubbish. This is a topic of propaganda!" Mike shouted.

"Mike, we did not come here to discuss this. There is another urgent priority. Do not waste time. Do not divert topic. Nobody can stop me this time. I am not going to write any speculation or fiction. This is a simple narrative of facts that happened in my presence. My book will be a memoir about the government."

"The White House didn't allow you to do so. It is illegal and against the non-disclosure protocol. The Senate will take action. We will put sanctions on you and drag you to the court."

"You guys are in an authoritarian regime. Continue misusing the sanction legislature for your own choice. I do not care. Do not threaten me, Mike. Mind it, there is a specific long chapter on my Arctic supervision. I briefly touched base with my few tasks in handling resource mobilization for the 'polar bear' military coverage. But I hadn't named anybody yet, nor had I disclosed 'polar bear'. These pages are still in my raw manuscript. I have not included this yet in the final version. If you want, I can increase the length of the book and include some bad stuff. Do you want me to elaborate?" Bolton was shrewd.

"You are an outright liar!" Mike was extremely annoyed.

Bolton shouted, "I will illustrate the assassination of Denmark's PM, too. What do you judge? Is it a lie?"

Mike exploded in anger, "You are a sick puppy! A born traitor!" Mike picked up the glass from the table and threw it to Bolton. The glass was heavy and missed his head. It was dramatic and happened suddenly. Mike started shouting even more.

The atmosphere changed.

Bolton was angry, "How do you block me? On what? I have not released my book yet! It is only a manuscript!" Bolton shouted with a smile.

Mike controlled his anger and tried for a beneficial deal, "Tell me your price. I will speak to the PM." Mike was still seething.

Bolton knew his deal. He didn't take much idle time in replying, "I want the nomination of Dy PM candidature in this election."

"America is a democracy, Bolton."

"But the public is not aware of machinery. Do you want me to reiterate which AI data analytics company was hired in the last election for manipulation? Or would you rather me describe the blueprint of deliberate malpractice being implemented for the mail-in postal ballot voting system and logistics towards this election, too? I know everything. Do not play around with me."

Mike realized that Bolton was going deeper and breaking the gates, "Give us a couple of days. Candidature for Deputy PM has not been announced yet. We will internally debate on this."

Bolton, being a National Security Advisor, was connected to the core administration, and he knew serious confidential information. Mike knew that Bolton became a risk to the authorities.

Chief opened up, "Bolton is second in command in the 'polar bear'. He has two other important trump cards in his fold. Those are not just manuscripts. He does not need to write a book for this. He is a witness and has evidence." Chief turned to Bolton.

Bolton was carrying a small envelope in the pocket of his long suit.

"Here are a few. Carrying a pen drive or data card is risky at this moment. I took some prints for your reference." He placed a few photographs on the table. These were some clips from the CCTV footage of the tunnel at the time of the accident of Denmark PM. Floyd stole this earlier from a government server. There were pictures just before the convoy entered the tunnel. And there were a few pics post-explosion. His death was reported as an accident due to a blast of the engine and severe injury. This was still under investigation.

"I want to explain this," Den said after being quiet and observing for quite some time. "If you all see that there were almost equal gaps between the covering cars who were covering the PM from the front and behind. This is a usual practice. But inside the tunnel, this was changed. The car in front accelerated the speed, and the car in behind slowed down. The gap increased. And the explosion happened."

Mike inquired, "You seem to have witnessed this."

"I saw the video footage."

"Quite obvious. So, are you working for Bolton?"

Den didn't say anything.

Bolton continued, "An explosive was fitted in the engine, and the electric wearing was compromised. Once the PM got into the car and locked the door, the door was locked in such a way that he could not open it anymore from the inside. The preparatory process and second attempt to buy Greenland from the Danish government started. The Senate approved starting the US consulate in Greenland. China is putting pressure on the Faroe Islands to secure an order for the island's 5G network. Frequent American delegations have landed on Nuuk, and Washington is reopening its consulate there after more than sixty years of absence. Safe and encrypted lines of communication are being established between Copenhagen, Nuuk and Torshavn, the capital of the Faroe Islands. The situation is dramatic. Kim Kielsen, PM Of Greenland's Sovereign Administration, has decided to run for another term as chairman of Siumut, Greenland's main political party. All these are heading towards one single priority point at this moment. Deputy PM- Minik was supporting us though. But all these would not have been possible except one thing. We had to eliminate the Danish PM. It was unfortunate for Washington and Britain that execution got delayed, and he passed the approval resolution for Nord Stream Two by that time."

Mike laughed at him, "Your storytelling is excellent."

Bolton gazed at everybody and replied after thirty seconds, "I can tell this story accurately because I ordered the assassination. I am C2 of 'polar bear'."

As if the nuke exploded here in the boat. Bolton admitted further, "Assassination recruit came from the Danish Naval base at Kangilinnguit (Gronnedal) in the south of Greenland. He is a CIA asset. We convinced him to fit the bomb and malfunction the door switches of the target car."

"But who ordered you?" Den asked.

Bolton took a slice of bread and looked at Den. He then turned his eyeballs to Mike and then Chief.

Chief resumed, "Bolton, we want your files. These secrets are required to be classified at this moment. And I mean both of the secrets."

"Kelvin Floyd and Jeffrey were hired to spoof the Denmark government's database to push a revised version of the Nord Stream Two contract. They were supposed to revise terms in favor of the US. Few critical license requirements were supposed to be included in the final signed term sheet so that the project would get delayed and stuck in a legal trap. Additionally, there was a plan to explode the Nord Stream Two pipeline. Arrangement for the malfunctioning pressure system of North Stream Two was also supposed to be done by Floyd, but they double-crossed everyone. The terms were revised in favor of Germany, and the system malfunctioning was bypassed intentionally. Now, nobody would stop it from completion and commissioning."

"Germany will balance it out," Den smiled. "The chancellor will give some deals to buy US LNG as well. She visited Bavaria last week to meet Mr Soder. Washington is influencing Mr Soder to become the next Chancellor candidate. There may not be any surprise if the CDU party nominates the defense minister, who is also a close friend of both Madam and Soder, as the next chancellor candidature in case Madam Markel decides to step down. This may be an interesting turnaround. There will be a good balancing deal very soon. What do you say, Mike?"

"We will not let the Nord Stream Two happen. Let the election of Poland continue because they are going to impose heavy penalties on the subject of disconnect in consortium formation for Nord Stream Two. We will have to put a tight bottleneck on it."

"So your candidate is winning there also?" Bolton asked, but Mike ignored him.

Chief replied, "I, too, have a new but better deal, gentlemen. Beijing has a deep Middle East plan. They will invest at least 400 Billion for Tehran to build oil and gas infrastructure and for manufacturing SEZ. In exchange, Iran will supply them with energy. China will set up manufacturing factories for the assembly of goods with the help of cheap labor and use belt-road transport routes to market this to the Middle East and Europe. Washington does not want to lose Europe to the hands of China or Russia. If Nord Stream Two cannot be avoided, you better try China. I am okay with revoting the US resolution for all-out sanctions over Iran. However, if they agree to bypass the Dollar and take the crypto or gold route, then this sanction may not work effectively. I cannot guarantee that part."

"What do you want?" Mike asked.

It is as if players on the chessboard were cleverly waiting for the next possible turn, and they had to think of alternatives in advance or with the changing situation. Politics is not a sport. Participants in global politics are shrewd because they know that they may not get a chance for a plan B."

Chief grabbed the chance to get straight into the deal. He took two long puffs and started, "Bolton is working for me. I mean, he agreed to certain terms. He is disclosing a few crucial secrets. This is the tip of the iceberg, though. My dear friend, this is a give and take. One demand is to get him the Dy PM candidature. Decide fast, Mike.

"Do not come in between us. Mind your business, Chief," Mike shot back.

"I have only one year left to complete my term at the UN. I am not sure whether I should volunteer for this organization or go back to Portugal. I want to take a rest and might get far from politics and diplomacy. This is the opportunity for all of us to launder our crime and image. I am talking sense, so think and decide. This is a beneficial proposal. Otherwise, we would never reach a consensus." Chief took a halt.

"Are you negotiating? Do not waste my time, Chief."

"Keep your patience, Mike. You are no exception to this. We all know the truth. You guys have built this Nexus so well."

"Please do not bluff and spoil the time."

"Of course it is." Chief was changing his expression and became louder now. "From its very inception, it has been presented as if this organization was built in a federal and democratic structure. In actuality, this was formed as a closely held consortium for mutual benefit and authority. Who built it? The so-called Allied force winners and destroyers. Who has been bluffing, Mike? It is your United States who has made themselves custodians of power consciously? Your contribution and decision within the UN are never unconditional. You took no shame to conspire for your own terms based on those conditions. Surprisingly, the charter was never reformed. Power still remains within the five permanent seat holders. This organization is used with all possible arm's length and beyond just to establish supremacy and economic dominance in a polarized manner. This is modern-day colonization, my dear friend."

"Do not be so emotional. We have been contributing on a large scale to UN activities and law-making."

"Yeah. On the one hand, you export war and blood. On the other hand, you present a fountain of peace. This is an intelligent hypocrisy."

"You are crossing the line," Mike warned.

Chief was in a different mood. He ignored it and continued, "The UN is facing a severe budget deficit and may run out of money at any time. Operating expenses and the peacekeeping budget are being survived based on a volunteer-funded bank. Member states have delayed committed contributions. The White House had canceled funding for UNESCO, UNICEF and the Population Fund. Our major spending on Humanitarian assistance, Development programs and Peace-keeping operations are at stake. The secretariat is not allowed to publish these reports and statistics. Do not take us for granted anymore, Mike. Enough is enough."

"You have fallen in love with the United Nations, Chief", Mike provoked.

"You and your PM are playing dirty business."

"I reiterate, Chief. Shut up your mouth. Do not test my patience."

"Your arrogance and cleverness are ruining a lot of crucial initiatives. With-draw your veto from the appointment of judges in WTO. Let the organizations function on global need and sovereignty. Do not influence it to make it your government agency. For God's sake, stop it. All members supported the appoint-ment of Ngozi Okonjo-Iweala of Nigeria as the next WTO Chief. She is the most imminent choice. However, only the US opposed her and nominated the South Korean candidate for its own diplomatic exchange package. You guys have put sanctions on the investigative officers in ICC. You guys have withdrawn from WHO, the Paris climate change commitment, the Comprehensive Nuclear Test Ban Treaty, the Open Skies Treaty and whatnot. Do you think this is justified? Is this democratic?" Chief yelled.

"These are state decisions and conscious calls. The next call awaits. It is a matter of time, and we will ensure the death of your beloved UN very soon. The Charter of the 'League of States' is almost ready. This will replace the United Nations soon. Whatever happens, we will not let anybody interfere with this agenda by whatever means."

"The World is not a USA monarchy. It is a waste of time to debate with you, Mike. Actually, I do not have any deal. I thought to make you realize that you are doing wrong things, bad things, nasty things."

"But I have a deal, Chief. Don't be so emotional with the UN. Be practical. I offer you a better deal. We would delay the League of States process till you retire. Enjoy your remaining one year and return back to your country, Portugal, thereafter. Do not try to compete with the US. You may not be able to cope.

We have multiple tasks, so please listen to me patiently. The Arctic Development Bank is a proposed financing arm for civil and marine construction surrounding the US-Canada Arctic coastline. Another recommendation was to build new strategic deepwater ports and the expansion of existing ports in the polar territory. However, "Kawerak Inc." filed a lawsuit against this for potential threats to local natural resources and the Indigenous people who depend on those resources. They claimed that heavy construction and business traffic would affect the environment. What do you think? We stop all businesses and keep appraising this kind of regional tribal government! The Kawerak presented a marathon list of recommendations for improvements on oil-spill readiness, air pollution, potential interference with subsistence hunters and vulnerability of cultural resources. The matter was escalated in the UN forum. There was a hold order from the International Court of Justice for our construction projects. Even expansion and buildup plans for a few Arctic ports were put on hold by the US Army Corp of Engineers (USACE). We are pushing the agenda for final clearance, but without a firm commitment and effort from your side, things would not move in our favor."

Chief knew that Mike was a master negotiator.

Mike asked directly, "Withdraw all such hold orders. The Port expansion plan of the Arctic Development Bank is an extended part of the 'polar bear', as you also know very well. Favor us for the Polar Circle."

Chief relighted his pipe. He likes sophistication, so he uses a 'butane lighter'.

"One more thing, Chief. Lomonosov Ridge, which is a 1700-kilometer mountain beneath the sea, is ours. Dismiss the claim of Russia and Greenland, approve Canada, and we will take care of Canada in favor of the US. We are anyway donating Canada for their desired permanent seat in the UN."

"Mike, hope you are not dictating the negotiation."

"Canada is final, Chief. Do you have a choice? We will fix our choice either here or in a new league. Then you will see better from the pavilion who dictates!"

"You guys are devils."

"Don't be emotional. It is politics. 'Polar Bear' failed. We will soon catch hold of the sabotage." Mike looked at Den and then turned back to Chief. "We will not lose Greenland nor the trans-polar region."

"There is no harm in the US going very aggressively for the Arctic! But you are desperate for wrong things!" Chief argued back.

Mike expressed a sly smile, "The Arctic is the new battleground. Winning on the roof will drive terms for lands."

This was another battleground here inside the Barge. It was a private cold war. Four people faced off against each other. Everybody had a story, but all those stories coincided with a big conspiracy event. Everybody had a deal to settle. And one was a master conspirator among these gentlemen.

The grandfather clock of the cabin rang six times. This was the time for high tea. Chief called the attendant. The attendant was already ready and served Tea and Coffee to the center table.

Mike was extremely shrewd by nature. He now started commanding the meeting. He played the trump cards effectively. Things were in his grip, and everybody was aware of the fact that Mike was powerful. It is a known fact that the White House is run by him. Without his ideas and interventions, critical political or economic policies of the White House are not formed. He is the second in command after Mr PM and a loyal right-hand man. Mike was a businessman. He was an army officer and then started aerospace manufacturing. His experience with defense stakeholders was deep, which helped him to become a champion lobbyist in the White House. Gradually, he influenced bureaucrats and senators to grab orders in the oil field equipment business. He became the natural choice of another business tycoon turned politician, like the present PM. Mike's political career grew by grabbing influential and heavy posts within a very short time. Mike was made Director and head of the CIA. He brought his business partner as CIA COO too. After a stint as CIA head and loyal contribution to his master, Mr PM, Mike was promoted as the Secretary of State.

Chief attempted to make tea for all the guests, but Mike asked him to stop.

"I do not take hazardous items for security reasons. Who guarantees that you do not poison me?" Mike accused.

"Nobody loses a golden goose. You are my guest. I am not you, so no worries. We will take a sip first. You make your choice. There is no compulsion, and I can order something else or more if you wish." Chief poured the tea into two cups and handed one to Den. Bolton does not drink tea or coffee.

Den took the first sip and then broke the silence, "I do not have any deal, Sir. I have prepared a file for you. Obviously, I could not carry the full draft due to obvious risks, but I carried some portion of it. This may interest you. Furthermore, this would help us to reconcile the conspiracy."

"Conspiracy! Who is the criminal?" Mike was angry. He started yelling at Den. "I rescued you, Den, and you betrayed us! You betrayed our government! You yourself were caught red-handed on an espionage charge. However, it was the right act that you confessed the name of the main mastermind. Thanks for your wit." He motioned Chief, "We would ensure a tough extradition prosecution. You are a fugitive. Surrender as a witness, and we will guarantee your security."

Den listened patiently. His chin was tight. He knew the bad, hard truth. He then replied, "It was all made up, Mike."

Mike jolted, and could sense the surprise. Den continued, "You played a drama in Ethiopia, and we played one in Svalbard. The investor meeting was first scheduled in Svalbard, but later it was changed. You trapped your two targets in an illusive meeting in Ethiopia, along with the roleplay of proxy characters. Recent critical equations between China and Russia and their probable nexus, which are yet to be established and proven in public, were brought on stage very cleverly, and it was recorded by a hired journalist. Backstage, the original meeting happened in Neom, Saudi Arabia. Please correct me, if I am going wrong!" Den smiled little.

"You mean, it was pre-planned that the outcome of the covert meeting would automatically come out in public! What rubbish!" Mike exclaimed.

"Who hired Walter? He delivered his bit. He published the article 'The Covert Meeting' correctly, as per the dealing. But his full and final payment of one million was unpaid. I appreciate that Walter demanded the same in the right way. I hope you realize that even if you buy the COVID-19 file from him, there is competition. Someone may offer him a better deal to expose the information. Either way, you will lose money or your reputation."

Now, Mike's chin became tough, his eyeballs were cold, and he was becoming a cold-blooded fox.

Den didn't stop, "Walter was not aware that the Ethiopia meeting was a made-up event. He was doing his task, but he doubted Medkev. The room was dark, so it was really difficult to be sure about someone and to recognize the face accurately. He intentionally fell down over him and discovered that the chairperson was not Medkev. Actually, there was no real character in the room except four: Jour himself, Taylor, Oskar and myself. Jour started blackmailing you for the release of the final payment. He prepared another investigation on the COVID conspiracy. Instead of meeting you directly, he took Bolton's help. Bolton introduced him to Chief, and you were already running after him. Naturally, once Chief discussed this deal and this private meeting today, you were excited to catch the business, but you didn't realize that the syndicate had a mole in the system."

Den looked at Bolton and started again, "Thanks to Bolton. He was the double cross. Bolton was leaking information about the 'polar bear' to Chief. Chief planned to infuse his trustworthy security person with an Interpol Intelligence Officer into the meeting. Oskar was given the charge to cover me, and Bolton managed to get him in. Bolton helped to arrange entry passes as well."

"But I was not aware of the last-minute plan, the kill order," Bolton replied.

"I was aware from day one that you are a traitor, Bolton." Mike blasted.

"You betrayed me too, Mike." Now Den blasted on Mike, "You betrayed the entire globe, the global ethos, the systems, the states. You even betrayed your own man, Taylor."

"Taylor was an old horse. His job was over. He suddenly changed his attitude, and he was opposing us. He started blackmailing us and threatened to spoil the sport."

"He didn't take his friend's murder lightly. He knew that his employer plotted the assassination. This was a political move. It was obvious why he revolted."

"What do you mean?"

"Use and eliminate if the team is a risk to the government. This is a simple fundamental of politics. Isn't it!" Den stated.

"Government! You are crossing the line, Den!" Mike yelled.

"I will show you one paper. Hold your nerve for the roller coaster." Den opened his bag and showed a two-page printout. It was a copy of an email that PM wrote to Mike, Bolton, Stephen Miller- the Senior Policy Adviser and Michael Cohen- his personal lawyer. This was the PM's most trustworthy and dependable inner circle. The latter two were engaged in Election, so they were not engaged in 'polar bear'.

"I am bothered about Europe and done with Saudi. I don't mind if they are collateral damage in the mission. We have to restrict our regional enemies. We can play divide-n-rule to keep Europe fragmented and the Middle East disturbed. Build a representation instead of a presence. Consolidate European allies in favor of Britain's command and Middle Eastern allies in the camp of Israel. We only intervene there in terms of the double face. One face is political and diplomatic interference. The other face is to supply arms and economic support only to strategic allied countries when needed. Build up the need.

Eurasian consolidation of the Muslim Brotherhood in the leadership of Turkey and Iran is the emerging threat. Form a dedicated mission for Eurasia and activate it discreetly. Involve the CIA. My business lies in East and South Asia now. So, our power in machinery and resources should be concentrated towards that territory for the next decade. It is not Atlantic. It is now the Pacific and Indo-Pacific where we focus our camp.

The Arctic is our next top priority because we should reach out to the east through a better route. Russia is building up. We cannot wait for our natural turn to happen. Melt the ice and form a firm NWP. Nato will not prioritize the EU anymore. Rather, they will mobilize to the Arctic. Our newly formed IPTO will cater to the Pacific. My defense budget and resources will now concentrate on the Pacific. We need safe passage there and need to safeguard the market. Ancillary efforts are already being carried out for our immediate single-point enemy. Now, this is America's moment to stand up as an Arctic nation and for the Arctic's future. Additionally, if the virus is also effective, this will change a lot of equations. Prepare it now and manage the escalation."

The email was dated three years ago.

Mike was a strong-minded professional. He does not lose his cool, even in tough times, but he realized that for him, it was a tough time now. He looked at Bolton and Chief with outrage, returning to Den, "So this is a team! Who sponsors it? UN or Russia or China! Are you an intermediary?"

Den smiled. "Unfortunately, I haven't sold anything yet. I am not a political broker or getting paid, Mike. But yes, I procured information. The information is an eye-opener to the roller coaster conspiracy. Sir, you better sit tight at this moment. I only showed the prelude. I will take you on a joy ride."

"I guess we assembled here for settlement, but you guys teamed up with a vested interest," Mike showed his annoyance.

"Team!" Den took a long breath. He realized that a sly person never gives up easily and keeps trying underhand tricks to gain favor. Mike was a wily fox.

Den went ahead, "Recruiting the assets and operatives were done very intelligently. C3, Alex Navani, was given supreme authority to supervise and spearhead the 'polar bear' while also working on committee recruitment. He was Russian. However, he was an opposition strongman in the Russian command. C7, Taylor, was an interesting recruit. He was a skilled but equally crazy and moody person. He was used for his rich experience in underwater site construction. He hates Russians, so it didn't take much time and effort to convince Taylor that the mission was for American supremacy. This would challenge Russia in the Arctic. He was injected with white American pride and sentiment. Later on, he had several confrontations with his line supervisor, Navani, as he was Russian. He could not change his racist habit. The matter escalated to the management, as he was unmanageable, but what made him more furious was the killing of his friend."

Bolton said, "It was not known that Denmark PM and Taylor were close friends. This assassination was an official decision."

Den replied, "Political murder is always an official decision but executed unofficially. That incident broke Taylor completely. He revolted, and he had to pay the price."

Mike shouted, "What's going on here? Would you complete this drama?"

"We are reviewing the facts, Mike. Please calm down. You already achieved your goal! The resolution for the independence of Greenland from Denmark has almost been granted. This is the first step to decoupling Greenland from the old legislature. Now, the US can re-propose a purchase offer. You are on schedule. You should be happy!

"Stop the nonsense! Don't accuse the Government!" Mike again shouted.

"Of course it is. C2 will confess this correctly." Den turned to Bolton, " I hope you do not mind, Sir, as I addressed you by your code name," Den smiled.

Mr Bolton acknowledged and then replied, "Recruitment was done carefully. Starting from C3 to C7, they were outsiders. They are from Russia, Armenia, Israel and Canada. Identifying the double-cross players was not an easy task. The idea was to mitigate the risk of losing one's own perception. To do this, the respective country would be questioned, and the case would be put in extradition. Even if the person is caught, the White House would get a clean note. However, working with such outsiders, even if you buy them at a high price or break them through deep emotional reasons, you still have risks. This is the risk of leakage or double-crossing. The Government cannot afford it. From day one, it was clear that ultimately, the asset would be used and thrown away."

"Nobody knows the killing better than you, Bolton," Mike laughed at him.

"I always played in a war zone. Boosting war was my job. We don't fight just to achieve peace and security. Sometimes, war conflict is a commercial requirement. Don't you know this, Mike, being in the defense business for so long? I never interfere in civil conflict. Government-directed covert killing is usually executed by intelligence agencies, not the army."

Mike didn't say anything. His ears and eyes were red. However, He was not able to explode. Chief was still silent.

Den kept eleven photos on the tabletop. These were Chief, Mike, Bolton, Navani, Dr. Bunn, Ted Mateen, Eric Nichols, Taylor, Floyd, Sir Jodman, Denmark PM and Den himself.

Everybody's eye was over the table now. Den picked up a blue marker and sequentially wrote the operative code from C2 to C7 on the face of the respective photo. Only C1 was yet to be mentioned. At this point, the choice was funneled into limited options between Chief and Mike. He now took a red marker and signed a cross at the bottom of Taylor, Sir Jodman and Denmark PM. He also put a cross on his own picture and then marked a tick with a green marker. "I could escape. It was my luck, but these guys could not."

"Do we know this old man?" Chief asked after a while. He indicated towards Sir Jodman.

"Surprised that your person injected the nerve agent, and you refused to identify him now!"

"What rubbish, Den!" Chief showed annoyance.

"Kim Kielsen, Greenland's PM, has been spying. Satellite and security surveillance was also monitoring my movements. The syndicate is so cruel and desperate that they don't take chances. They eliminated every single risk. A local medical attendant was assigned to go to his house in the name of blood collection, and he was injected. It was reported that he died of Coronavirus. His dead body was also buried in isolation, but believe me, he was innocent. He didn't know anything serious about polar bear', nor was there any risk from him. His friend Taylor didn't disclose anything to him at that time. However, Sir Jodman kept trying to convince Taylor to realize that he was trapped in a geopolitical crusher. Specifics were not known to him. His voice was always working for the truth, climate victims and tribal rights. He was a rebel and a local hero. It was extremely unfortunate. It is easy to say that he was collateral damage." Den was very upset about the unnecessary murder of Sir Jodman.

Den then pulled the photo of Chief, halted for a few seconds, looked at everybody once and marked C1 on top of the face. The bomb was detonated.

Den already finished one cup, and he poured another half cup for himself. This was the first flush of fine Chinese tea. Mike usually, in this kind of situation, takes tea or coffee. He takes six to eight cups of tea daily. It is his habit. For security reasons, he hadn't taken one yet, but he now requested Den to prepare a cup for himself.

"Finally, you are convinced, but please do not trust my hand. I can poison you. I request you to prepare for yourself." Den replied with a mild gesture.

Mike smiled with utmost pleasure, "You already identified who ordered to poison you."

Mike prepared a cup for himself. He did not take sugar cubes. His brain was relaxed and now he could cherish the drink. Nobody in the room said anything for five long minutes.

Chief was annoyed. He was fat, but the present situation was not burning the fat from his body. Rather, it increased his blood pressure. It fluctuated. Bolton's walrus mustache fits well with his peculiarity, and his two wolf eyes were still freezing cold. It was difficult to assess him, too. Mike was also fat, but his blood pressure looked steady now. He was enjoying his first flush tea.

The center stage was ready to welcome another shock. Den already revealed the chief as a mastermind criminal. But the best was yet to come. Den had to expose the proof.

Den resumed, "Gentlemen, have you concentrated on that three-year-old dated classified email? There were two specific lines:

'We cannot wait for our natural turn to happen. Melt the ice and form a firm NWP', 'Additionally, if the virus is also effective, this will change a lot of equations. Prepare it now. Manage the escalation.'

It meant everything. Business houses need to be very visionary in making decisions with precision and correct speculation, and so does Washington. The Spread of Coronavirus is a biological weapon. Explaining its consequences in global trade and economic slowdown would take at least a few hours. Let me get straight to one specific agenda of this man-made genocide. Negative fuel prices have already started dragging Russia, the Middle East and some OPEC countries into a sudden death situation. The fracking shale industry of North America is also deeply affected. But before its gradual death, along with the bankruptcy of a few big brother fuel companies like Zonmobil or Chevron, the US had prepared itself. Large secret SPRs are built with undisclosed reserving capacity, but that's not all. Oklahoma and Texas started buying unsold oil consignments at high discounts and oil futures in the cheapest possible deal ever. Storage is created now. This will be used in the emerging value chain of blue ammonia renewal energy."

Mike countered, "Don't you know that we are almost done with Saudi? Now they themselves have to grow without the US."

"I know the clever game plan," Den said in return, "This is a giveaway to establish your Middle East agent, Israel. Anyway, the Whitehouse is trying to consolidate the Middle East in the hands of Israel. People are calling this a 'peace deal'. You also know jargon and reality are different. For the white house, it is a balancing act and pressure tactics. You are isolating Iran and Palestine with the help of Saudi-Israel dealings. The US, anyway, cannot decouple Saudi. In the era of baby boomer oil purchases against petrodollar, arms sales are old methods. The balance of trade is getting revised. They are pushing Saudi Arabia to establish direct trade with Japan. If the use of fossil fuels is reduced, the economy of the Middle East will collapse. Agreement to sell blue ammonia at dirt-cheap prices to Japan is their natural choice at this moment. This is actually a trick. The US compelled Japan to become a middle agent in exchange for military and naval protection in the Pacific. One-half of those goods will be used for captive consumption by Japan, and the residual is re-sold to the US. They, in turn, would sell the goods at higher prices."

Mike opposed, "You imagine big and seem to know everything. Don't you know that these are bogus?"

"I know the deal in Neom."

Chief didn't say anything. Bolton was also silent. They were listening. They all knew that Den analyzed this bad stuff correctly. Truth was no longer a stranger.

Blue ammonia is a feedstock for blue hydrogen, a version of the fuel made from fossil fuels with a process that captures and stores CO_2 emissions. The future of Energy lies in hydrogen-based blue ammonia. Japan is taking the lead in this segment, and China also gave a surprise pledge in this line. Washington took a shortcut. A pandemic was created. Fossil fuel was bought in stock at heavily subsidized prices to take advantage of the future value chain. On the one hand, they continued the arbitraging oil trade, and on the other hand, they were maturing themselves and the market for future trade of hydrogen energy.

Mike was losing patience, "Will you end your fiction now!"

"Yes of course. We just read the first few chapters. There is a final chapter on Arctic Supremacy. Have patience, Mike. I shall read out the thriller for you all." Den replied and took a pause for a few seconds.

He tried to read the minds of Mike and Chief. Intelligence was a unique identity and a complex affair of humans. Both Mike and Chief were extremely sharp in some form. It was not easy to read their minds. Den knew what to elaborate on at this moment.

Den resumed, "Can you deny that the US started in the Arctic late? When a scientist predicts climate change, it is based on research. However, when a businessman predicts climate change, it is speculative, purposeful and linked only to the business agenda. The US always believed that thick ice and inhabitable extreme weather conditions of the Arctic made the choice for America tough, at least in the northwest territory and northwest passage. There was no hope. There was no priority. Naturally, American policy and focus has been slow and indifferent in this region, but the enemy country is already in a commanding position around the polar belt. Russia in particular has an edge, not because of the resource-rich large continental shelf surrounding the Arctic Circle, but because of long ice-free seasons. This geographical advantage made Russia stronger economically and politically for the North Pole. Geography is always one of the key influencers in shaping the political and economic fate of a state. The Russian flag was hosted beneath the center of North Pole water in 2007, and things changed in Washington thereafter. They decided to evolve. They realized the significance and future consequences of geopolitical hegemony surrounding the Arctic Circle. It is better to be late than never."

Den took a pause, "Please allow me a cigarette." He lit his cigarette and continued, "The Senate made the Arctic a top priority for their agenda. National Oceanic and Atmospheric Administration, ie. NOAA, reported that by 2050, the Polar Circle will be almost ice-free in the summer. Can the US wait? Obviously not. The prelude of this second chapter of the mission was framed to remove the hostile blocks. It was planned to melt the ice faster, no matter if it damages the environment, natural and marine resources or any other tribal inhabitants. Once it was determined by the government to pursue the agenda and backed by business houses, there was no care about the environment. Going to the Indo-Pacific market has to be quicker, less costly and safer for future trade. Asia would play a vital role in the future world order. Holding on to supremacy in the trade value chain is of utmost priority. So, Japan, Taiwan, South Korea, Australia, India and Vietnam have been made key strategic allies in the East with quick revision of US policy along with a few business deals. Vietnam is being nurtured as an alternative labor resource in the global manufacturing and supply chain. Without the Arctic, this ambition is not possible. Correct me if I am going wrong!" Den poured warm water into his glass and sipped. And he concentrated on his smoking.

Chief, Bolton, and Mike could easily make out that Den was going in the right direction, but the truth was harder, stronger and stranger.

Chief opened up after a long while. After his name was revealed as 'C1' in front of everybody, he didn't say anything. He was hosting the meeting for everybody's benefit. The agenda was a settlement. "Dynamics and Interest in the Arctic differ for each country. For Russia, it is mainly resources and revenue from the North Sea Route shipping corridor. Deployment of military infrastructure in that zone is a complementary checklist. For China, it is easier, faster and more economical to have a trade passage to Europe. For the US, the Northwest Passage is the future marine highway in the East. Naturally, they are supporting and investing heavily in Canada as an immediate intermediary for Allie in this journey. The Arctic was more of a priority than Suez now, but withdrawal from Suez was a bad idea. This would confront Middle East partners in Israel and Saudi. So, France & Britain picked Djibouti to challenge China, and the US picked Ethiopia with all-out support and investment to challenge the disturbance in North Africa and the entrance point to the Mediterranean. This was a critical combination. It was a well-thought-out plan."

"You are an old pig. Have you lost your mind? Do you expect the US to lose the battle to competition? We are the superpower not by fluke or chance but by planning. We deserve this." Mike stated, humiliating Chief.

"A plan of massacre to stay relevant in business! nuke explosives in the Arctic is indeed a big plan," Den replied sarcastically.

"Ask Chief. You caught him, right? I am not the planner."

Chief was walking around the room. He replied in annoyance, "Global warming is a viral fever. Industrialisation and the consumption economy are viruses. It is fatal. The North Pole is melting, and the Arctic is melting faster. This would devastate the ecological balance of the Earth. It is as good as pushing the end of the human race closer. It is definitely man-made. Don't you really know who has done all of this? Who has planned 'polar bear'" Chief asked for Mike.

Den also cornered Mike with pressure tactics. He fired at Mike, "Planting nukes to fast-track the melting is a global crime, Mike. I caught Chief consciously. So that we could give you a chance, now it is time to catch the real monster fish and slap it on the face."

Den picked up the marker and crossed out the C1 on the photo of Chief. He now wrote C1 on the face of Mike's photo and marked the circle.

Everybody became quiet. This was a storm. This was dramatic. The demon mastermind lawmaker behind the big conspiracy was finally exposed. He was Mike.

Mike paused for a long minute and then sneered at Den, "So ultimately, you caught me!" His face was red, and his jaw was tight. Eyes and ears were warm with anger. He asked, "But why did you require so much of these dramatic scenes? Bolton might have told you all. Do you realize that you cannot prove it? Your sabotage unplugged the 'polar bear', but it ultimately helped to erase the main lead. There was no explosion, so there was no crime."

Den replied with a mysterious smile, "Bolton and Kelvin Floyd came at a much later stage. I took their help to consolidate the facts, not the leads. I caught you long before that."

Bolton also nodded his head to agree with Den.

"Your first mistake was to hurry in eliminating Dr. Bunn. You didn't want me to reach out to Dr. Bunn before you did. Your men could not manage the assassination well, and they left loose ends."

"Make your storytelling tighter. Be more convincing," Mike had enough stamina to defend and debate. He did not give up so easily, whether he was right or wrong.

"Have some more patience. You lied by saying that he was arrested and taken into army custody for a confession, but here it is," Den showed the death certificate of Dr. Bunn, "See the date? I accessed this timely through my channel. It came to me by chance. Your second mistake was very immature. As per you, Dr. Bunn confessed about secret oil reservoirs in the North Slope and a nuke in Oklahoma. It was not needed, though. By that time, I already had specifics from Taylor's dairy and satellite imagery to spot the exact locations. I was speculating about some nuke plots. I became sure that you were misleading. You actually misled me from the beginning. Chief wanted my assignment in Svalbard. After the Katowice conference, he asked me to go to Svalbard immediately to solve the labor dispute, but you wanted me to stay back in Hong Kong to spy in a Chinese camp. You didn't want my presence in the action circle. Very clever indeed."

"I was getting leads on the said Arctic campaign that a big-scale conspiracy is being cooked. The surrounding diplomacy was very unusual on some occasions. I was curious that something was going on," Chief replied.

"Oskar, the undercover cop, did a great job. His team silently penetrated into the arranged area, kidnapped a participant and replaced the person with Oskar. It was not an easy task." Den continued, "The Ethiopia meeting, along with the false characters, were anyway proxy of the original investor meeting in Neom. Oskar played a double proxy. You were very close to accomplishing your agenda, Mike.

I really started perceiving the event as real. The roleplay was very accurate. Most importantly, I really misunderstood Chief initially. It was not a simple play. It was a real illusion."

Den's eyes were almost red, as if his entire body was pressing a load on nerves and brain cells. It was a mix of his anger, annoyance, hatred and nervous agitation. He saw the wristwatch. He knew that he only had 30 more minutes. After that, the reaction would start.

Den resumed. Den was talking straight to Mike, "I appreciate your wit, Sir. Taylor was poisoned because he had to be eliminated. His usage was over. I know that there was no poison in my cup. Actually, it was a nerve agent. The idea was not to kill me upfront. Rather, the plan was to disrupt my system with nerve agents for some days to ensure a halt in the investigation. It was required to smoothen the last mile job of the detonation successfully."

Mike is still holding onto his nerves. He laughed, "I wanted you to live. You are a secretariat while color staff. There is another sophisticated method for your death, my dear friend. You should owe me for your survival!"

"You camouflaged my brain with false information and misleading roleplay. You wanted to use me in soliciting and spreading manufactured information. This would have benefited you in gaining political control," Den replied.

"Sometimes spoiling the enemy in their own program is more profitable than elimination. It is a business rule."

"Mike, you were actually very close", Chief replied. "When you disclosed your wish to me that you wanted a trustworthy guy to attend a secret business meeting in Ethiopia and your nomination is Den, believe me, I took this as an opportunity. I was very sure that it was a trap. However, I was also sure that Den would manage it in his own way and be able to win. I didn't know that you are such a clever devil." Chief turned to Den, "Sorry, my boy. Knowingly, I had put you at life risk. I should have avoided this."

"Don't be sorry, Sir. It was a turning point. Without that blow, we perhaps would not have ever come closer to this conclusion," Den replied with a gesture.

Mike again shouted, "What's going on? Where is the conclusion? Who is concluding? Where is the proof? I am not here to waste further time by listening to all this nonsense," Mike tried to wind up.

"I am the guest, Mike", Chief ordered with a firm voice. "The captain will not listen to you. None of your men will be able to reach out. I know your satellite is monitoring us. A missile could be triggered from the surveillance drone, but do you really mind giving your life along with us for this silly meeting? Do not create a scene. Be patient. Sit down. You have ten more minutes. Thereafter, you will be released automatically." Mike returned to his chair. Bolton was silent because he knew that the submissions of Den and Chief were correct. Chief's eyes were also red, but this is due to anger and physiological reactions. The eyes of Den and Mike were red because of chemical reactions caused by a nerve agent.

Chief resumed, "I was not sure about the game plan. It was at an infant stage to speculate anything sitting far away in the city. My age and my chair do not permit me to investigate. I was almost sure that the big game had some root in Svalbard, and therefore, I thought to consciously deploy Den to that region. Den does magic when he works in the field. I keep telling him that he should have moved into a field agent job or intelligence role. He is wasting himself here in the secretariat role. It is boring, cumbersome and thankless." He smiled towards Den with pleasure. "He is my boy."

"Mike, I will give you some surprises. You must be searching around for the reason why the detonation failed. You perhaps could not digest this yet," Den replied to Mike. "We Floyded the system in Svalsat. We mean Kelvin Floyd, another recruit who, after the murder of his brother, turned to revenge. He knew the full architecture of the launch code system, so he could successfully break the door and push the bug. Thanks to the fact that you were hospitalized, else it would have been difficult for me to bypass and escape to Svalbard. In Svalsat, it was all pre-planned. I was not caught. The machine was already installed in the server room. I just attempted a roleplay as per plan. The police arrested me and sent me to the custody of the Norway intelligence branch. After this, Remi took over. She and her friend General Morten Lunde designed the expedition to sites to collect field information and visuals. We got Oskar on the team as well. However, we kept the task discreet. Any leak would have spoiled the plan. I was released soon after, and I came back to New York. It was all made up."

"Interesting indeed", Mike heard patiently.

"Even when the malfunctioning task was done successfully, we did not want to take a chance. We had to stop the detonation. After the espionage news broke out, we were sure that the syndicate would postpone the detonation for some time. We were buying time, but you guys were really desperate to execute. The button was triggered instead of deferring it."

"I wanted to postpone," Mike's face was serious. He realized that Den was very close to the conclusion of the investigation.

"So, who was more desperate? Your boss!"

"Do not cross the last line. It may harm you, Den." Mike said, angry.

Den now exploded. "How do you do more harm when you have already exhausted all your resources and attempted to do the same? You guys didn't bother to use the bio-weapon for the Covid genocide. You guys didn't mind putting the entire marine life and polar fate at risk for the sake of business and political will. You didn't think twice to eliminate the risk elements. A liar, a mastermind monster! Now, I will show you to your last door of death."

"Shut up, you bastard!" Mike shouted at Den.

"Here it is, your death certificate." Den pulled a file from his bag. "I prepared this for you, Mike, your final nail in the coffin. This will elaborate the Launch code log and trail from specific PAL. It has proof that the launch instruction was triggered from Mr PM and then you. Witness and version of Bolton, Floyd and Navani are also included."

Den earlier marked a cross on the picture of Navani. Now, he marked a green tick on Navani. "He was escaping to Belarus, and he was injected with a V-grade nerve agent while in flight."

"So a deadman will also confess for your file?"

"A half-dead man. He survived by luck. He, being the main supervisor and commander of 'polar bear', has gold mine information. Remi took charge of convincing him to confess. He should unmask his masterminds who ordered everything. Navani is safe and taken into secret custody now."

Mike seemed to lose, ultimately. His blood-clotted eyes were gazing straight at Den. He was almost at a standstill with a sense of failure, fear and anger.

Den continued, "There was no report lodged in the police station about the housekeeping staff, who was killed in the bathroom at the Katowice conference. Den investigated this missing link. He was the only earning member of the family. The family was completely ruined. it was his fate that he was just present in the bathroom that day without even being bothered about the conversation. He was perhaps concentrating only on the housekeeping task. Trust me, he was never a risk to you. He was a simple ant, but you didn't spare him. Politics is so cruel. Politics doesn't care."

Den again saw his wristwatch, "Ohh, it is almost time, Mike. There may be a few more minutes before both you and myself fall ill," Den smiled with pleasure.

Drama has escalated to its peak.

"I kept a few blank pages as the last chapter. Kelvin Floyd will help you to log in with your password and fingerprint into your handset. He will help us to Floyd into your handset and execute my last chapter. I need the call and message log of you and Mr PM. Then the proof file will be completed."

"Are you drunk?" Mike asked, fumbling. Mike already started feeling drowsy and his blood pressure started fluctuating.

Den replied, "I am poisoned. But this is not toxic. This is a G-grade nerve agent. This is a mild enzyme. Very soon, this is going to disrupt my nervous system and organs. I need to rest for a couple of months. I came after taking an antidote as well. This grade will not kill us but affect the nerves and organs to malfunction with peculiarity."

"You are a drug addict!"

Den was firm, "I was addicted to unmasking the 'polar bear'. However, the job is done. By the way, thanks for ultimately agreeing to the courtesy of accepting a cup of tea from the host. You were initially adamant with fear of poison. So I diverted your concentration and started accusing Chief. I marked him as C1 at first. You thought you were the winner, and the truth would be spoiled in due course. Bolton and Chief didn't take tea for their age. I took the chance. Without someone having the tea in front of you, you would not have been convinced to drink it. I am okay with being a tiny collateral damage in the sphere of this conundrum. But we wanted a conclusion with truth. To inform you before you lose your control, a Nerve agent was mixed in the tea that we both had."

***

Mike wanted to stand up and strike back, but he was not able to gain sufficient energy now. He realized that he was in deep trouble and losing his fate. Chemical reactions started acting.

Chief slapped on the face of Mike, "I hope your satellite does not capture this, and your men won't get to know. You deserve this."

Den assured Mike, "Don't worry, Mike, this will not kill you. Killing you was an easy choice, but spoiling you is more toxic to your fate. You said it is a business rule. We levied the same protocol on you. Your 'polar bear' failed. The PM is not happy with you at all. This is high time for an election. After this, you would malfunction. We will release the file in a classified way only within a close group, a few diplomats, the UN Security Council and the White House. Do you think your employer is going to keep you? They would show no mercy in keeping the threat. They will kick you out, and once you are unplugged from the system without having position and power, we will either kill or use you." Den was also affected by this time. He started fumbling. The play was complete. It was a curtain call.

***

Floyd was hiding inside the engine room. He came upstairs, plugged an external chip inside Mike's handset and held Mike's finger for a fingerprint. A forensic chemical was brushed on top of the key touchpad to identify the highlighted screen spots for buttons. All the relevant data were copied within ten minutes.

Booster vaccines were arranged well in advance. After this was injected, the chance of recovery was faster. At least this would make the patient immune. However, the drug reaction and behavioral impacts remain for a longer time, at least for a couple of months. During this period, the patient loses memory, voice control and other normal brain functions. Floyd knew how to use the injection, so he injected both Mike and Den.

Rewind

Few Missing Dots

UN Climate conference in Katowice, Poland

The hall was full. Mike was addressing the audience. Den took a pause and went outside for a short time. Time was monotonous, and everything was business. He wanted to come out of the suffocation for a few minutes. Mike finished his speech, and Nikolay was next.

Mike used this time to go to the washroom and pinned Taylor, "Time to pee". Taylor was sitting in the row in front of Den. Taylor also pinned Dr. Bunn, who was waiting in the reception. Dr. Bunn came from Georgia to Poland for this visit. They have a quick but serious business to finish. They could not meet publicly. All three gentlemen assembled in the washroom. A fourth person came inside. He was representing Mike. He handed over a heavy suitcase to Dr. Bunn. It was his final installment. nuke shaft installation was completed as per design in all three sites.

Mobilization of the nuke balls was the only thing left, which would take place in the last leg. The bag was tight with gold bars. Sometimes, this old trick of offline smuggled items is more effective than paying through a modern laundering route of telegraphic transfer to bank accounts of shell companies. Mike called both Taylor and Dr. Bunn in person because there has been a disconnect and misunderstanding between these two. Mike thought to mediate this. Work might be impacted if the team was not cohesive.

Mike was annoyed with Taylor because he was very slow at uninstalling a few oil rigs across the Northwest Passage of the Canadian coast and the western coast of Greenland. It was part of the divestment business plan of Zonmobil and a few other American and European Giants. The future of fossil fuel is fragmented and will have to be diversified with immediate effect to remain in business. Climate and environment are secondary. The primary immediate agenda was to find feasible, meaningful alternatives. It was obvious that oil refineries and seabed mine owners did not easily agree to withdraw. They had to be compensated in the deal. All these companies were hard investors. Compensation for other avenues, like renewable energy and seabed mining of rare earth elements or shipping, was a must. This ensured that the investors didn't back out. Zonmobil was forced to compromise in the withdrawal. Removal of a few of their oil rigs was in exchange for a committed investment and profit sharing in the planned mission and future business prospects in the Arctic.

Mike insulted Taylor in front of Dr. Bunn and threatened to disqualify him from the task. Taylor was aware that getting disqualified or kicked off from this kind of secret mission meant a life threat. He simultaneously threatened Mike that he would disclose the conspiracy. The government, on one side, was representing an attractive proposal and propaganda to build a climate fund contribution, and on the other side, was withdrawing from the Paris Agreement for the committed reduction of greenhouse gas emissions. Taylor slapped Mike, not caring that Mike was the second-in-command in Washington and the right-hand man of Mr PM.

The conversation and confrontation were not lengthy and happened within a close group of the three. There was supposed to be nobody in the washroom, but it was bad luck for one housekeeping staff member, who was stuck in the last latrine cubicle while he was repairing a commode. Taylor was agitated with the behavior of Mike and lost cool. He came outside to the lobby and collided with Den. Den was passing through the lobby and was returning to the hall. Dr. Bunn also departed. Mike washed his face, which was still angry and red. He was revengeful.

He discovered that one housekeeping staff was already inside and perhaps heard and saw everything. He was quick to make brutal decisions. He pinned his men to take care of the boy in the washroom. After Mike left, two men came within a minute and injected poison into the housekeeping staff.

Svalbard

A year back and the prelude of the conspiracy.

The mastermind flew from Olavsvern naval base with a military chopper to attend the meeting. It was Mike. The executive team assembled together to discuss and fix the blueprint for 'polar bear'.

Nuuk

Navani, C3, was annoyed with Taylor's slow progress. Zonmobil was supposed to remove a few specific oil rigs in the northern territory as per their plan. They could not do this officially. So, Taylor was kept in charge of accomplishing this discreetly. After the nuke explosion, the oil rigs, which were stationed very close to the nuke sites, might carry the risk of fatal damage. Zonmobil had to protect the equipment and assets to rehabilitate. Hence, the removal was planned. Taylor was not able to manage this, and Navani had to answer to Mike and Bolton on the overall progress of the mission. He was also under pressure to complete the stages in a timely manner. He ordered a sabotage. They created technical damage for man-made oil spills to showcase temporary suspension of the oil rigs.

Mike, Navani and Bolton assembled for a quick field meeting. Sulemani was eliminated. Denmark's PM was killed. Everything was on schedule. The report spotted Taylor as a disloyal asset. The report also spotted Den as a vulnerable person. His movement and interference in the matter, as well as his constant connection with Sir Jodman, who was a friend of Taylor and Denmark's PM, compelled Mike to conclude that Den was a threat to the mission, and so was Sir Jodman. Mike didn't take a chance. He first ordered his team to kill Sir Jordan. Den was an exception. He was an active Secretariat officer. A lot of top diplomats knew him. Mike wanted to mislead him into a predefined illusion so that he would solicit lies in favor of Mike and his Govt. It was a clever masterstroke. Mike scripted a proxy meeting for Den in Ethiopia.

Neom Meeting, Saudi Arabia

The original consortium meeting took place in Neom, Saudi Arabia. Three private jets landed one after another in half-hour intervals on the runway of the newly built Neom Bay Airport. It was midnight. Four heavyweights Mike himself, The Saudi Prince, Israel PM and Mossad Chief reached the destination.

Neom is Saudi Arabia's bet to survive beyond fossil fuel. The city, called 'Line' is dreamt of flying taxis, robot maids and an artificial moon in the middle of a desert wasteland. The future is being built at the cost of a new investment paradigm.

There were other critical crises that still occurred behind the curtain. The crisis of life. Urban development cannot happen without the displacement of natives.

The 'Huwaitat' tribe, which has spanned throughout Saudi Arabia, Jordan and the Sinai Peninsula for generations, have been living in the Middle East before the founding of the Saudi State. At least 20,000 members of the tribe now faced eviction due to the project, with no information about where they will live in the future.

***

It was a full house. The whole 'polar bear' team and the investor brigade assembled in one place.

Mr Dick Tillerson was the chairperson of Zonmobil, the world's largest oil and gas company, which has had an influence over Washington lawmakers for decades. But now they were bleeding, and time had changed. Zonmobil was a leader in climate change denial, opposing regulations to curtail global warming. They funded organizations, critically opposing the Kyoto Protocol and undermining public opinion against the scientific consensus that global warming is caused by the burning of fossil fuels.

They even used to lead the Global Climate Coalition of Businesses opposed to the regulation of greenhouse gas emissions and influenced Washington to withdraw from the Paris Agreement. They had to mislead climate information to stay in the business of fossil fuels. The situation has changed. Now, they need to diversify to survive. So, they are investing a big bet into Arctic marine infrastructure, buying and building ports with public and private models and shipping. They need huge funds for this. A stake was being sold for its Arctic and North Sea assets to the Norwegian-Italian joint venture "Var Energy". However, Var alone will not be able to raise funds to pay the full amount. They brought a new partner. The US-brokered this deal, and the new partner was 'Saudi Aramco', another oil giant.

The Saudi Prince himself was present. He was the host, but the meeting was spearheaded by Mike. The US pressed Aramco to support Zonmobil, and in exchange, the US was investing in building Neom. The Saudi Prince had no interest in the Arctic. The US was not buying enough oil from Saudi Arabia anymore, so they had to negotiate with their US counterpart to compensate for the oil trade in exchange for Nemo's investment. The bailout package of Zonmobil by Aramco was a high-ticket deal. So, the deal and compensation were equally high. The Saudi Prince, additionally, demanded protection assurance from the US against Iran and Turkey. Riyad, in turn, agreed to compromise with Israel in a Middle East peace with a trade deal to isolate Iran from the Middle East, to play neutral for Turkey in Eurasia and to cut off Palestine from Israel permanently. International affairs are give-and-take, and this is always a marriage of convenience.

When the interests and purposes of two competitors complement each other, they find out ways for an amicable deal. For the US, political stability in Saudi Arabia is more of a priority than its economic stability. So supporting aid to build Neom and arms sales to fight against Yemen is actually a small agenda for the White House. Their major agenda is a peace deal with Israel. Through this, the US wants to bring the fragmented Middle East under the leadership of Israel. Obviously, it is also important to balance and negotiate the supremacy of the Middle East while shifting from Riyad to Jerusalem. On the other hand, the Saudi Prince knew that the Arab Spring was still not over and this had just started. Unrest of Tunisia, Egypt, Libya, Syria might resonate with Saudi Arabia anytime. This was the best time to compromise and make political friendships with Bahrain, UAE, Qatar and even with their all-time rival, Israel. It made sense at this point.

The Israeli PM was also present. The order of the Middle East had changed, and now it was in the hands of Israel with the support of the White House. Time was in favor of Israel's camp to dictate future terms. Terms needed to be tightened because Israel will see the presidential election very soon, and the chair needed to be retained.

Another crucial agenda was also discussed in this meeting. A similar future city like Neom was being planned for the Arctic region. 'Polar bear' was a prelude and preparation to open up the Arctic for future business and trade. However, it was equally necessary to establish settlers and populations in some key choke points of the region for their sustainability and active participation. So, the township corridors were planned. They discussed the first blueprint of the idea. A similar concept of 'Neom Line', which is a three-layer city along with ecology and residence in the first layer, market in the second layer and transport corridor in the third layer, was in the plan. But unlike Neom, this Arctic city would be built vertically instead of underground. The same contractors of Neom were being hired. The American company Bachtel for project management and Aecom for the city's backbone design have already been awarded the contracts under the table.

***

Journalist Khashoggi opposed this. He brought a personal fight to the global stage and started criticizing the Saudi Prince in public. It was a big bet for the Saudi Prince, and obviously, they could not afford a leak or obstacles. Khashoggi was killed while in private government custody. First, they cornered him through a bureaucratic trap. Khashoggi was in Istanbul to apply for political asylum. He already got hints that he was not safe in the US or Saudi anymore. Riyadh sent a hit squad to the Saudi consulate in Istanbul. Khashoggi had to collect some official documents from the consulate, where he was murdered in the presence of the official hitmen.

Turkey opened the investigation file and managed to curate sensitive CCTV footage, trail and proof to substantiate that it was a political murder and the Saudi Prince himself was the mastermind. So, this also became a prime agenda for the Prince to now settle. So, Mossad Chief was called. A tripartite negotiation was done in this meeting for a mutual trade-off between Israel, Turkey and Saudi Arabia. The parties compromised to the respective tune of future benefits and agreed to settle on a few crucial issues. The spider web of 'Arctic conspiracy' had spread wide and thick. It changed the equations and friendships of multiple governments and several geopolitical businesses.

***

The CEO of Arctic Capital, Minnesota, was taking part due to their interest in port investment. Chairperson of a drilling and mining company partnered for upcoming contracts and huge business opportunities ahead of exploring the Arctic resources.

After Denmark's PM was killed, it was easier for shipping giant Maersk to grow the shipping business throughout the Northwest Passage with the ambition of gaining more market shares. The managing director of Maersk was also present. Billions of funds were approved, raised and being invested for this epicenter of the future. Collaboration of Companies and Governments were made ready to grab the business.

Mr Boris Churchill was present as well. He was a well-known international broker in pharmaceutical dealings. However, most of these deals are backed by political sponsorship and of large scale. These pharmaceutical brokers drive this industry to formulate new demand and supply of drugs. The Nexus was almost ready. However, both the COVID-19 virus and antivirus formula were stolen and mishandled.

Mr Churchill intermediated the covert deal with Astra Pizer and Moder Pharma to develop the first COVID vaccine on mRNA technology, but the vaccine formula, via the hand of China, reached first to Russia. Russia would take the first moving advantage to launch the first vaccine. However, the complementary business was on schedule. 'Becton Dickinson & Company', one of the world's largest manufacturers of needles, syringes and medical supplies, was ramping up with collaboration of Astra Pizer. Stock prices of these giants sky-rocketed. These companies had to donate a portion of the estimated revenue to 'polar bear'. It was a precondition of their deal. The consortium was a well-thought-out memorandum.

The investors and the masterminds assembled together and reviewed the progress of the 'polar bear' before they agreed for the consensus on the final lap of the conspiracy.

Norad - Cheyenne Mountain Complex
Launch Centre L.1.0

This was the finishing line. The core execution team Dr. Bunn, Ted Mateen, Eric Nichols and Mac Metesky sat together underneath the mountain bunker and reconciled the last-minute action points and checks. Taylor was replaced recently by Mac for completing underwater sites. The confirmation meeting was held a day back in Neom, Saudi Arabia. The consortium agreed on a consensus for the final stage and gave permission. Now Navani and Ted Mateen were going to deliver the key authorization envelope to the second and third launch centers,

L.2.0 and L.3.0, respectively. They will also visit the satellite centers for final checks.

Abkhazia: The autonomous border of Georgia on the bank of the Black Sea

Three teams came to catch Dr. Bunn, who was in a political asylum. Den himself wanted to reach out to Dr. Bunn as soon as possible. It would be a major breakthrough to understand and defuse the conspiracy if he was able to catch him. Den was getting help from Dr. Bunn's partners. Mike also sent his men to Abkhazia to find Dr. Bunn. However, Mike sent his men to eliminate Dr. Bunn before he was caught by his opponent. Although Dr. Bunn changed his old number, Mike had access to his new number. He was tracked and cornered. The weapon used was the same this time as well. It was a V-grade nerve agent. There was no postmortem since it was reported as a death caused by Coronavirus. This was a similar arrangement as Sir Jodman's.

Mike lied to Den that Dr. Bunn was arrested and kept in safe custody, but ultimately, the truth was revealed. Den got the information from the two masters of the smuggling gang, Sumbat Tonoyan and Dr Hrant. Their man Scot spotted Dr. Bunn one morning before he was caught in the hands of Mike's men. Dr. Bunn was buried in a local graveyard. Scot had good local connections and collected a copy of the death certificate. The reason for death was false. He convinced the doctor and medical staff to reveal the truth. However, Mr Sumbat and Dr. Hrant were happy about the death of their partner. They were not bothered about the cause of the death. It mattered to Den the most, and this incident compelled Den to doubt Mike for the first time. This lie gave him direction. The episode was clear after Kelvin Floyd met him in New York and confessed. Floyd convinced Bolton to team up and reveal the secret. The picture of 'polar bear' became brighter after Den met Bolton at his house in Michigan.

Michigan

Den met Bolton in his house along with Floyd. Chief and Remi were also present on that day. Convincing Bolton was not an easy task. He is a self-centered, stubborn person. He usually does not break his interests or benefits and doesn't explore beyond his scope. However, exposing Mike was the right opportunity for him. He agreed to team up and disclosed untold stories about the conspiracy they planned and executed.

Now the time for conclusion. Five masterminds discussed the blueprint to catch the mole in the trap. To complete the file, they had to investigate further into the site locations to collect field information. The arrangement was not easy. They rehearsed the drama of plotting the false arrest of Den by Norwegian police. Mr Gaup's influence and good relationship with the Monarch of Norway helped the game. The younger brother of King was also very close to Remi. Together, they convinced Lieutenant General Morten Lunde, head of the Norway Intelligence Service, to support the game. After the arrest, keeping Den in the mainland of Norway in the custody of the Royal Navy was the plan. They bypassed the PM and police to avoid leaks.

Lutvann, Oslo - Norway Intelligence Service's new headquarter

The investigation crew was visiting the nuke test sites and Petroleum reserve sites. The submarine was coming back from the Northwest Passage. Den was in safe custody. General Lunde sent Oskar to Den in private. Oskar rushed into the cabin of Den. He had to get him alone for a few minutes. He got a scope. Oskar got an instruction from Chief. He carried a piece of paper. He placed it at the bottom of the coffee mug. The plan for the final meet and the invitee list was written on it. The appointment was fixed near Chief's house in New York. The false arrest of Den and expedition of the witness was only known to General Morten and Oskar other than Den. The submarine crew and the other Naval officers at headquarter were not aware that the entire arrangement was made up.

'Polar bear' failed. Consortium investors, Corporations, and whoever had invested in this mission for business prospects would ask for a return or refund. There was no single party to the conspiracy. Mike had to manage the government as well. After all, this was government-sponsored. His job, reputation and position were at stake. Mike was in deep trouble and would be questioned by his senior authority. He feared being terminated. He was waiting for a turning point. That was when he got a call. It was Remi.

The call did not turn his fortune in his favor but rather provoked him to move towards the final conclusion. Remi called Mike for a deal. Although Mike knew that she was not trustworthy for him because she was helping Den, Remi offered an exchange. Mike was desperate to eliminate all his risks, whether he was Navani,

Floyd or Den. Remi proposed a mutual settlement. Walter had an extremely sensitive file on the spread and coverup of the coronavirus. He wanted to sell it at a price. This might interest Mike. Chief convinced Bolton to settle his piece with Mike as well. Floyd was in the custody of Remi and underground. Getting together was set up with Chief. Mike realized that he better buy this opportunity, so he was convinced, and inevitably trapped.

The last mile before the War

On way to Svalbard

After the injection, the table was rearranged with a drink platter as if there was a casual get-together between four friends. Drivers and security teams were called to escort Mike to his home. He was reported drunk and lost sense. So Den was.

***

It has been one month since the last meeting in New York. Both Mike and Den were still recovering, but this will take some more time. Mike, even after gaining sense, may not take any official action. His cover was blown, and he was exposed. He had to carry this fear for life. His behavior had a lot of anomalies due to the side effects of the nerve agent. He lost all usage value for the system. Additionally, he now became a liability for the administration. Naturally, the White House decoupled him. He was removed from all positions and power and Mr PM used him as a scapegoat.

Mike was now a failed case by himself and would have to strive to find means, shelter and a new godfather to survive. His stardom, authority and political power were destroyed forever.

***

Den's right side had mild paralysis, but he was able to respond and move only with his left side. Remi and Den were in a chopper flying from Tromso to Svalbard. Floyd was waiting near the Archipelago airport. In the last month, Remi completed the pending works on behalf of Den. She collected a lump sum amount from climate activists around the world and transferred the money to the family of the housekeeping staff in Poland. She also flew to Nome and returned Taylor's diary to his daughter. She told the truth of what happened to him.

She met the wife of Sir Jodman, as well, in Nuuk. However, she didn't tell the truth there. The wife might not take the shock easily. The emotional effort was probably too selective and tiny as there are thousands of such families across the globe who are left behind to a dark, uncertain destiny after this kind of innocent murder. The rule of these government killings is simple and common. Use and eliminate. These low-stature people and their families are collateral damage in bigger games. The games of politics.

Remi completed the last chapter of the file, which contained extremely sensitive and confidential information and communication between Mike and Mr PM. They will keep the file in the safe vault of the Arctic World Archive for the next few months. They have to wait for the US election to be over, or else people and the media might press this as propaganda. At the right time, they will detonate the bomb and publish the file. Svalbard is the most geopolitically secured, Remilitarized and insulated territory in the world. However, this status quo is as of now. Nobody knows if war starts someday, whether related countries and their governments will stick to the same protocol of sovereign peace land for Svalbard or this will compel to change.

The chopper was running over the frozen Arctic Circle. Although the ice bed was not completely frozen anymore. Climate was changing the landscape, and with the increasing temperature being linked to prolonged wildfires that grow more severe every year, the thawing of the permafrost was now faster. Climate data shows that the Arctic is one of the fastest changing ecosystems on the planet, with serious consequences for wildlife and marine life, while the melting sea ice contributes to rising sea levels worldwide. Temperatures rising beyond the threshold will lead to worsening hurricanes, floods, droughts and wildfires, as well as agricultural disasters that could shrink the world's food supply. But this will not stop. The human race is aggressive and would fast-track its own extinction.

Den had fallen asleep, but when he opened his eyes, Remi was looking at him. She smiled.

Den asked, "What are you thinking?" He had to raise his voice as they were inside the helicopter.

"I am thinking what a herculean task that you just had to overcome. Did you realize how phenomenal it is?"

Den looked at the briefcase. It has his file. Everything happened all of a sudden. He was hooked on to the game by chance. He was dragged into the critical mass and trapped. It would have been an easier immediate choice for him to escape, but he didn't let it go. He gambled, put his life at risk and reached the epicenter of the conspiracy. The file was prepared with precision, relevance and detailing. It needed to be kept with utmost secrecy and security before it is placed in the wrong hands.

"After this, I want to quit my job from the Secretariat. This has become boring for me. I expressed this earlier to Chief."

"You are exceptional, Den. Please hold on to it." Remi stated.

"I am a misfit in Secretariat. I fear for myself that one day I will be mentally corrupted, like others, by pursuing habits of stereotype diplomacy. I negotiate and reconcile for a sponsored agenda of member countries. This is the rule of diplomacy. I want to be free, Remi. I want to wear a Blue helmet again."

"Peacekeeping!"

"Yes, of some kind. I want to go back to the field."

"You are on a wanted list. You will be underground for a longer time now. The government is behind you. After the file is de-classified and published, do you think that you would get a nomination from any government?"

"I don't have a country, Remi, nor have any blind nationalism at the cost of humanity. Citizenship doesn't mandate me to be patriotic nor political."

"It will be unfortunate to leave you. We need you in system, Den."

"I need a change."

"You saved the Earth by deferring the catastrophe at least for a few years. It is not only stopping the 'polar bear', but identifying the mastermind and cornering him with the proof and detailed evidence is a masterstroke. The conclusion is exhaustive. They now have to put the agenda of the League of States, diluting the United Nations and other similar parallel agendas, on the back burner for the time being. This unmasked a lot of big brother corporations and dark nexus. You are brave, my son. May God bless you."

"You correctly said, it is deferred. The problem is much more complex than it appeared. We alone cannot fight a military or political battle. The devil politics are bigger and stronger. But we can build up the Secretariat capacity with people's support and strength to stand firm."

"What is that?"

"To transform the UN into a true democratic organization."

"That is next to impossible. You cannot cope with the political pressure."

"I know it is difficult. In the next general assembly, Chief is going to propose a resolution for a revision of the charter. The proposal is to include independent experts to draft the revision in favor of people, peace and nature. This will then be a fair trial. The resolution will propose to break the five-member permanent seat monarchy."

"Crazy stuff. You are again putting your hands in the fire. Do they invest in the budget if they don't get the desired dividend?"

Den smiled, "Something needs to be framed. This is make or break. This change has to happen now before another war. The victors of the next global war are going to be more lethal. We may not get a chance thereafter. The UN has managed to survive for a long period of time. Surviving through the Cold War and the initial challenges of the formation of new age competition has been commendable for the UN so far. But world order is not just bipolar nowadays. Earlier, the bipolar conflicts were more predictable, and the powerhouses used to settle among themselves. However, now conflict is more fragmented and regional. The future is going to be more intrinsic and challenging. The Security Council should not be dependent on the mercy and legislature of the five-power framework. It cannot survive. I want the United Nations stand true and more affirmative for the people."

"Den, I want you to get better soon. You need rest first."

"Remi, war is inevitable. Once you push somebody to failure, he may either give up or retaliate. But if you keep pushing somebody very hard from all corners to their last wall, they will either dismantle or revolt. We have both scenarios at the present time. The Arctic is a make-or-break for America. We pushed their mission to failure. They will retaliate for sure. On the other hand, trade tariff war, sanctions and prohibition of 5G and technology value chain are not a simple decoupling decision by the White House. It is not just a simple fact of a decade-old marriage of convenience between the US and China, which suddenly has gone bad. Pushing Bejing and CPP from all corners to restriction and reduction will ultimately give birth to a much superior demon. A large-scale war. It may be a natural choice for China to trigger the war. The probability of Russia or Germany playing neutral is high. If it is a direct war by Bejing, then obviously, the plot will be Indo-Pacific. If it is indirect or through a political alliance, then Turkey or Iran may probably trigger the escalation on behalf of the new emerging brotherhood with the help of China. Most interestingly, the US themselves would want a large-scale war. Oil prices, fuel economy and military business may not survive without a global war now. This is a matter of survival of supremacy. Control on the Arctic and Indo-Pacific will define the order."

It was going to be 'midnight Sun' outside. The sun never sets during the summertime in the North Pole. Both saw beyond the window to the ice shield of nature. Ice was not white. Everything will turn gray. Nature is beautiful. But time is not.

There is no need for time travel to imagine the future of the North Pole. Spectacular species like polar bears, walrus, seals, reindeer and whales may not survive. Nature governs our Earth. Now the economic mafias are the new governor of the World. The Arctic will turn gray from white. Indigenous tribes will be pushed further to extinction because corporations and governments will seize their land and homes by that time.

There will be heavy marine traffic over the crisscross shipping highways through the northwest passage, northern sea route and transpolar route. Under ocean mining for rare earth elements and drilling of new fossil fuel patches are going on in full swing. The Arctic will be very busy and developed. The top of Earth will be populated with modern cities and business townships. Each piece will be heavily guarded by respective government stakeholders and their corporate tenants. The new world order will now be determined not by the West or East. The world will now look at the Arctic as if it itself is a new, busy planet.

Den was absent minded for some time. He was still looking through the chopper window. His health was not keeping well. They will reach Svalbard within next half an hour. He was thinking something. He broke the silence after some time. "We could just defer the program. This never unrooted the threat. Destiny is imminent. War is coming."

"The World War?" Remi asked.

"It is more complicated."